MW01135355

A Taste of Sin
Kate Hawthorne

Copyright © 2019, 2020 Kate Hawthorne
Edited by: Aly Hayden

Cover Design: AmaiDesigns
www.amaidesigns.com

A Taste of Sin

SECRETS IN EDGEWOOD
KATE HAWTHORNE

DEDICATION

For Melinda.
Thank you.

ONE

REED

REED MATTHEWS POWERED down his computer and switched off the lamp on the corner of his desk. He pushed his chair away and stood, collecting his blazer from the coat rack near the door to his office and shrugging it up his arms. He put on his messenger bag, the worn leather strap resting comfortably on his shoulder.

"Take care, Susan," he said, stepping into the main office. He closed his office door behind him and passed by his secretary's desk.

"Have a lovely evening, Principal Matthews!" Susan called after him. He turned and found her smiling, every strand of her gray hair tucked into place, much like it had been every day for the past four years they'd worked together. He returned her smile and tipped his chin, pushing through the front doors of the office and into the parking lot.

The evening air was thick and balmy, sweat instantly beginning to bead at the base of his neck by the time he reached his car in the staff parking lot. He'd never felt comfortable using the assigned Principal space near the front. Instead, he reminded the staff that all were equal in God's eyes, and maintained a first come, first served parking spot policy since he'd begun his tenure at Our Lady of the Mount Catholic High School.

Once his car was unlocked, Reed looked around the parking lot, squinting his eyes toward the practice field to the south, making sure all the students had left campus for the evening. Confident there were no children left to see him dressed so unprofessionally, Reed took off his jacket and hung it on a wire hanger he kept in the back seat.

He rolled the sleeves of his white dress shirt up, tossing his messenger bag onto the passenger seat and climbing into the car. His stomach rumbled, the sound filling the quiet space. Pulling up to the stoplight at the intersection of Grand and Devonshire, Reed narrowed his eyes at the strip mall down the street.

Chinese.

Mexican.

Italian.

All in one place. It was one of his favorite one-stop shops for his Friday night takeout. Reed was diligent about cooking at home, doing his best to spend his money carefully and put as much as he could into savings. Since he lived alone, he didn't mind eating alone. Saturday through Thursday, he prepared himself a meal for two, eating one portion at his small dining room table and packaging the other for his lunch the following day.

Fridays were the night he splurged, normally working on a three-week rotation between Mama A's, Pina's, and Star Garden. He'd had Star Garden last week, which meant it was time for pasta, but his stomach protested at the idea as he maneuvered his car into a parking spot equidistant between Mama A's and Star Garden.

Reed tapped his fingers against the steering wheel, his eyes darting from restaurant to restaurant. It wasn't like his world would get turned upside down if he had Chinese food two weeks in a row, and besides, the barbeque pork fried rice sounded like a really good idea.

There had been a birthday party for one of the teachers at school, and Reed had indulged himself with a slice of cake just before two in the afternoon, so the idea of eating pasta as a follow up didn't sound appetizing in the least. If he went with the rice, it would be less filling.

Mind made up, Reed turned off the car and stepped out, locking the doors and heading toward Star Garden. The jingle bells over the door rang as he walked in, and the owner, Lisa, turned to greet him, her face morphing into a look of shock when she saw him.

"Reed." She smiled. "I didn't expect you for another two weeks."

Reed approached the counter and pulled his wallet out.

"I had a late snack," he shared.

Lisa raised an eyebrow, picking up a pen and her order pad. "You still want your usual?"

"Of course."

Lisa scribbled down his order, which was barbeque pork fried rice and General Tso's chicken. She clipped it onto a spinning order wheel and sent it to the kitchen, then she passed him a clear plastic cup.

"Thanks, Lisa." He handed her a twenty dollar bill.

He returned his wallet to his back pocket and took the cup to the fountain, where he filled it with water, no ice. Reed slid into the booth closest to the register to wait for his food, taking small, measured sips while he waited.

The restaurant wasn't busy, but it wasn't empty. There was a family of four at a booth across from him, the children most likely middle school age. Reed lamented the fact that he hadn't at least rolled his sleeves down, aware of the importance of presenting a professional impression for parents in the community.

He didn't recognize the family though, so he assumed they most likely were not Catholic, as he hadn't seen them at mass before either, but that didn't rule out the possibility of the children being enrolled at Our Lady in the future.

Reed fidgeted with the cuff of his shirt, debating on unrolling it, when the bells above the door chimed, introducing another customer. Reed took a deep breath and flattened his hand against the table, leaving the sleeves rolled. It was too late to save face now.

"Dominic, how are you?" Lisa greeted, coming out from around the counter.

"Better now," the customer, who Reed assumed was Dominic, answered.

Lisa made a squeaking sound, and Reed poked his head out from the high-backed booth to find her wrapped up in the customer's arms. He picked her up and dropped her back on the ground, a smile on his face that sent a shockwave straight through Reed's entire body. It was a smile he recognized, he knew that much, but he couldn't immediately place it beyond the familiar feeling that it roused in his gut.

Lisa stepped out of the way with a laugh, revealing Dominic, who looked very much like a priest, dressed in familiar black with a crisp white collar. Reed narrowed his eyes, well aware if he was a priest, Dominic was no Catholic priest.

"Everything ready?" Dominic asked, walking with Lisa to the counter.

Reed watched him go, trying to figure out why he felt a sense of longing every time this stranger's voice rattled around in his ears.

"Just about." Lisa hoisted two large catering trays from the kitchen pass and set them on the counter in front of Dominic. "Are you all ready for tonight?"

"It's either going to go super well or really awful," Dominic said with a laugh.

"Hi, Father," a young voice called, drawing Reed's attention to the family in the booth across from him. One of the children who was tucked against the wall was waving his arms wildly around.

Dominic turned, offering up that familiar smile again.

"Hey there, Cameron." His eyes appraised the other people at the table. "Calvin, Mr. and Mrs. Meyers, how are you?"

"Oh, just enjoying a nice meal," Mr. Meyers said, patting his stomach dramatically. "What about you?"

"I'm about to." Dominic tipped his head toward the catering trays. "I take it you won't be joining us tonight?"

Mrs. Meyers blushed and looked down, embarrassed.

"No, no," Dominic chided. "None of that. You don't need to feel bad for not coming."

"We'll be there next month," Mr. Meyers promised.

Dominic held his hands up in concession. "Only if scheduling permits. While it's important to attend on Sunday, I'd never begrudge anyone for missing the Friday night movie, even though your dinner could have been free."

Dominic winked, and Reed's heart sank.

There was no way.

It couldn't be.

After so many years.

Reed slid a shaking hand to his cup and raised it to his mouth, hoping the water would cure his parched tongue. It felt like he'd swallowed sandpaper. He closed his eyes, praying for suggestion and guidance.

"Just waiting on one more tray for you, Dominic," Lisa said, and Reed made a note that she didn't call him Father, like the Meyers family did.

"You've got time. We aren't due to start until eight."

"I think it's just lovely what you're doing over there," Lisa told him.

Reed dared to open his eyes, focusing on the back of

Dominic O'Halloran's head while he conversed with Lisa. Reed broke out in a sweat, the confines of the restaurant more overwhelming than the thick May air outside. He swiped at his temple, yanking a napkin from the dispenser at the end of the table to dry his hands. He wadded the damp and flimsy paper into a ball and set it carefully next to his now-empty water.

He prayed that his food wouldn't be done until after Dominic had left, because now that he recognized the man, he wasn't prepared to face the onslaught of emotions bubbling inside of him. Everything from jealousy, to rage, and pent up... *something* that he couldn't put his finger on.

"It's only a movie night," Dominic said with a deep laugh. "I'm just working to engage the community outside of the two hours we spend together on Sundays."

"Well, you've definitely breathed new life into St. Paul's," Lisa said with a small laugh.

The bell in the kitchen dinged.

That was why Dominic was wearing the collar. He wasn't Catholic. He was Episcopalian. St. Paul's was the church on the other end of town, across from Our Lady. The spires matched each other for height, in a dominating sort of way, the Catholics and the Anglicans keeping a careful eye on the happenings in the growing town of Edgewood.

Reed, of course, prayed daily for the Episcopalians, hoping that their engagement with the Lord was enough to see them through the pearly gates at the end of the days, although he wasn't ever certain his good word would be enough. He'd become fond of the members of town, whether they were part of the Catholic congregation or not.

"Your food's ready, Reed," Lisa called, her voice carrying over Dominic's shoulder.

Reed pinched the bridge of his nose between his thumb and forefinger, taking a deep breath before standing. Dominic turned to make room for him to reach the counter, his face morphing into shocked recognition.

"Reed?" he croaked, his baritone voice cracking on the single syllable. "Reed Reilley?"

"Matthews," Lisa corrected, handing him his to-go bag.

Reed nodded, unable to look up and meet Dominic's stare, which felt as heavy on his shoulders as it had when they were younger.

"Formerly Reilley, then," Dominic corrected, eyes wide. "Is that really you?"

Reed's right leg weakened, his foot tapping out a nervous beat against the floor that he wasn't able to stop. He reached out to brace himself against the counter. Dominic leaned forward, a strong hand wrapping around Reed's forearm. His touch burned with the memory of a childhood Reed had spent his entire adult life trying to forget.

"Nic," Reed mumbled, shaking him off.

Dominic took his hands away, shoving them into the pockets of his well-pressed black slacks.

"Sorry," he said. "But, Reed. Is that really you?"

"Do you two know each other?" Lisa asked, leaning over the counter, eager for gossip.

"I think…" Dominic started to say, stopping himself and taking a step backward.

"Yeah." Reed cleared his throat and risked a look at Dominic's face. "We were in foster care together."

"Foster care?" Lisa chirped. "I didn't know either of you were adopted. How lovely to reconnect then, after so long."

Reed swallowed, Dominic's eyes intent on him, and so dark, they looked like polished obsidian. It was a stare he remembered, eyes he knew. The emotions in his stomach twisted, an uncomfortable confusion burning its way through his bones.

Reed lived a careful and calculated life, but the feelings he'd had toward Dominic when they were children had been anything but. Dominic had been his best friend, his only friend, the two of them housed with the same foster parents for over a year, until Reed had been adopted just after Nic's fourteenth birthday.

Margaret and James, his adoptive parents, had been kind and gracious, also devoted Catholics, who'd raised Reed up in the church they'd attended their entire life. He'd been old enough to choose for himself at that point, but agreed to attend mass because he liked the rigidity and structure the Catholic faith offered.

They had been wonderful parents, as tolerant and patient as they could be after taking in a thirteen-year-old orphan, and Reed woke up missing his makeshift family every single day. James had passed years ago, but Margaret had always been there for him, like a mother should.

He'd long ago stopped waking up with that same yearning for Dominic. Or so he thought.

"Reed was adopted," Dominic told Lisa, tilting his head toward her while keeping his eyes focused on Reed. "I never was."

TWO

DOMINIC

"I NEED TO GET GOING," Reed stammered, snatching his bag of food out of Lisa's hand and grabbing his receipt off the counter.

"Reed." Dominic tried to stop him, but he was gone.

Dominic closed his eyes, his entire body covered in gooseflesh like he'd just touched a ghost, and in a way, he had. It had been a lifetime since he'd seen Reed Reilley—or rather, Reed Matthews. He was thirty-four now, and Reed was adopted when Dominic was fourteen, so over twenty years.

Dominic had often wondered what had become of Reed after he'd been adopted. They'd known it was coming and of course had made plans to stay in touch, but that was all before cell phones had become prevalent, and neither of them really knew what sort of home Reed would be moved into, whether they'd have internet or what kind of rules they'd have. As it was, the dial-up at their foster parents' house was unreliable on a good day.

He'd been so excited that Reed was getting a family, not ever stopping to think about the implications—that he'd be losing his brother, his best friend.

"Dominic." Lisa's voice behind him sounded like it was

coming through an echo chamber. He shook his head and turned, plastering a smile on his lips.

"All set here?" he asked, taking his wallet out to pay for dinner, but Lisa waved him off.

"Janice already paid when she placed the order," she told him.

"Oh," Dominic said blankly, nodding. "Right, of course she did."

He put his wallet away and held his arms out. Lisa flung a towel across them and stacked the catering trays.

"You sure you've got this?" she asked warily.

"On second thought," he said with a small laugh, "can you come open the doors for me?"

Lisa rolled her eyes and grabbed his car keys from the counter, jogging to get in front of him and open the door. She helped him to the car, and once the food was situated in the trunk of his late-model Honda, he passed her back the towel in exchange for his keys.

"You sure you don't want to come tonight?" he asked, straightening his collar. "We're watching *The Shawshank Redemption.*"

Lisa laughed and stepped backward onto the curb. "You've already sermonized me about the symbolism in that movie. I'm good, but thank you, Father O'Halloran."

Dominic scoffed at her use of the honorific title.

"I can tell when I'm no longer wanted," he teased.

She smiled at him fondly. "You're always wanted and you're always welcome here."

"I appreciate that, Lisa." Dominic patted his pockets to make sure he had everything. "Oh! Do you have the receipt so I can give it to Janice?"

"It was on the counter; did you not take it?" She glanced over her shoulder toward the restaurant.

"Reed must have taken it," Dominic realized.

"Oh, crap," Lisa said. "I can go write you up another one."

"It's fine," Dominic stopped her. "I'll come get one this week. I want to make sure I have time to get everything set up before the movie starts."

"I'm sorry."

"It's alright," he said with a wink. "You're forgiven."

Lisa made a shooing motion with her hand and turned on her heel, leaving Dominic alone in the parking lot. He watched her retreat into the restaurant, his eyes following her to the booth Reed had been sitting in. She leaned over the table and picked up the cup he'd been using and a crumpled napkin, and disappeared into the kitchen.

And just like that, all trace that Reed had even been there was erased.

Dominic rubbed at his chest, his smartwatch vibrating against his arm. He tapped the screen and scrolled to find a text from Janice that was just a picture of an hourglass. He rolled his eyes and lowered himself into the car, heading across town to St. Paul's.

Janice was waiting for him in the parking lot, bouncing from foot to foot with a worried look on her face. She was at his door before he'd even gotten the car turned off.

"It's about time you're back," she said.

"I wasn't gone that long," he grumbled, shoving his keys into his pocket.

He popped the trunk and unloaded the trays of food, Janice slamming the trunk closed and trailing behind him into the church auditorium.

"The tables are set up over there," she said, pointing toward three six-foot folding tables under a window.

"I can see, thank you."

She followed behind him, unfazed by his comment, fiddling with the tablecloth, even as he lowered down the trays of food.

"Do you think you should put the rice after the entrees so

people don't fill up on starch?" she asked, more to the room than him.

Dominic cast her a sidelong glance, and she mumbled something before disappearing out of the room. He huffed out a laugh, loosening the lids on the trays of food but leaving them on enough to hold the heat in.

A look up at the clock indicated it was half an hour till eight. That meant he had enough time to pop back into his office before the movie night was scheduled to begin. He locked the auditorium door behind him, walking quickly across the church campus and letting himself into his basement office.

He rested his back against the door, hand still curled around the knob. It was then he realized he was shaking. He flattened his palms against the cool wood of the door and closed his eyes, only to be immediately assaulted with memories involving Reed and tire swings over streams in the woods.

Dominic covered his face with his hands, sucking in a gasping breath of air. His knees trembled and he leaned forward, his elbows landing on his bent legs. His ass stayed firm against the door, the only point of contact to hold him standing.

Why was he shaking so much?

He tore his hands away from his face and held them in front of him, turning them so the tops were visible. A plain gold band around his right ring finger reflected the fluorescent light of his office. He took the ring off, holding it in his palm and rubbing the metal with his finger. He slid down the door, landing on the thin and worn carpet with a thud.

Raising the ring to his mouth, he pressed a kiss against the warm band before sliding it back around his finger. He had a tan line from it now, he'd been wearing it for so many years.

"I found him," Dominic whispered into the empty room.

There was, of course, no reply. Just an oil painting of the crucifix behind his desk. Dominic narrowed his eyes at it and sighed, dropping his head onto his knees.

In all his life, he'd never expected to see Reed again, realigning his wants and goals to exclude him once he'd turned twenty. He'd figured by the time he was twenty or twenty-one, Reed would have been almost nineteen, and if Reed hadn't tried to find him by then, he probably never would.

Dominic had spent his twenty-first birthday packing up his final memories of a life he'd never have. That night, he closed the door on Reed and opened a bottle of Jameson, never looking back. At least, that was the lie he told himself. He thought about Reed often—more than he'd admit to anyone. Haunted memories aside, he knew it was unbecoming for a member of the clergy to have a drinking problem, so he kept *that* secret.

He scoffed, dropping his head against the door of his office. He didn't have a problem. Not now. All he had was a bottle of whiskey in his desk that he drank alone sometimes. He'd negotiated himself back down to no more than one glass a night, and that hardly constituted a drinking problem. He was *allowed* to drink. Hell, he was allowed to do a lot of things that he didn't choose to indulge in, so whiskey wasn't a huge vice as far as he was concerned.

A knock on his door startled him, and he flew to his feet, brushing the remnants of carpet off the back of his legs.

"Who is it?" he asked, clearing his throat.

"It's time for the movie, Father."

Janice.

Dominic pushed up the cuff of his shirt, his watch lighting up with the time. He shook his head, shocked half an hour had already passed.

"I'll be right there," he called.

Dominic retreated to the small bathroom in the corner of his office, splashing water on his face. He studied himself in the mirror, the lines around his eyes that weren't there last year, the patch of gray hair that had taken root just above his ear.

With a sigh, he turned off the water and the light, locking his office behind him and joining Janice and the rest of his congregation in the auditorium.

He was pleased to see about sixty percent of the normal Sunday crowd had gathered. They were arranged around tables in their familiar groups, shoveling food into their mouths when he arrived. The projector screen was dropped below the stage, and Janice had moved the lectern off to the side.

"Good evening, everyone," he greeted, and was met with a chorus of hellos in return. "I want to thank everyone for coming. I know it's a Friday night."

There was a spattering of laughter and throat clearing.

"I know what we're doing here tonight is a little bit out of the norm, maybe a little, dare I say, progressive." He paused and waggled his eyebrows. "But I think it's important for church to be a community that extends beyond afternoon tea on Sundays. I wanted to have this movie night as an opportunity for us to not only fellowship together, but to maybe see a little bit of how the Word is active around us even when we don't realize it."

He took a drink of water before continuing. "There's a ton of biblical imagery in books, music, and movies, but I wanted to start with movies since they're the most fun."

More laughter, a little more robust than before. Dominic took that as a good sign, so he carried on with his pre-planned speech.

"With a show of hands, how many of you have already seen *The Shawshank Redemption*?" he asked.

About thirty hands went up. He nodded, smiling and clasping his hands together.

"That's great. So, for those of you who haven't, you can cover your ears if you don't want a spoiler, but one of the most famous scenes in the movie is after Andy escapes, and he tumbles into the river on his knees." Dominic extended his arms out to his sides, much like the crucifixion in his office. "And he holds his arms out like this, and the water rains down on him. What do you think that scene represents?"

There was a moment of silence before someone raised their hand, looking around to see if anyone else was going to answer.

"Yes, Jordan." Dominic pointed toward Jordan Chambers, one of the few single men who attended St. Paul's.

"Baptism?"

"Bingo!" Dominic clapped his hands. "And baptism represents what? Rebirth. Being reborn in the love and care of Christ."

Jordan nodded and looked proud of himself.

"There's some other imagery in this movie, but I'll leave it to you to see if you can find it. Janice, can you get this going?" he asked, pointing toward his secretary at the back of the auditorium.

She gave him a double thumbs up and turned off the lights, then pressed play on the laptop connected to the projector.

The opening credits rolled and Dominic snuck toward the back of the auditorium, taking a seat in the corner. Janice brought him a plate of food that he hadn't asked for but ate anyway.

Halfway through the movie, he found himself wondering what Reed had ordered, if he'd gone home and shared his meal with someone or if he was alone. He scratched his temple, glancing down at his watch to check the time. He was still, even after a month, getting used to the time difference from Maryland, where he'd been living.

He'd just moved to Edgewood five weeks prior, after taking the open position at St. Paul's. He'd been told the church wasn't necessarily struggling, but had a dwindling attendance, especially in comparison to Our Lady of the Mount, the Catholic church at the other end of town. While the neighborhoods were definitely segmented, Edgewood wasn't what most people would consider a small town. It was smaller than the big cities around it, but large enough you weren't always up in everyone's business.

The previous pastor at St. Paul's had been older, a staunch man with a white mustache as thick as his eyebrows, and he'd left the call to go live with his son in Florida. Dominic wondered what Florida was like in June. How bad was the humidity? Edgewood was thankfully a pleasant, dry heat, nary a mosquito in sight.

His daydream was interrupted by applause and the lights coming back on. Shoveling a final bite of forgotten dinner into his mouth, he jogged back up to the lectern. Hands flew up, waiting to be called on, and the room hummed with excited chatter.

"Alright," he said, scanning the crowd, "who wants to go first?"

THREE
REED

REED ATE EXACTLY two bites of his dinner before giving up and pulling the emergency bottle of vodka out of his freezer. The booze wasn't something he'd ever have bought for himself—it had been a Christmas gift from the teachers at school his first Christmas on staff. He'd accepted it graciously, tucking it away in his freezer for reasons he couldn't have named at the time.

But he was glad he'd kept it. Reed unscrewed the cap, holding the bottle by its long neck, while he stared at the neatly-arranged row of glasses in the cupboard over his sink. If he used a glass, that meant he was committing to a night of drinking alone. If he just took a swig from the bottle, it was more of a one-and-done event.

He set the bottle on the counter, eyes darting between it and the glasses, before finally removing one and closing the cupboard softly. It didn't need to mean he was going to be up all night drinking, it just meant he wanted to maintain his dedication to decorum and manners.

He poured what he assumed to be an ounce of vodka into the glass, twisting the cap back onto the bottle and pushing it toward the back of the counter. He picked up the glass and swirled the small amount of liquor around, dipping his nose down to see if it had a smell. He scrunched his face and pulled back, noting vodka did have a smell.

Reed's body trembled with another unwelcome memory of Nic. He raised the glass to his mouth and swallowed the contents of the first drink. He pinched his features together and smacked his lips, the flavor of the vodka strong and tart against his tongue. The liquor burned, and he could feel it sliding down his esophagus.

Reed coughed and rubbed at his chest, somehow hoping he could work the vodka into his gut where it wouldn't sting him so intensely. The burn finally settled, and Reed set the glass down on the counter, bracing himself against the edge and closing his eyes.

Clear as day, his mind was assaulted with a picture of himself at thirteen with Nic, freshly fourteen. He was already so much taller than Reed then. It had been Nic's birthday, and someone in his class had given him one of those small gift bottles of Smirnoff. Nic had been so excited when he got home, showing it to Reed in secret, then waking him up and dragging him out to the roof just before midnight.

"It's still my birthday," Nic tells him, twisting the cap off the tiny bottle.

"Barely," Reed laughs.

"Share this with me," Nic says. "I've been waiting to celebrate with you all day."

Reed's cheeks heat from the attention.

"Cheers." Nic smiles and raises the bottle to his mouth, drinking half of it. He passes it to Reed, and Reed wraps his lips around the edge where Nic's have just been. He swallows the small amount of vodka that is left.

"Happy birthday, Nic."

Nic wraps his arm around Reed's back and pulls him close. They bump together and Nic looks up at the sky, a small smile on his face, then he rests his head against Reed's shoulder and closes his eyes.

Reed blinked, the memory unwelcome and painful. He rubbed at his eyes with the heels of his hands, feeling his unease develop into a feeling more forceful and foreign, like anger. Reed liked things a certain way. He *needed* them a certain way, and who was Dominic O'Halloran to think he could move to town and patronize the restaurants Reed ate at and make friends with people like he had any right to do so? Reed had lived here longer. The families in the town were his, the welfare of their children, his own to manage.

It was just like Nic to do something ridiculous like become a priest, and an Episcopalian one, no less. Reed reached under the collar of his dress shirt, feeling for the gold chain he wore. It had been a gift from Margaret the day he'd been baptized into the Catholic faith, and it meant more to him than anything else he owned.

Reed's gut churned, more memories that he'd long since buried trying to filter to the surface. Against his better judgement, he poured another glass of vodka, relaxing his throat so it would slide down easier than the first drink had.

The burn this time was more welcome, as though it were searing away the indecent thoughts and ideas he'd harbored as a child. He knew more now, knew better, and even as he tried to remind himself of that, his mind showed him the broad lines of Nic's back as it stretched his starched black shirt.

Black shirt with a white collar.

Reed poured himself another drink.

And he prayed.

Two pours later, Reed focused his blurry stare on the untouched plate of fried rice he'd neglected earlier. He stumbled toward the table, pushing the bag out of the way. His receipt fluttered to the ground, and he bent over to pick it up, his head muddled with vodka and confusion.

He slapped the piece of paper onto the table, picking up his fork and shoveling a bite of rice into his mouth. The pork tasted delicious, and he groaned, taking another bite. He gripped the side of his plate to stop it from turning—because the whole room was turning at this point—and his eyes were drawn to the thick Sharpie lines of Lisa's familiar writing on the receipt.

The receipt that wasn't his.

Nic's name was scrawled across the top with a phone number. Reed crumpled the paper into a ball, throwing it across the room. It bounced off the T.V. with a little show, dropping onto the floor in front of his entertainment center. Reed glared at the ball of paper, shoving more and more rice into his mouth until the rapid spinning of the room slowed to a crawl.

Reed pushed his chair back, and it clattered to the floor. He stalked toward the living room, leaning over to grab the receipt but tripping over his feet and landing in a heap on the floor, the receipt just in front of him. He unfolded the mess of paper, smoothing it against the hard wood of his living room floor, and he lay there, staring at Nic's name and the seven digits after it.

He'd spent so many years wondering what it would be like to see Nic again. If they'd be able to pick up where they'd left off, or if it would be like meeting a stranger. And none of those questions had been answered tonight. Nic had the appearance of a stranger, but his presence the comfort of a familiar friend.

Even as Reed pushed himself to a standing position, stumbling toward the kitchen to pour himself a glass of water from the tap, he felt warm with the recognition he'd had when his eyes locked on Nic's. He'd felt warm elsewhere, too, but those weren't appropriate feelings to have toward another man, and he pushed them aside.

He fingered the chain around his neck and finished his water, putting the glass in the basin of the sink. He returned the vodka to the freezer, the idea of washing it down the drain only a fleeting one that he pushed to the side before it had even fully formed. Reed closed his eyes, and it was Nic he saw.

With a pained grimace, he made his way to his couch, dropping onto one of the worn leather cushions with a sigh. He pulled his phone out of his pocket, spinning it in his hand, debating the merits of what he was about to do.

Reed hadn't ever really taken to the idea that touching himself was wrong. He'd been brought to the faith as a horny teenager, and there were only so many things he was willing to offer up to the Lord. At the time, self-pleasure hadn't been one of them. As he'd gotten older and remained alone, it had been easy for him to push those carnal feelings to the side. At least, it had been until now.

His cock had been half-hard since his first drink tonight, and Reed hated it. He wagered if he could just take care of it, the problem would go away. The feelings about Nic would go away. Again.

Reed glanced toward the far wall, making sure his curtains were closed, and he opened a web browser on his phone, pulling up a popular free porn site. He popped the button on his slacks, freeing his cock from the confines of his underwear before scrolling down the front page of the site, hoping to find something that would catch his attention.

What caught his attention, though, was not the scantily-dressed woman in a nun's Halloween costume, but the man with her, familiar black shirt torn open at the chest, white collar still in place around his neck. Cursing himself, Reed tapped the video and fast-forwarded to the middle.

The nun was on her knees, mouth full of cock, and the camera was trained on the man's face. He didn't look anything like Nic; he was blond and tanned, and his hands were far more slender than Nic's were now. Reed opened his mouth and pressed his tongue down, closing his eyes and listening to the sounds of the blow job and the man's satisfied groans.

He fisted his cock, and his entire body shuddered. It had been so long since he'd taken himself in hand. Months, maybe even a year, but here he was now—with one off-schedule Friday night and a palm full of precum. He knew it wouldn't be a long, drawn-out affair, his fist working roughly against his shaft for less than thirty seconds before he spilled, cum spurting from his cock and falling against the buttons of his shirt and the creases of his slacks.

He tossed his phone onto the couch beside him, dropping his head back with a defeated sigh. The orgasm had been useless and empty. He found himself feeling as bereft as he had before he'd even started to drink. Reed wiped his sticky hand down the leg of his slacks, making a mental note to throw them away instead of taking them to the dry cleaners.

Angry at himself, he kicked free of his ruined pants, discarding them into a messy pile on the floor. Next to him, his phone still blared the sounds of the porn he'd put on, and he furiously stabbed at his screen to quiet it. He closed his eyes, chest heaving with exertion and face damp with tears.

Reed rubbed his eyes with the outside of his forearm, sniffling and gasping, trying to fight back the onslaught of moisture that was building just behind his lashes. What had he done? What were all these thoughts? He'd banished Nic and those indecent childhood daydreams years ago. It wasn't supposed to be his life.

He'd gone to school and gotten his masters. He'd taught for years before accepting the principal position at Our Lady of the Mount. Four years he'd been there, offering guidance and counsel to students and families alike, working with the clergy to ensure the religious well-being of every child that walked the halls. Some of the staff had joked that Reed should have entered the clergy, with his devotion to his faith and his perpetual bachelorhood.

In the face of reuniting with Nic, he could lie to them, but not himself. There was a reason he'd remained alone for as long as he had. The things Reed wanted, and the way he wanted to live, it didn't align with the things he believed. His existence was a daily struggle between his heart and his eternal soul.

Reed sobbed, covering his mouth with his hand, the sticky residue of his release dragging over his lips. He cried harder, collapsing forward, his forearms against his knees, and he cried for everything he'd lost, and everything he'd never allow himself to have.

FOUR

DOMINIC

DOMINIC WAS sound asleep when his phone rang. A quick look at the digital clock on the nightstand indicated it was just after one in the morning. He didn't recognize the number, and he fumbled around the screen to answer the call.

"Hello?" he mumbled, voice thick with sleep.

He was greeted with silence.

"Hello?" he asked again, sitting up in bed, blinking the dark room into focus. He could hear someone breathing on the other end of the line. He pulled the phone away from his face to make sure the call hadn't dropped, then returned it to his ear after seeing the number was local.

Dominic scratched at the corner of his eye, fairly sure he knew who was on the other end of the call. He swallowed and stayed on the line, matching the caller's silence, even as his heart accelerated and his palms turned clammy.

"Nic." Reed's quiet voice filtered into his ear.

Dominic closed his eyes. It had been years since he'd allowed anyone to call him that.

"I go by Dominic now," he said softly, heart aching.

"But…" Reed's voice was raspy and hesitant. "Are you not my Nic anymore?"

Dominic pressed his fingers against his eyelids until he saw stars in the dark. How long had the answer to that question been yes before it had become a no?

"How many years has it been?" he asked with a sigh.

"Twenty," Reed answered. "Give or take a few days."

"What do you want, Reed?"

The question hung in the air between them, the words filling Dominic's room until he felt like the answer he'd spent his life hoping for was closing in around him. He flung his legs out of bed and stood, walking across the room and throwing open one of the small windows. The late-spring air was balmy and did little to alleviate the pressure that surrounded him.

"I drank tonight," Reed told him, seeming to change the subject.

"So did I."

"Don't you live on the church grounds?"

"I do."

"Do you drink often?" Reed asked, clearing his throat before adding, "Father?"

Dominic turned and rested his ass on the windowsill before sliding down to the floor. The warm breeze rustled his sheer curtains around him, tangling through his hair like fingers.

"I drink enough," Dominic admitted.

"That seems… not becoming of a man of the cloth," Reed countered, his words echoing with the slightest slur.

"I'm not Catholic," Dominic reminded him.

"Oh, I know." Reed chuckled. "You couldn't have snuck into town if you had been."

"Why is that?"

"I'd have known," Reed said cryptically. "I'd have seen you."

Dominic rubbed absently at his throat. "Are you a Catholic now?"

Reed made an affirmative noise in his throat.

Silence.

"You're up late, Reed." Dominic turned his face to the side, staring at the soft comfort of his bed. He pushed off the wall, returning and tucking himself back under the sheets. His head sank into the feathery cushion of his pillow, the phone still cradled against his ear.

"I was thinking was all," Reed replied.

"About?" Dominic rolled onto his side and watched the a.m. indicator on his clock blink in time with the seconds.

"Your fourteenth birthday," Reed admitted.

"What about it?"

"I thought..." Reed began to answer but trailed off into another lapsed silence.

Dominic wanted to know what Reed thought. He wanted to know if it in any way matched up with the numerous and varying thoughts Dominic had had himself.

"Nothing," Reed answered.

"Tell me," Dominic said sharply, his voice louder than he'd intended, but as insistent as he'd planned.

Reed sucked in a breath, and Dominic heard it tremble.

"Nothing," Reed reiterated, his voice slightly less slurred than before. "It's nothing. I shouldn't have called."

"It sounds like something," Dominic told him. "'Nothing' doesn't warrant drunk dials at one in the morning."

"I'm not drunk," Reed said quickly.

"You're slurring."

"I'm not drunk *now*," Reed amended.

"Why were you drunk earlier?"

Dominic heard glass clinking and what sounded like a refrigerator opening and closing. Reed made a sound like he'd just swallowed something, and Dominic was fairly certain Reed was on his way to being drunk again.

"Reed," he said. He had been awake long enough that he

could make out the shapes and shadows of his room now. The way the streetlight played off the curtains and reflected off the framed photos on the wall. The emptiness of the other side of his bed.

"What?" Reed asked, sounding surprised to find himself on the phone.

"Why have you been drinking?"

"Do you have a wife?" Reed answered with an unrelated question.

"No wife," Dominic told him.

"Girlfriend?"

"No."

"Boy—" Reed stopped, not asking the follow-up.

"No," Dominic answered anyway.

He closed his eyes and subconsciously rubbed the heel of his hand down the length of his semi-erect cock. Reed's hesitant and scratchy voice in his ear was doing things to him. He had no right to get hard listening to his teenage crush fumble around twenty years of absence to avoid asking the question he really wanted to ask.

"Are you gay, Reed?" Dominic finally asked it himself. "Are you thinking about the way you held my hand until the sun came up on the last birthday we spent together?"

Dominic had thought about that night frequently. The way he'd rested his head on Reed's shoulder after they'd shared a tiny bottle of booze he'd gotten from a kid in his homeroom, and the way Reed had taken almost half an hour to press their palms together, letting their fingers slowly notch into place. He'd oftentimes remembered the way his teenage cock had hardened, wanting more than either of them was prepared to give.

"No!" Reed answered. A quick and brutal denial, followed with a softer and less certain, "I'm not gay."

"Are you sure?" Dominic dared to ask.

"I'm not gay," Reed said again.

"I am."

Silence.

Maybe he'd said too much, but what did he have to lose beyond the same thing he'd lost two decades before?

He could practically hear Reed mentally berating himself on the other end of the call.

Dominic sighed. "It's late, Reed. You should get some sleep."

Reed didn't acknowledge what he'd said, so after the minutes on his clock ticked over to one-thirty, Dominic ended the call.

Twenty minutes later, he was still awake and there was a demanding knock at his front door. He slipped out from under the covers and grabbed his robe, which he'd left tossed over a chair in the corner of his bedroom. He tied the terrycloth belt around his waist and wandered toward the front door.

He gripped the doorknob and hesitated, all of his muscles tense with the understanding that he somehow innately knew who was on the other side, and that opening it was going to change both of their lives forever.

Another insistent knock.

With a deep breath, he pulled the door open, revealing a disheveled-looking Reed on his porch in a matching cotton pajama set. He was so beautiful. The sight of Reed still lodged Dominic's heart in his throat, just as it had when they'd been kids and Dominic was trying to make sense of the feelings he had toward his best friend.

His only friend.

Reed looked over his shoulder toward the street, even though the church house Dominic lived in was set back on the church property.

"Can I come in?"

"Are you sure that's what you want?" Dominic asked, even as he stepped aside to make room for Reed to enter.

"I don't want to be seen on your porch at two in the morning, I know that," Reed answered, stepping into the space Dominic had made for him. "But I'm not sure I want to, no."

Dominic pushed the door closed after Reed had cleared the threshold.

"Then why are you here?" he asked, scrubbing a hand through his hair.

Reed looked around Dominic's sparsely-furnished living room, eyes lingering on the stacks of boxes he'd yet to unpack.

"I don't know," he admitted, looking up at Dominic with his lower lip held tightly between his teeth.

Dominic yearned to reach out for him, to smooth the worry lines around his eyes away, but that wasn't his place. It hadn't ever been his place, and with Reed proclaiming he wasn't gay, it didn't look like it ever would be.

"You look like I could use another drink," Dominic sighed, turning on his heel and heading into the kitchen.

"What?" Reed asked.

"Nothing." Dominic pulled a bottle of Jameson off his counter, pouring himself a double and putting it back in one swallow.

"Can I get one?" Reed asked, lingering in the doorway to the kitchen.

Against his better judgement, Dominic took another glass out of the cabinet and poured a shot for Reed. He passed Reed the glass, their fingers grazing against each other and sending a bolt of fire through Dominic's body. He pulled his hand away, wrapping it around his own glass, and breezed past Reed back to the living room.

He collapsed onto his couch, the fatigue of being up since one in the morning finally settling in his bones, but he wasn't about to throw Reed out. A small part in the back of his head said he should offer Reed counsel, but the larger and non-chaste part of himself preferred to be selfish, not that Reed would appreciate or want religious advice from an Anglican anyway.

The idea of that conversation made him smile.

"What?" Reed asked, standing just past the arm of the couch, whiskey in hand.

Dominic looked up at him and huffed. "I was just thinking about whether I should offer you counsel in your time of need."

"Who said I'm in need?" Reed asked, before adding, "Besides, you're not Catholic."

Dominic rolled his eyes, then let his lashes flutter closed. "I knew you'd say that."

The cushion beside him shifted, and he opened one eye, watching Reed settle as close to the opposite arm as he could.

"And *I* say you're in need. I mean, why else would you show up at a priest's house at two in the morning if not for some earth-shattering religious turmoil?"

He lifted his glass, taking a small sip and letting the whiskey burn around his mouth before swallowing. His muscles relaxed as soon as the Jameson settled, so he took another drink.

Reed coughed, and Dominic opened his eyes. Reed was red-faced, the glass of whiskey empty, but at some point, he'd adjusted his body, and Dominic found the space between them smaller than a minute before. Reed set his glass on the coffee table, angling his body toward Dominic in the slightest before picking at something on the leg of his pajamas.

"You told Lisa you didn't get adopted," Reed whispered.

Dominic looked away and rolled his eyes, not wanting to have this conversation this early, but also unable to deny Reed anything.

"No," he confirmed. "But you did. Tell me about that."

Dominic hoped he could change the subject, maneuver Reed's train of thought into safer territory.

"Yeah," he said. "Margaret and James."

"I remember. Were they nice? I mean, I remember meeting them, but were they nice after you moved?"

Reed nodded. "Yeah, they were."

"Did you have any brothers or sisters?"

"No."

"Oh." Dominic finished the remainder of his drink, then set his glass on the table beside Reed's and sat back against the couch.

Somehow Reed was closer again, or maybe Dominic had moved. He wasn't sure.

"Where did you move to?" Dominic asked. "After you were adopted. I don't think I ever knew where they lived."

Part of Dominic hoped it was somewhere far away so he could let the distance be a tangible thing that had warranted their separation, but somehow, he knew it wasn't.

"Cherry Grove," Reed answered quietly, like he knew how the fifteen miles from where they'd been fostered to where Reed had moved with James and Margaret wouldn't be enough to justify the divide between them.

"That's nice." Dominic cleared his throat and forced a sideways smile.

"Can I get another drink?" Reed asked.

Dominic nodded, and Reed was up, in the kitchen and back before Dominic could even reach for their empty glasses. Reed dropped back onto the couch, even closer to him than before, the bottle of Jameson in his hand. He raised it to his mouth and took a swallow, passing it to Dominic, who took the bottle from him but set it on the table instead of drinking.

They sat in silence, side by side on his couch for what Dominic was sure had to have been another twenty years. The sun crept through the window in the kitchen, casting shadows down the hallway toward the living room.

When Reed's finger brushed against his, he didn't startle; he only stilled, holding his breath for every minute it took Reed to work their palms together. Tears bloomed in Dominic's eyes and he spread his fingers, ever so slightly making room for Reed, breath caught in his throat the entire time.

FIVE

REED

NIC'S HAND was hot against his. Reed was sweating, and when he realized what he'd done, he froze. Nic flexed their fingers together and stilled. Reed could hear his heartbeat in his ears, a loud and insistent battering. He knew what was happening was wrong, but how could it *truly* be wrong? Nic's skin felt so good against his.

"Is this what you were thinking about?" Nic rasped, "when you were thinking about my birthday?"

"Yes," Reed whispered.

"It's been so long," Nic said aloud, like it was meant to be a thought, not a statement.

"I didn't think I'd ever see you again."

Reed looked down at their hands, pressed together in the space between their thighs.

"I'm in my pajamas," he observed, suddenly not aware of how he'd gotten here. Had he driven or walked? Taken a car? Did he run?

"You are," Nic confirmed, extending a finger toward Reed's leg and dragging it down the red plaid cotton.

Reed shivered. Nic adjusted himself on the couch and settled, the space between their legs closing. He rested their still-joined hands on top of their thighs.

"Is this okay?" he asked.

"Uhm…"

"I can stop," Nic said, even though it sounded like a lie. He tried to pull his hand away, but Reed clapped his other hand down over their clasped fingers.

"No!" he protested, voice loud.

"Alright."

Reed made an inventory of the living room in the parsonage, from the basic couch they were sitting on to the flat pack entertainment center against the far wall, stacked with unpacked movies and a flat screen T.V. There were no pictures on the walls, no decoration or trinkets to be found.

"Reed." Nic cleared his throat and turned his body to face him.

"Yeah?"

Nic untwisted their fingers and set Reed's hand on the cool material of his pajamas, patting the top of it before pulling away.

"It's late. Or, early rather, and I'm tired." Nic's voice sounded it, like it was weighed down with a lifetime of could-have-beens. Reed feared if he replied, his would sound the same. These hours on the couch were nothing more than a cruel tease of all the things Reed would never be allowed.

"Oh, right." Reed stood up and smoothed down the front of his pajamas, finding them tighter around the crotch than before. He clasped his hands together in front of himself, hoping Nic didn't notice.

But of course he did.

Nic's stood. His nostrils flared and his eyes narrowed, but he said nothing.

When had Reed's dick hardened? And how inappropriate for that to happen, sitting on the couch with a man he'd once considered his best friend. Reed closed his eyes.

His cock was hard over a man.

"It's not sinful," Nic said quietly, addressing the unspoken worries that bounced around Reed's head.

"I know," Reed agreed, swallowing and nodding. "It's only sinful if I act upon it."

"That's not what I meant," Nic corrected. His body wavered, leaning forward toward Reed, even as Reed took a step back.

"I'm Catholic."

"You're a member of a congregation." Nic rolled his eyes. "I have a Masters in Divinity."

Reed glared at him. "You have no right to judge my understanding of my own faith, Nic."

Nic held up his hands and took another step backward, shoulders bumping into the wall. "That's not what I meant."

"It's exactly what you meant."

Nic sighed. "We all believe in the same ideas, Reed. If my God isn't going to judge me for lying with a man, then yours won't either."

"You don't know what you're talking about," Reed ground out, jaw clenched. He rubbed his eyes with the heels of his hands.

"Alright," Nic conceded with a sigh.

"You were saying it was time for me to go," Reed hissed, gesturing to the front door with a shaking hand. His eyes flicked between the patch of chest hair visible from the split in Nic's robe to the doorknob a few feet away.

"Right." Nic cleared his throat and moved away from the path to the door so Reed could approach. He wrapped his fingers around the knob and twisted, the door inching open.

It was daytime now, no doubt, and he saw his car parked along the curb. He winced, closing the door.

"What time is it?" he asked, reluctantly turning to face Nic.

"Nearly six."

"I can't." Reed let go of the doorknob and wrung his hands together. "Someone might see me."

Nic eyed Reed from the top of his head to his feet, a small smirk pulling at the corner of his mouth. "You don't want anyone to see you sneaking out of the good Father O'Halloran's house in your pajamas?"

"Do you have some clothes I can borrow?" Reed asked, chewing on the inside of his lip.

"Yeah." Nic sounded defeated. His shoulders slumped and he turned, heading toward a hallway a few feet away. He gestured for Reed to follow him.

It turned out to be a short hallway, only three doors before it ended and turned into a hall closet. The door on the left was closed, the one on the right cracked open, revealing what looked to be a standard bathroom. Nic continued to the last door on the right, pushing the door open and flicking on a light.

The bedroom was unpacked more than the living room was. A standard looking bed, flanked by matching nightstands. A tall dresser across the room, and some framed art on the walls. The lone window was framed by sheer white curtains that billowed in the early morning breeze. Nic slammed the window closed, batting the curtains out of the way, then he pulled open a drawer in his dresser and rifled around, producing a pair of dark jeans and a white undershirt.

"Will this do?" he asked, holding the clothes out toward Reed.

"It's casual," Reed said, trying to remember the last time he'd gone out in jeans.

"It's not pajamas," Nic countered, still holding the clothes between them. "You only need to walk to your car, Reed. It's not like you have to tromp across town."

Reed reached out and took the clothes from Nic's outstretched hand.

"Thanks," he mumbled. "I'll just…"

Reed wagged a finger toward the bedroom door, indicating he meant to go change in the bathroom.

"Sure," Nic agreed, collapsing onto his bed and resting his head in his hands.

Reed lingered, the veins and lines of Nic's arms revealed when the robe slid toward his elbows, then he cursed himself and retreated to the bathroom. He closed the door quickly and locked it, slamming his back against the thin pressboard material. He couldn't catch his breath, and he struggled to get a good inhale. It had been so easy to breathe around Nic. How could something so mundane, and so necessary, be so difficult now with the walls between them?

Reed divested himself of his pajamas, folding them neatly and setting them on the toilet seat. He wasn't wearing any underwear, and Nic hadn't given him any; not that Reed would wear Nic's underwear even if he had. Shoving his feet into the borrowed jeans, Reed pulled the soft denim up his legs, zipping up the fly and adjusting his cock so it didn't abrade. The movement was enough to make him harder, and he groaned, pinching himself around the base of his shaft to quell the blood flow.

He slipped the well-worn shirt over his head, the smell of an unfamiliar detergent lingering in his nostrils. Even under the clean linen smell, there was something decidedly Nic about the odor. Reed rubbed the hem between his fingers and looked at himself in the mirror.

There were bags under his eyes and a noticeable scruff on his cheeks. His brown eyes were tired, and it looked like he'd been up for days—not just hours—longer than normal. He turned on the taps and splashed some water on his face. It didn't help at all. Nic's shirt was too big on him, the vee of the collar dipping down his chest, the arms loose, just another reminder of how strong and broad Nic had become since they were kids.

There was a soft rap against the door.

"Are you alright in there?" Nic's voice called quietly.

Reed pivoted, grabbing the door and yanking it open. Nic tumbled into the space, his fingers wrapping around Reed's arms to steady himself. They both stumbled backward, Reed's back slamming into the towel bar, and Nic's chest pressing against him.

They froze, painfully aware of the sudden and unintended proximity, and Reed painfully aware of the thick cock sticking through the terrycloth of Nic's robe and prodding his thigh.

"Are you not wearing anything under that?" he rasped.

Nic shook his head rapidly.

The muscles in the back of Reed's neck tightened and he swallowed. He could feel himself shaking—with what emotion, he didn't know. Nic was back in the room, though, and Reed still couldn't breathe. He opened his mouth to suck in a breath. Nic's hands were still around his arms, his palms clammy against Reed's skin. Their faces were side by side, with Nic's breath dusting over Reed's cheek in a rapid flurry.

Reed dared a glance at Nic, finding the irises of his eyes nearly obscured by round, black pupils. Reed's breath hitched in his throat, and Nic's hands tightened in response. The only thing Reed could hear was Nic's breathing. Movement between his legs reminded him of Nic's indecent response to the situation, and Reed squeezed his eyes closed. Nic's cock dragged across the fly of Reed's borrowed pants.

"Reed," Nic rasped.

Reed shook his head, eyes closed.

"Reed."

"No," Reed begged, even as he tipped his head to get closer.

Their foreheads bumped, noses rubbing against each other, and the rough stubble on Reed's face dragged across Nic's chin.

"Reed," Nic said again.

"I can't," Reed said, begging for Nic to understand.

"Can we just pretend, then?" Nic asked, his eyes closing and his long brown lashes fanning out against his cheeks.

"What?" Reed croaked.

Nic looked like he was in pain, his face etched with lines and worry around his eyes. He nodded, leaning his head closer toward Reed's, their mouths sharing the same air now.

"Pretend," he repeated, the request like hellfire against Reed's mouth, "like it's my birthday again. God, Reed, all I wanted was to kiss you."

Reed closed his eyes, feeling his lash line dampen unexpectedly, the agony in Nic's voice like a bullet straight into his chest. All Reed had wanted as a teenager was for Nic to have everything and for them to have everything together, even though at the time he hadn't understood what that meant.

It was clear now, though. With his back against a towel bar, with Nic's strong fingers wrapped around his arms and their mouths almost touching, cocks hard between their legs, it was clear what the feelings from his youth had meant then. Less clear what they meant now.

"Pretend," Reed repeated, his voice cracking on every syllable.

"Yeah," Nic agreed, his thumbs stroking up Reed's arms, under the cuffs of the t-shirt.

The jeans tightened between his legs, his cock hard and angry now against the fly. He swallowed, needing to release the tension somehow before it built inside of him and exploded into something frenetic and violent.

Reed flexed his fingers at his sides, balling them into fists and relaxing, over and over again. Nic's breath kept blowing across his mouth. Reed's lips were dry and chapped now. He opened his eyes, the want in Nic's enough to set a forest on fire.

Reed physically ached, his heart, and his body, and his soul at war with what he believed, and what he wanted, and what he knew in his bones he needed. Nic hadn't moved beyond his thumbs, which stroked tight circles around the front of his arms, the pads of his fingers pressing hard into Reed's triceps.

Reed took a deep breath, his flesh winning over his soul.

"Happy birthday, Nic," he whispered.

Nic groaned and closed the space between them, his lips pressing softly against Reed's parted mouth. Reed's entire body seized before his muscles weakened and softened, the release of the tension he'd been holding immediately evident. He melted into Nic's hands, and Nic kissed him, then, truly kissed him. His tongue dipped into Reed's mouth, licking at his teeth and his gums, sliding against his tongue.

Reed sighed, his mouth falling open to allow Nic more, and Nic took it, releasing one of Reed's arms so he could cup the back of his head. He moved him to a different angle, pillaging his mouth with an eager tongue. Reed couldn't stop his body from bucking forward, his cock rubbing against Nic.

He moaned into Nic's mouth, and Nic's fingers tightened in the mess of Reed's hair. It hurt, and Reed gasped, his cock shooting off into his borrowed jeans. Reed sobbed through his unexpected orgasm, pouring his anguish and his pleasure into Nic's mouth until his body stilled.

Nic slowed the kiss, pressing his lips chastely against the corner of Reed's mouth before pulling away. His cheeks were flushed red, and his lips were swollen. Reed raised a hand between them, ghosting his fingertips across Nic's lower lip.

Nic exhaled and shifted, the adjustment pressing Reed's spent cock against the damp material between his legs.

Fuck.

What had he done?

He tore himself away from Nic, unable to meet either of their reflections in the mirror.

"I've gotta go," he whispered, voice trembling.

"I know," Nic agreed, stepping out of the way and making room for Reed to flee.

SIX
DOMINIC

AFTER A MUCH NEEDED MID-DAY NAP, Dominic trudged across the church grounds toward his office. He needed to make sure his notes were in order for service tomorrow morning. Janice had left a copy of the bulletin in the box outside his door, and he collected it before letting himself inside and locking the door behind him.

The office, which until this moment had always been a place of refuge for him, now felt claustrophobic. The walls too dark, too close, the furniture too old. He tipped his chin down and passed by his desk, dropping the bulletin on the leather desk pad and moving toward the side wall to open one of the windows.

He closed his eyes, the breeze gusting over his face. It was still warm, even as the sun was on its way toward the horizon. Summer hadn't even started, and he was ready for it to be over. For the first time in weeks, he longed to be back in Maryland.

After he'd aged out of the system, he'd stayed with his foster parents for a few months until he got a plan together. He knew that wasn't the normal experience, but he was lucky that he'd developed a good relationship with Carol and David. They'd been nothing short of wonderful through his teenage years, especially during his broody and miserable post-Reed months.

He twisted the gold band around his finger and returned to his desk, dropping his weight into his creaky leather desk chair. He powered on his laptop and dragged his finger around the mousepad while he waited for the screen to light up. With his other hand, he flipped open the bulletin.

Here I am, for you called me.

Dominic glared at the scripture from Samuel and flipped the bulletin closed.

His computer lit up and he opened his word processing program, scrolling through the sermon he'd prepared to ensure everything made sense and was in order. Finding it to be satisfactory, he pushed back from his desk, lacing his fingers together behind the back of his head.

If he closed his eyes, he could still see Reed's kiss-swollen mouth. So he did.

His cock thickened against his leg and he shifted his weight, only to then find himself thinking about Reed coming in his pants—in Nic's pants—as if they really *had* been teenagers. Dominic licked his lips, wondering what Reed's cum tasted like.

With a deep breath, he opened one eye, the agony of Christ's crucifixion bearing down on him from the opposite wall. He groaned. As Reed had pointed out, he wasn't Catholic. He was allowed to engage in sexual activity, even with someone of the same gender if he so chose. The Episcopalian church as a whole wasn't necessarily on board with homosexual clergy, but St. Paul's was. He'd made sure of it, reiterating to Bishop Jenkins every time they'd spoken before he agreed to come here.

There was just something about having a hard-on under the crucifixion that seemed in poor taste. His cock grew thicker, in obvious disagreement. Dominic closed his laptop and left his office, satisfied everything was as in order as it would get for tomorrow. He was always thankful for Janice, his diligent, if not overbearing, secretary, who made sure of it.

He decided to take a walk toward one of the small church gardens normally set aside for quiet reflection after prayer time. It wasn't really a garden so much as a small patch of grass under a magnolia tree with a white iron bench. It was uncomfortable by design, and he had the fleeting thought of replacing the dated bench with something a little more welcoming.

He wiggled his phone out of his pocket, texting Janice to remind him about it on Tuesday, then scrolled through his favorites until he reached the contact he was looking for.

"Dominic," Carol answered after the third ring. He could hear the smile in her voice.

"Hey," he greeted, always choking up on the *mom* that he knew she wanted to hear.

"How are things? Shouldn't you be getting ready for tomorrow?"

Dominic could hear dishes clattering around in the background.

"I'm ready for tomorrow," he told her. "Are you busy? I thought I'd get the call in before you had to set up for bridge."

"I'm fine, sweetheart. Geraldine couldn't come help me today so I was just getting started a little early is all."

"Did she cancel?" he asked.

"She hasn't been feeling well," Carol said. "She's an old bitty."

"You're not necessarily a spring chicken," he told her with a laugh.

"Watch your mouth, young man," she chided, huffing an exasperated noise.

Dominic listened to her clang around in the kitchen for a minute, trying to remember exactly how old Carol was. She'd been fifty when he was thirteen, and he was almost thirty-four, which put her just shy of seventy. She was getting old, but he knew Geraldine was older, and that was a small comfort he allowed himself.

"Are you still there?" she asked, breathless after a minute.

"Of course."

"Good. So, to what do I owe this unscheduled phone call?"

"I don't call you on a schedule," Dominic disagreed.

"You call me every Tuesday morning," she countered. "Sometimes Thursday, but never on the weekend."

"I know you have bridge!"

"It doesn't matter," she said soothingly. "I'm just happy to hear from you. So tell me what warrants this out of character phone call."

"The weirdest thing happened last night," he whispered.

"Dominic? Are you there?"

He chuckled. "Sorry, I'm here. I'll talk louder."

"Alright, sweetheart."

He swallowed, the words he wanted to tell her lodging in his throat.

"I found Reed."

"What was that?" Carol asked for clarification. "I could have sworn you said you'd found Reed."

"I did," he said louder. "I ran into Reed last night."

"Well." Dominic could picture Carol patting her chest while she contained herself. "How was that?"

Dominic scoffed. "He's Catholic now."

"And you're Episcopalian, so you've both found Jesus."

"Yeah," he agreed, "but he's *Catholic* Catholic."

"A priest?" Carol sounded horrified.

"No," he corrected. "Definitely not, but he's very Catholic, if you get my meaning."

There was a small silence and Carol made a tutting sound on the other end of the phone. "I'm sorry, sweetheart."

Dominic leaned back on the terribly uncomfortable bench and closed his eyes. Carol had been as supportive as she could be after Reed had been adopted. She and David had taken his attitude changes in stride with his hormones and given him space to sort out his feelings, while still being as present as they could be.

"It was good to see him," Dominic told her, skirting around the rendezvous they'd had in his bathroom at sunrise. Carol didn't need to know all the details of his life, but she'd want to know about Reed... after all these years.

"Are you going to see him again?"

"I don't know," he told her honestly. "I'd like to, but he seems not entirely interested in the idea."

That was vague enough to not be a lie.

"Oh, I'm sorry dear," Carol sympathized. "Does he live in Edgewood, or were you somewhere else?"

"He's here," Dominic answered, clearing his throat.

"I see."

"Anyway," he said, brightening his tone and forcing a smile. "It's fine. That was a long time ago."

"It was," Carol agreed, even with a hint of worry in her voice.

"It's fine," he repeated.

"Okay, sweetheart."

"I'll let you get back to set up. Be careful and have fun." He stood and stretched.

"I will," she chuckled. "I love you, Dominic."

"Love you, too." He ended the call and slid his phone back into his pocket.

He made his way out of the garden, veering toward the parsonage instead of his office. Dominic kicked his shoes off inside the door, padding down the hallway to the bathroom. Reed had left his pajamas behind when he'd fled in the morning, and Dominic had set them on the counter, unsure of what to do with them.

He wanted to call Reed. He wanted to see him again. To touch him again. But he knew Reed didn't want any of those things, and he didn't want to push. He'd never want to take something that wasn't freely offered to him.

His phone buzzed in his pocket and he pulled it out again, assuming it was Janice following up with outdoor furniture samples already, but it wasn't. It was a local number he'd only seen once before and promptly saved to his address book.

Reed: You have my pajamas.

Me: I do.

The three dots indicating Reed was typing a message appeared and vanished no fewer than four times before his next message came in.

Reed: I need them back.

Me: I know. Do you want to come and get them? I'm home.

Reed: Not really.

Me: Is it because of me, or because I'm home?

Reed: Yes.

Me: What do you want me to do then, Reed? Mail them to you?

Dominic bristled, wondering how terrible it must be to live the life that Reed had built for himself. This closet where he not only hid his preferences but had tied himself with public appearances and structure so he had no chance to ever just relax and let go.

A vision flashed into Dominic's head of all the ways he could make Reed let go, if he'd only be given the chance. He inhaled sharply, fisting the thin cotton of Reed's pajamas in his hand.

Reed: I don't know.

Dominic groaned, sitting on the closed lid of his toilet, Reed's pajamas still tight in his fist. He dragged them off the counter, toward his face, and he inhaled, the scent of Reed filling his nostrils. It was the same as when they'd been younger, an indescribable smell that reminded Dominic of home, only now it was laced with a little more starch than before. His insistent cock pulsed against his leg, reminding him he was fighting his own war when it came to giving Reed the space he wanted.

He swiped out of the messaging app and dialed Reed's number. It rang four times, picking up just before voicemail.

"Nic." Reed's voice was quiet and scratchy, like he was pained to use it.

The rasp sent a bolt of arousal straight to Dominic's cock, and it pushed harder against his pants, so he worked the fly down and freed his erection from the confines of his underwear.

He must be a sight—sitting on his toilet with a hard cock and a fistful of pajamas in one hand, phone pressed against his face with the other.

"What do you want to do about your pajamas, Reed?" he asked, leaving no space for Reed to interpret his question as anything besides what it was.

"I…" Reed started to say, then stopped. He exhaled heavily into the receiver and it reminded Dominic of the way he'd breathed into his mouth when they'd kissed.

He grabbed his cock, using Reed's pajamas as a buffer, and stroked his length with one long and slow pull. The cotton dragged over his slick crown and he gasped, trying to muffle the sound.

"What are you doing?" Reed asked.

Dominic didn't want to lie, but he knew he couldn't tell the entire truth.

"I'm just sitting here," he exhaled heavily, "with your pajamas in my hand."

He worked his cock quicker, tightening the material around the head of his dick like a cage. His cock leaked against the fabric every time Reed gasped on the other end of the line. Dominic listened to him breathe, his balls tightening.

"I'm off on Monday," Dominic practically grunted. "You can get them then. I'm sure you're busy with church tomorrow."

The idea of Reed on his knees, praying and begging forgiveness for his transgressions, made Dominic hard. He thought about how unraveled Reed must feel right now, how he'd be turning to God to put him back together instead of Dominic. His muscles tightened.

"Alright," Reed whispered.

"What happened this morning wasn't wrong," Dominic gritted out through clenched teeth, his orgasm working itself into a bundle of energy at the base of his spine.

"Nic."

"It's godly, to know someone in that way." Dominic's arousal was evident in his voice, even to his own ears.

"Are you alright?" Reed asked, his voice laced with speculation. "You sound…"

"Sound like what?"

"Like you're in pain."

Dominic clenched his eyelids together and came, hot spurts of cum jetting into the red material of Reed's pajamas. His entire body bucked, folding forward so his arms rested on his knees, his back bowing through the rest of his orgasm.

"I am," he agreed, finally able to catch a breath.

"What's wrong?" Reed questioned, voice ever quiet, like he didn't really want to know the answer.

"I ache," Dominic admitted, "with want."

He tossed Reed's soiled pajamas into the tub. He'd need to wash them before Monday, although the idea of *not* was also tempting.

"Goodbye Nic," Reed said in reply.

The call disconnected and Dominic tossed his phone onto the counter, spent cock resting soft and heavy against his leg.

SEVEN
REED

"PRINCIPAL MATTHEWS!"

Reed plastered a smile on his face and turned around.

"Mrs. Ollingham," he greeted, knowing it had been her based off nothing more than the shrill screech of her voice.

"I wanted to speak with you about Catherine's grades," she said, shuffling her feet until she reached him.

Reed's eye twitched, but he remained calm, tilting his head in what he hoped was an agreeable manner. He fidgeted with the cuff of his blazer while he waited for her to catch up.

As far as masses had gone in Reed's life, the one he'd just walked out of had been about as unsatisfying as they'd come. He'd prayed—no, he'd *agonized*—over what had developed Friday night and Saturday morning, choosing to contemplate through the entirety of the prayer time after communion.

He couldn't get Nic out of his head. He'd slept terribly after their phone call on Saturday—in the wrong pajamas—his brain racing with memories and promises and could-have-beens that never were.

"My door is always open Mrs. Ollingham, but it's a little late in the year to have this discussion, isn't it?"

Catherine Ollingham was a junior and one of the students who needed a little extra attention. She'd been a good student before, but had been acting out the past few months. As a result, her grades and her attendance had suffered. She was approaching dangerous territory.

"Rachel Davidson was not interested in having the discussion with me," Mrs. Ollingham tutted.

Rachel was Catherine's fourth-period statistics teacher, and she was at her wits end with managing Catherine's disruptions.

"Ms. Davidson did try to breach this topic during conferences in the spring. She had even presented an improvement plan, but advised me after we'd approved it that you hadn't accepted it. There was a time to do something about Catherine's behavior, Mrs. Ollingham, and it's come and gone."

Even as the words left his mouth, Reed regretted them. He'd never cared so little about the welfare of his students or their future, but there wasn't room in his head for things that now seemed as trivial as whether Catherine got her act together or not. Reed sucked his tongue across the front of his teeth, the taste of the communion wine still fresh.

"That doesn't sound like you, Mr. Matthews."

Reed imagined if Mrs. Ollingham had pearls, she would have clutched them.

"Classes conclude in less than one week," Reed reminded her. He squared his shoulders and straightened his tie. Mrs. Ollingham narrowed her eyes and glared at him. Reed bit back a caustic remark, finding himself tired for the first time of being held responsible for the actions of every student under his care.

He was only one man, he could only do so much.

He was... just a man.

"We are traveling in July and Catherine will not be able to attend summer classes. I'm sure you understand."

"Would you rather her repeat the year?" he proposed, scrunching his nose and looking away.

Mrs. Ollingham gasped.

Reed scratched the back of his head and took a deep breath.

"I'll speak with Catherine tomorrow, but this isn't a guarantee that anything can be done at this point," he said, resigned.

"That's all I ask," Mrs. Ollingham replied, even though her tone was a clear indicator she assumed the discussion was final and their summer travel plans would remain intact.

Reed gave her a curt nod and continued his walk home.

It was barely ten. He wondered how Nic's sermon had been received on the other side of town. Reed was curious how different Nic would be in the pulpit from Father Cowart. Reed scoffed. Nic probably didn't even wear the proper vestments. Everything about him exuded casualness and ease. Nothing like the formality and structure Reed expected on a Sunday.

At home, he shrugged out of his blazer and hung it back in his closet, then removed his shoes. He arranged them on the rack, stripping down the rest of the way and slipping into a pair of workout shorts. He padded into the kitchen and opened his fridge, the leftover Chinese from Friday taunting him from its paper takeout boxes.

He yanked open the crisper drawer and grabbed a bag of bean sprouts and snap peas and a package of thin cut beef from the top shelf. He heated oil in a pan and chopped the beef into smaller pieces, then groaned.

His entire schedule was off. It was supposed to be stir fry for lunch Sunday because he should have had pasta on Friday, but he'd had Chinese instead. Angrily, he turned the stove off and shoved the vegetables back into their bags. He scraped the meat onto the pink Styrofoam tray it'd come in and covered it with foil, putting it all back into the fridge.

Reed trudged to his bedroom, pulling a pair of khakis and a polo from his closet to redress. He would just go out for lunch, then go to the store tomorrow after work as he always did and get things back on track.

He figured swinging by the supermarket deli would be a safe bet, and he could just grab a sandwich and some chips. He debated the merits of doing his shopping today, but his schedule was already in enough turmoil as it was.

His attention was focused on the slab of roast beef behind the glass when he heard a deep chuckle behind him.

"Reed."

His blood chilled and he froze, not turning around.

Nic stepped beside him.

Reed cursed himself, promising to never deviate from his schedule again.

"Hey, Father O'Halloran!" The butcher behind the counter greeted Nic with a wave.

"Good morning, Jimmy. How are you?" Nic responded.

"Doing well. What can I get for you?" Jimmy rested his elbows on the counter and waited for Nic to answer. Reed bristled at the oversight.

"He was first," Nic said, tipping his head toward Reed.

"Oh, right," Jimmy corrected. "What can I get for you, Principal Matthews?"

"Principal?" Nic raised an eyebrow.

"Four years. Our Lady of the Mount," Reed answered, turning his attention to Jimmy. "Roast beef sandwich on sourdough with cheddar cheese."

"Toppings?"

Reed shook his head. "Just the sandwich."

"Condiments?"

"Just the sandwich," Reed repeated, forcing a smile.

"That sounds like a boring sandwich," Nic stage whispered.

Reed snapped his head to the side and glared up at Nic. "It's the way I've always gotten it."

"No it's not," Nic said, laughing.

"What?" Reed sputtered. "Of course it is."

Nic shook his head. "Not when we were kids."

"I used to eat a lot of things when I was a kid that I don't eat now," Reed countered.

"You used to say the bread was too dry without mustard."

Jimmy slid a packaged sandwich across the shiny metal display case. "Is that all for you, Mr. Matthews? I didn't expect to see you here on a Sunday. You normally do your shopping on Monday, right?"

"I still do," Reed told him. "My weekend was a little… disrupted."

"Right." Jimmy smiled. "Well, enjoy your lunch. What can I get for you, Father?"

"Reed can order for me," Nic answered, his voice teasing.

Reed smashed his sandwich between his fingers.

Jimmy shifted his attention to Reed.

"Give it your best shot, Principal," Nic said quietly from his side.

"You can order your own lunch," Reed bit out.

"I could," Nic agreed. "But I'd rather you do it."

Reed narrowed his eyes on the crisp white collar around Nic's neck, finding himself overcome with the urge to strangle him with it.

"Turkey and provolone on rye with mustard." Reed forced the words out, finding them on the tip of his tongue after being nothing more than a long-forgotten memory.

"Good job." Nic's tone was congratulatory. He rested a hand against the small of Reed's back and Reed jumped, pulling away.

"Don't," he warned.

He spun on his heel and retreated toward the cash registers, paying for his sandwich with shaking hands and getting back to the safety of his house as soon as he could.

———

THERE WAS a soft tapping against his office door and he looked up, finding Catherine Ollingham's face poking through the crack.

"Catherine," he said, clearing some papers from his desk. "Come in."

She skulked into his office, dropping her backpack on the floor and collapsing into a chair.

"My mom said to come see you." She huffed a breath upward to blow stray hairs from her eyes.

Reed's first instinct was to correct Catherine's horrible posture, but he reminded himself that he wasn't her parent. He tapped his fingers against the edge of his desk.

"She did," he confirmed. "I ran into her after mass yesterday."

"You mean she accosted you," Catherine corrected.

Reed raised an eyebrow. "She wanted to talk about you."

"That's all she wants to do," Catherine said, folding her arms over her chest.

"Do you know why that is?" he prompted.

Catherine mumbled something.

"Pardon?" Reed tapped his ear with his finger.

"If she isn't trying to get me to go to confession, she's trying to get me to talk."

"What does she want to talk with you about?"

"She doesn't want to talk *to me* at all. She wants to talk *at* me."

Reed couldn't help but note what an accurate observation that was in regards to Mrs. Ollingham.

"She's worried about your grades," Reed told her.

Catherine scoffed. "She's worried about her trip to Africa."

Reed dropped his head back and looked up at the ceiling, taking a steadying breath before returning his attention to Catherine.

"Would you like to talk with me?" he offered.

She glared at him. "No."

"I'd like to know if there's anything going on," he told her.

"Your grades have been suffering, and you seem much unhappier than you were in September."

"I'm fine," she said caustically, a mocking smile on her face.

"Catherine."

"I don't want to talk to you about it," Catherine shouted, standing up from her seat and grabbing her backpack. "I'm fine. It's fine. Just everyone leave me alone!"

Catherine fled the room, leaving Reed's office quiet and smelling like floral perfume.

The end of day bell rang through the school, echoing through his office. With a sigh, Reed stood, stacking all of his papers on top of his laptop and locking them away in his desk. He collected his jacket from the coat rack by the door and picked up his messenger bag, locking his office behind him.

"You're leaving early today, Principal Matthews," Susan observed from her desk.

"No," he corrected her. "I'll be at the car line like always. I just didn't want to come back to the office after everyone was gone."

He adjusted the strap of his messenger bag in front of his chest.

"Are you pleased with how the year has gone?" Susan asked him, twisting a pen in her hand.

"Of course," he told her. "We only have three days to go."

"Three days," Susan echoed.

He cleared his throat. "I should get to the parking lot."

"Of course. Have a good evening." Susan waved him off.

Reed observed the student pickups as he did every day, then satisfied everyone was accounted for, he crossed the lot toward his car, repeating the routine of double checking for students before hanging his jacket in the back.

He drove across town to the supermarket, collecting a cart from the corral in the parking lot and starting his shopping at the bread aisle, which happened to be the aisle farthest from the produce. He appreciated that the store had been set up to allow for customers to shop up and down every aisle, saving the refrigerated items for last. The market in Cherry Grove had the produce in the front and the freezer aisles in the middle. It drove him up the wall as a teenager, when he'd return home with Margaret and his ice cream would have already melted.

A shopping cart clanged against his, and he was jarred from the memory. His instinct to apologize was caught in his throat when his eyes locked on the other party involved in the collision.

"Hey there, Reed," Nic greeted with a smile. "You shop here too?"

EIGHT

DOMINIC

DOMINIC WAS FAIRLY sure Reed didn't curse, but he sure looked like he wanted to. He had to admit, coming to the store today wasn't something that he'd *had* to do, but he'd take whatever opportunity he could to see Reed again. Besides, it wasn't like Reed was running him off completely. He was still talking to Nic, answering his texts...

"Of course I shop here," Reed ground out. "It's the only store on this side of town."

Dominic smiled, tapping Reed's cart out of the way and wandering toward the bagels.

"It is, isn't it?" He stopped his cart and grinned.

"You don't even live on this side of town," Reed grumbled.

"I have your pajamas. In my car."

Reed's eyes widened and he flailed his arms around. "Would you keep it down?"

The discomfort and guilt in Reed's voice were so thick, it stopped Dominic in his tracks. What was he doing? This was wrong of him.

He shook his head, disgusted with himself, and abandoned his cart.

"You're right, Reed. You know where I live when you decide you want your things."

"Nic," Reed protested, wheels on his cart creaking.

"No." Dominic held his hand up, light reflecting off the band around his finger. He clenched his hand into a fist and shoved it into his pocket. "I'm sorry."

"I don't…"

It sounded like Reed was telling him to stay, but he had already put too much space between them. He turned and shrugged, a casual smile on his face to mask his displeasure.

"I forgot my shopping list anyway."

He spun on his heel and returned to his car, banging his head against the steering wheel until it hurt, then drove back to the parsonage.

He'd barely gotten the front door closed behind him when there was an insistent knock from the outside. He knew who it was, and he debated if opening it up was the best idea. Dominic wasn't a fool. He'd joined the clergy after graduating from seminary, and he'd never really planned on or cared about having a partner.

He was allowed. The rules of the Episcopalian church were decidedly gray when it came to a stance on gays in the clergy, but the parishes he accepted positions at were always welcoming. Reed's reappearance in his life had spun his ideas about his future into a tailspin, but after a moment of fleeting hope, he knew it would have been better if he'd never run into Reed again at all.

Dominic ignored the knocking and kicked off his shoes, padding down the hallway to his laundry room. Reed's pajamas were folded neatly on top of his dryer, free of evidence of their earlier misuse. He returned to the front door as Reed's knocking turned frantic. Dominic opened the door a crack, blocking entry with his body.

"What are you doing here, Reed?" he asked.

"You can't just…" Reed flailed a bit, his face pinked from the exertion of it all.

Dominic held out Reed's pajamas, and he snatched them away, folding them into a smaller ball and tucking them under his arm.

"I'll leave you alone, Reed. I'm here to stay, but I can shop on the other side of town, so you don't need to worry about that," Dominic promised, feeling defeated and alone.

"Nic," Reed protested, but Nic held up his empty hands.

"It was good seeing you again," he whispered, pushing the door closed between them and locking it.

Dominic turned and pressed his back against the door, head thumping heavily against the wood. Reed called his name, but Dominic squeezed his eyes closed and covered his ears with his hands, tipping his head forward so his chin rested on his chest. He clenched his jaw together, eyes dampening with angry tears. He shoved off the door, offering a frustrated shout into the empty room before retreating to the point in his house farthest from the front door—the kitchen.

He pulled the bottle of Jameson down from the cabinet, the one he and Reed had shared just two days before, and took a swig, not bothering to dirty a glass. It burned the whole way down, and he shook his head to clear it before pouring another shot straight down his throat.

Dominic contemplated calling Bishop Jenkins to ask for guidance, but the room was swimming by the time he'd thought to appeal for spiritual help. One more swallow of whiskey and Dominic found himself sprawled out in the middle of his living room, half dressed and half drunk. He was aware time had passed; the room was dark, an evening breeze filtering around the room from the open window in the kitchen.

His phone buzzed in his pocket, and his heart sank.

Fucking sank.

He knew who it was.

"No," he said into the emptiness of his living room. He shook his head from side to side, rolling it across the floor.

The buzzing stopped, then immediately started again.

"No!" he protested, louder this time.

The buzzing wouldn't stop, the spinning wouldn't stop. He pried his eyes open and tried to focus on the ceiling, but it swam around his field of vision. Dominic ached. His body, his soul, his heart. To have had Reed so close again, within his reach, only to have him held away by tenets of a religion that wasn't even his own. Dominic had made his life choices carefully, always leaving a window open in case he found someone to love, in case he found Reed again.

But Reed hadn't done the same.

Reed...

Reed wouldn't even admit that he was gay, or at least bi, even as he collapsed into Nic's arms and cried out his orgasm into Nic's mouth.

The incessant buzzing.

He answered the call, not even looking at the screen. He put the phone on speaker and dropped it beside his head.

"I can't do this with you," he said in lieu of a proper greeting.

"What?" Reed's voice sounded choked and scared on the other end of the call.

"I respect your understanding of your beliefs," Dominic slurred, resting his cheek on the floor and trying to figure out which of the two cell phones in front of him was the real one. "I disagree with them, but they're yours."

"What do my beliefs have anything to do with any of this?" Reed asked weakly.

"Straight men don't kiss me the way you kissed me."

"You kissed me," Reed whispered.

"Okay," Dominic agreed. "Sure. I kissed you, and you came with your tongue in my mouth. I'm glad we're agreed that you didn't initiate the kiss, though."

"Why are you being this way?" Reed asked him, sounding hurt.

"What way?" Dominic accused.

"You're being so mean!"

"Oh, stop," Dominic bit out through clenched teeth. "I don't know what you think is going on, or what you think this is, or whatever, but I'm not a toy for you to just… fuck with."

Reed gasped as the expletive left Dominic's mouth.

Dominic rolled his eyes and nearly retched up the contents of his stomach.

"I feel a certain way when I see you," Dominic continued, ready to make himself clear for the first and last time, but was interrupted.

"How do you feel?"

"Lustful."

"Toward me?" Reed questioned hesitantly.

"Yes."

The call lapsed into a prolonged silence, until Reed's breathing grew louder, coming in rough and harsh pants through the phone. If Dominic didn't know better…

"Reed?" he asked, eyes focusing on the screen of the phone.

"What?" Reed answered, his voice distinguishably thick with what Dominic knew was want.

"Are you…?"

Reed whimpered, and Dominic's cock throbbed against his leg. The sound Reed made was as clear to his ears now as it had been on Saturday morning just before Reed had come.

"Reed." He cleared his throat to infuse his voice with some level of command. Maybe if he could convince himself he was in control of whatever was happening between them, it would hurt less in the end.

"Nic," Reed moaned, the single syllable of his name falling off into a drawn-out sigh.

Dominic closed his eyes, taking the phone off speaker and

pressing it against his face with both hands so they had some-thing to do that wasn't reach down his pants.

"I'm sorry," Reed whispered.

A minute later, Dominic heard him start to cry. Dominic rubbed his eyes with his thumb and fingers, pulling away to find his skin wet with his own tears. He uttered a curse and took the phone away from his face. He moved onto his knees, dropping the phone onto the floor and balling over into a folded prayer position. He curled his arms around his legs and cried into the space made by his body, hoping it was enough to muffle it from Reed's ears.

His body jerked with sobs, and he sank his teeth into his forearm, hoping the pain would be enough to still his tears. All it did was make his cock harder. He reached blindly for the phone, bringing it back to his ear. Reed was near hysterical, hiccupping and gasping for breath on the other end of the line. Dominic swallowed, wanting to go to him, to comfort him in some way. If only he could promise they'd be okay, or at least that Reed would be okay. He'd worry about himself later.

"Reed," he whispered.

Reed cried again, a howl of anguished regret that caused gooseflesh to rise across Dominic's entire body.

Let me come to you.

Come to me.

I'll fix it.

I'll be there for you.

For this.

Us.

All the things Dominic was desperate to say collided on the tip of his tongue and he swallowed them down into the bitter pit of his stomach, instead choosing the words that hurt him the most because he knew they were the ones Reed needed.

"Please stop calling me, Reed."

Dominic ended the call and turned his phone off, then curled into a ball and cried himself to sleep on the floor.

HOURS LATER, he woke up, his head feeling as heavy as a freight train. He was almost positive he'd been hit by one and it was still jammed into his skull. That was the only explanation for why he felt like he'd been literally wrung dry.

He blinked, the room slowly focusing, and his eyes narrowed on his powered-down cell phone. He was smacked with a painful reminder of the last phone call he'd had, and he swatted at the phone with a frustrated cry, batting it under the couch.

Dominic tried to stand but found his legs weren't ready, so he chose to crawl to the bathroom, flinging his body over the edge of the tub to turn the taps on. He slumped against the wall, the same place Reed had slumped days before, and waited for the tub to fill.

He maneuvered his way over the edge of the basin, lowering himself into the steaming water. He winced, skin immediately reddening as he submerged himself. It hurt, his entire body feeling like he'd lowered himself into a pit of flames, but he forced it, gritting his teeth until he adjusted to the temperature.

He'd allow himself this and no more. One last hour to think of Reed. One last fantasy. One last wank. He rested his sore head against the inflatable bath pillow behind him and fisted his cock, working the tender skin of his shaft under the surface of the water. His motions made waves, and hot water lapped against the edge of the tub, against his chest, his throat, as his strokes grew shorter and rougher.

Dominic imagined a life where Reed hadn't been adopted, where he hadn't joined the clergy, where they'd traveled the country after high school graduation like they'd always planned.

His balls drew up against his body, the heat of the bath intensi-fying the shivers that worked their way across his skin.

This wasn't new. He'd done this before. Wiping Reed from his mind thirteen years ago, only to find that he'd worked his way back in to Dominic's daily thoughts, even into his prayers.

Dear Lord, please let me find him, please let him be happy, please let him love me.

Dear Lord, please take this love away from me, it's too much. I can't bear this burden anymore.

Dear Lord, loving him is fucking agony.

Dominic tightened his hand around the tip of his cock, orgasm building inside of him. He closed his eyes, Reed's voice still loud in his ears.

Nic, he'd rasped as he came.

Nic, he'd cried as he realized what he'd done.

Dominic arched, back lifting from the bathtub, orgasm at the ready. He uncurled his fingers from the rim of the tub and pinched the tip of his cock so hard he shouted in pain, his orgasm wilting and retreating.

He wept, pinching harder until he was sure the need to come had disappeared. Only then did he release his cock. He gripped the sides of the tub until his knuckles turned white, breath heavy with the remnants of his want and burgeoning regret.

He rested his eyes and his heart until the water grew cold, and by then, it was a new day.

NINE
REED

THE DOOR to Reed's office slammed open, and a disheveled-looking Catherine stormed inside. She threw her book bag down onto the floor and flung her body into one of Reed's guest chairs with so much force he was surprised it didn't topple. Her eyes were red-rimmed and her lashes were damp.

Susan appeared in the doorway, a worried look on her face. Reed held up a hand to stop her, and she closed the door quietly, leaving Reed and Catherine alone.

"To what do I owe this pleasure, Ms. Ollingham?" Reed asked, setting aside his notes for the commencement speech that he was set to deliver in less than an hour.

He was impressed he'd been able to focus on his words at all, having gone over twenty-four hours without talking to Nic again. Which, on its own, shouldn't have even been that impressive. He had, after all, existed twenty years without Nic, but now that he'd come back, he was like air.

Poisonous air.

Nic had asked him not to call anymore, and he hadn't so far.

She leveled a sharp look at him, her eyes filled with rage, then promptly burst into tears. Reed shifted awkwardly behind the desk, not wanting to go to Catherine, lest anyone walk in and think something untoward was happening between them.

"Do you want me to go get Mrs. Carson?" Reed asked, gesturing toward the door and referring to Susan by her surname. "Or maybe the nurse?"

"No," Catherine answered, after her sobbing had quieted into what Reed would describe as a hysterical whimper.

"Are you ready to talk about whatever is going on?"

"Will you tell my mom?" Catherine chewed on her thumbnail.

Reed pulled a tissue from the box on his desk and extended his arm toward her. Catherine took the tissue and wiped her face, balling it into her hand and holding it close to her chest when she was done.

"Only if I feel it's something she needs to know," Reed assured Catherine, worried by now she was going to harm herself or someone else.

"I bet you'll think she needs to know this," Catherine pouted.

Reed leaned back in his chair, crossing his arms over his chest, his ability to maintain his put-together facade dwindling with every minute he went without Nic's voice fresh in his mind. This was unacceptable.

"Try me," he proposed.

Catherine swallowed, eyes darting around the room before settling at an arbitrary point on Reed's desk.

"Mary Francis says I'm going to hell," she whispered.

"Why on earth would she say that?" Reed asked, affronted.

Catherine sobbed, biting the side of her fist between her braces-covered teeth. She looked up at Reed, her entire face painted with torment.

"I think I'm a lesbian," she finally said.

Reed's heart skipped, a breath lodging in his throat.

He uncrossed his arms and flattened his hands against the

top of his desk, one hand tapping nervously against his desk pad.

"You think?" he asked.

"I haven't done anything!" Catherine cried, jumping out of her chair.

Reed motioned for her to sit back down.

"I didn't accuse you of that," he said softly.

Catherine worried her lip between her teeth and slowly lowered herself back into the seat.

"All I meant," he continued, "is that you said you *think*. I was trying to understand why you think that."

What he didn't say was:

Is it because you met someone who makes your heart slam into your ribs?

Is it because you've cursed your God for not taking the lust from your life?

"I don't know." She shrugged. "Like, no one asks straight kids that. How do you know you're straight? I just know."

"Fair enough."

He scrubbed his hands over his face, taking a deep breath and schooling his features.

"I don't want to go to hell," Catherine whimpered. "It's not even fair. I can't help this. Why should I need to live a lie? Why does God even care who I love? Is it love my neighbors only if they're straight?"

"Catherine." Reed scratched the side of his face, interrupting her protestations. "Some of these questions may be better suited for confession."

Catherine rolled her eyes. "You know what Father Cowart will say."

Reed pursed his lips, well aware of what Father Cowart would say, which was precisely why he'd skipped confession last week, although against his better judgement.

"Have you prayed over it?"

"Of course," she huffed.

There were a thousand words jamming onto the tip of Reed's tongue, all of them about scripture and verse to aid her in her search for truth, then the biting rebuttal that sounded a lot like Nic, saying...

There's another way.

"There's other ways," Reed said, reflecting on the stockpile of scripture indicating he was lying.

"What?" Catherine asked, her head snapping up. She blinked at him, chin quivering.

"Do you think your parents would love you less if you were gay?" he asked.

"I think they would because God would," Catherine answered him, the words acidic in the air between them.

"I'm not sure I have advice for you, Catherine," Reed told her regretfully. Who was he to act as any sort of moral compass with the feel of Nic's tongue still hot against his lips?

"Of course not," she spat, her face morphing from guilt to petulance with the speed and agility only seen in teenage girls.

She stood, snatching her bag off the floor with a dramatic exhale and flurry of movement. She was inches from his door when he stopped her.

"Catherine." Her name left his mouth like a plea.

She stalled, turning on her heel to glare at him over his desk.

"What?" she bit out caustically, her backpack half over her shoulder and her lips bared in a scowl.

"Maybe talk to Father O'Halloran." He forced the words out, and Nic's name scraped over his tongue like it was barbed. He winced.

"What?" She squinted at him doubtfully.

Reed lowered his voice, fisting his hands together beneath his desk.

"At St. Paul's," he amended.

Catherine searched his face, trying to see if his suggestion was meant to trap her. Reed forced his hands to relax and he held them above the desk, indicating he meant no harm. He hoped she couldn't see the divots his fingernails left in the flesh of his palms.

"See what he has to say about it," Reed suggested.

Catherine's glare softened in the slightest and she nodded, disappearing out of his office much quieter than she'd entered. Reed sat frozen behind his desk, his knee shaking out a nervous and violent beat under his desk.

"Everything alright in here?" Susan asked, poking her face inside.

Reed used one hand to push his jumpy foot into the floor and the other to pick up the pen he'd been using before Catherine's grand entrance.

"Of course," he assured her. "Catherine was just having a bad day."

"Very well then," Susan said with a small nod of her head.

"Are you going to be on campus until commencement?" Reed asked, desperate for a moment of peace.

"I was going to run home for a bit, but I'll be back before five. Is that alright?" Susan patted at the back of her French twist with a manicured hand.

"Of course," Reed answered, the relief in his voice evident even to his own ears.

Susan exited, closing the door behind her. Reed's entire body collapsed, like his muscles had given up the ability to support his bones. He slumped in his chair, rolling backward then leaning forward to rest his face in his hands. He listened to Susan bang around at her desk, then the familiar clack of her kitten heels as she left the office.

Reed's phone sat on his desk, and he regarded it warily, trying to ignore the number he wanted to call most of all as he scrolled to the contact he was looking for.

"Reed. What a surprise." Margaret answered the phone with a delicate laugh.

"Are you busy?" he asked reflexively. "I can let you go."

"Don't be silly. I'm here, and bingo doesn't start for an hour. What do you need?"

Reed huffed out a small laugh at the ease of his adopted mother's retired life.

"One of the students just came to my office," he told her.

"Is everything alright?" Margaret asked, maternal worry infusing her question.

"Yeah. Well, no. I mean. I don't know." Reed sighed.

"Did you want to talk about it?"

Reed rubbed at the crucifix around his neck.

"I don't know," he whispered, feeling very much like the scared child he'd been the first time Margaret had asked him that question.

It had been two days after he'd moved in with her and James, and Reed thought he would die for the way he missed Nic. His bones hurt and he didn't even want to get out of bed. Nic had been so excited Reed was going to have a family, but in hindsight, Reed would have taken foster care if it would have kept him with his best friend—even though he'd known his relationship with Nic was more than something that simple.

"Did you want to try?" she asked him, another echo from the past.

"Catherine is worried she's going to hell because she thinks she's gay," Reed finally managed to tell her.

"Sweet child. Did you tell her not to be ridiculous?"

"What?" Reed sputtered, spit catching in his mouth.

"Reed," she chided. "Don't you think that's an antiquated way of interpreting the scripture?"

"Not according to the Pope," he protested.

"Do you really think our Lord would forgive a murderer, but not a homosexual?" she asked.

"That sounds like something Nic would say," Reed said.

"Hmmn."

"What?" he asked sharply.

"Nothing, dear," she answered with a small laugh.

"No, tell me!"

"I just haven't heard that name in a very long time."

"He lives here," Reed grumbled, sounding as petulant as Catherine had earlier.

"Lives in Edgewood?"

"Yeah. I saw him a few days ago." Reed closed his eyes, the memory of Nic's angular back seared into his mind. A memory he never asked for and didn't want.

"Have you seen him again?"

"Yeah," he admitted.

"How did that go?" she pushed, in that maternal way he was all too familiar with.

"What are you really trying to ask me?" he ground out.

"I just…" Margaret sighed. "Oh, dear…"

"Margaret."

"Did anything happen between you and Nic when you were children?"

"Happen how?" he rasped.

She sighed. Loudly. She sounded annoyed. All in her motherly way, of course. "James and I always felt like there had been something more than friendship between the two of you. You were so invested in your relationship with him. We never asked you about it, but you're an adult now, and it seems like it's a conversation we can have."

"Something more," Reed repeated.

"Yes, dear."

"Are you asking me…" Reed couldn't even voice the question he thought Margaret was trying to ask him.

"I'm just wondering if you think you may be in a position to help Catherine navigate the feelings she's having."

Well, that was artful avoidance at his best, on both of their parts.

"I suggested she speak with someone," Reed answered.

"A priest?"

"Sort of," Reed said, a puff of judgement in his voice. "Nic is a priest."

"Ohhhh," Margaret whispered. "Is he at Our Lady now? With you?"

Reed barked out a laugh. "No. He's at St. Paul's across town."

"Isn't that interesting."

"Is it?" he countered.

"So, you suggested this Catherine girl go seek out the advice of someone who wasn't Catholic?"

"Yes," Reed answered through gritted teeth.

"Why would you send her there and not to Father Cowart?" Margaret asked the question even though she already knew the answer. Reed could hear the prodding certainty in her voice, even as he swallowed the truth back into his gut.

"You know what he'd say."

"I do," Margaret hummed thoughtfully. "And you must not agree with him if you've sent the girl across town."

"Nic has a more… open minded way of looking at things like that.".

"Mmmn," Margaret agreed. "I'm sure he does."

TEN

DOMINIC

DOMINIC NARROWED his eyes at the clock on the wall opposite his desk. It was nearly four in the evening, and only three minutes away from the end of his office hours for the day. He was looking forward to the sandwich he was going to make himself for dinner as soon as he returned to the parsonage and changed into something less starchy than he was currently wearing.

He barely heard the knock on his door, instead looking up when he heard the doorknob turn. A face he didn't recognize popped through the cracked open door, her eyes nervous.

"Come in," Dominic greeted her, standing from his desk and smoothing a hand down the buttons of his shirt.

The visitor took a tentative step into his office, not opening the door any wider than needed to squish her tiny body inside. Dominic sighed, still not recognizing the face, but familiar with the plaid of the girl's skirt, having seen it around town daily since he'd moved.

"I think you've found yourself the wrong priest," he teased, taking a seat on the couch that sat under his office window. He patted the cushion, encouraging the girl to come sit with him.

She stumbled through his office, sitting awkwardly against the arm of the couch. She flicked her attention to Dominic, then around his office, finally settling it on the hem of her skirt.

"Does it look familiar?" he asked her, wondering how much his office looked like that of Father Cowart at Our Lady of the Mount.

"Less crosses," she whispered, darting her eyes back up to Dominic's face. "Less agony."

Dominic chuckled. "That is a favorite of the Catholic church."

"Not your church?"

"We're not as stringent," he admitted.

"I talked to Mr. Matthews today and he said I should come see you."

Dominic tried to school his surprise.

"Do you know him?" the girl asked, looking up. Dominic realized her lashes were wet, her eyes red, and it looked like she had been crying.

"We're old friends," Dominic told her, folding his hands together in his lap. "But I don't know who you are. Can you tell me your name?"

The girl paled.

"You're not gonna tell my mom, are you?"

"Cross my heart," Dominic assured her, drawing an X over the left side of his chest.

"Catherine Ollingham."

"Hi, Catherine. I'm Dominic."

Catherine's eyes flitted around the room again. "Mr. Matthews called you Father O'Halloran."

"That's me," Dominic said with a nod. "Father Dominic O'Halloran. You can call me whatever you're most comfortable with. I'm not your priest, so I wouldn't expect that level of formality."

"It's respectful, though," she whispered.

"Again, Catherine. Whatever makes you most comfortable. It doesn't matter to me. What does matter is what's brought you across town. Did you want to talk?"

"I'm gay," Catherine blurted, her hands flying to her face and covering her lips. Her eyes widened and filled with fresh tears.

"So am I," Dominic assured her with a friendly smile.

A tear slid down her face, and she squeezed her eyes closed.

"I bet it's scary to know something like that about yourself and to know how it conflicts with the beliefs of your church."

She nodded.

Dominic tried to figure out what counsel to give Catherine, but he was also trying to figure out what had possessed Reed to send her to him in the first place. Reed had made it painfully clear to him with his actions and with his silence that his views on the church's acceptance of his sexuality was still an issue. Or rather, and maybe even worse, Reed still insisted he *wasn't* gay.

"It's not an easy thing," he told Catherine, unfolding his hands and holding his palms up like a scale. "You're raised thinking things are one way, but when you realize you may be the other way, it hurts. You're probably angry with yourself, and scared, too."

"Mary Frances says I'm going to hell," Catherine mumbled, swiping at her eyes.

"Well, I know my God isn't going to be the one who sends you there. I know that may be hard to believe, but I don't interpret the Word to say love your neighbor unless he's gay. Care for those less fortunate than you unless they're gay. God made us in his image, and his image is so unfathomably complex, it's ill-advised for us to think that he doesn't exist in all of us somehow."

Catherine looked doubtful.

"I'm gay," Dominic repeated. "And my church doesn't just *allow* me to be here. They've accepted me not only to worship but to lead the congregation and assume responsibility for their spiritual welfare. Do you think they'd allow that if my existence alone was cause for damnation?"

"No," she whispered, fidgeting with the hem of her skirt.

"Do you want to talk more?" he asked, getting the feeling that Catherine was dubious of his confession.

"Not right now," she answered.

"My door is always open. I imagine you can't join us on Sunday, but we have a movie night on Friday if you ever want to come. Everyone would love to have you. There's actually a couple members of the congregation who are gay that have been talking about starting an LGBT youth group. I'm sure they'd be willing to speak with you about it if you find them less daunting."

A smile flickered across Catherine's face, and she nodded. "I'd like that. Thank you, Father O'Halloran."

Catherine stood up and smoothed her skirt down, her eyes looking calmer than when she'd arrived at his office. Dominic followed her to the door, stopping while she adjusted the straps of her backpack.

"I'm serious, Catherine. If you ever need to talk to someone, I'm here, and I'm sure Mr. Matthews will be also."

"Thank you," she repeated, before tucking her chin against her chest and disappearing down the hallway.

Dominic closed the door behind her and took a deep breath. What on earth had happened to Reed that would have found him sending one of his students—who was obviously extremely Catholic—to him for guidance? That was probably the last thing Dominic had ever expected to happen, and he didn't know what it meant, but he actively fought the bubble of hope that was building in his stomach.

He had the idea to call Reed and see what was going on, but he stopped himself, remembering the last phone call they'd had and his own request that Reed not call him again. It wouldn't be right for him to be the one to reach out for something as trivial as this.

It was well after six by the time he pulled himself together and began the short walk to the parsonage. He'd spent longer in his office than he'd intended, staring at the wall while the light turned from blue, to purple, to red, then a bright gray after the sun had set. His stomach grumbling was the only other indication of how long he'd sat. He couldn't even remember what he'd thought about for the past two hours.

Dominic's breath caught in his throat when he reached his front door, finding Reed there in a crisp navy blue suit and tie that was the same plaid as Catherine's skirt. He was resting with his back against Dominic's front door, legs crossed at the ankle and arms folded over his chest.

"Aren't you worried the neighbors will see?" Dominic asked, pushing Reed to the side and unlocking the door. He stepped inside, leaving space for Reed to follow if he wanted. Dominic cursed himself all the way to the kitchen, listening to Reed's footfalls behind him.

"I'm pretty sure everyone is at the graduation party," Reed answered.

"Is that today?" Dominic opened his refrigerator and pulled out the supplies for his sandwich. It seemed far less appetizing now that Reed was filling his space.

"It is."

"Shouldn't you be there?" Dominic slathered two slices of bread with mustard. He hesitated before taking two more slices of bread out of the bag and dropping them onto the counter, leaving them plain.

"I was."

"And now?" Dominic folded slices of roast beef onto all four slices of bread, adding provolone cheese before closing them up. He shoved a plate toward Reed.

"Now I'm here," Reed whispered. He pulled the plate closer to him. "I don't like provolone."

Dominic took a bite of his sandwich, studying Reed's face while he chewed and swallowed. "You used to. But believe me, Reed, you don't need to eat it. What you do need to do, though, is tell me why you're here."

Reed winced and picked up his sandwich, taking a bite and chewing thoughtfully. After he swallowed, he answered, "You told me not to call you."

"I didn't mean show up at my house instead. I meant I didn't want to talk to you at all anymore."

"I deserve that." Reed looked away.

Dominic clenched his jaw, gazing longingly at his overdue dinner before dropping it onto the plate.

"Why did you send Catherine to see me?" He asked the question that had been burning a hole in his chest for the past three hours.

"She needed guidance."

"Don't you work at a church?"

Reed scoffed and angled a glare in Dominic's direction. "So do you."

"Yeah, well, we seem to have different beliefs." Dominic sighed. "I don't want to do this with you, Reed. I won't debate theology with you and how it applies or doesn't apply to who I choose to bed. Or who *you* choose to bed, for that matter."

"So, that's just it then?" Reed drummed his fingers across the countertop, his entire body exuding a nervousness that was so painful, Dominic nearly felt it in his own bones.

"What should it be, if not that?"

Dominic dropped his plate into the sink, sandwich still on top, and left the kitchen, retreating toward his bedroom. He worked his collar loose and popped open the button of his shirt, pulling the tails free by the time he'd reached the door. He kicked off his shoes, using his feet to propel them into his closet, and he loosened his belt, whipping it off.

He heard Reed suck in a breath, and Dominic turned to find Reed standing in the doorway to his bedroom, his eyes trained on Dominic's belt. His nostrils flared.

"What?" Dominic asked, throwing his belt on top of his dresser.

Reed's eyes followed it, even as he hesitated to enter the bedroom.

"What did you tell Catherine?" Reed asked.

"I told her my God doesn't care who I fuck." Dominic discarded his shirt into the hamper, leaving him bare-chested with his slacks undone.

Reed's eyes widened.

"In more appropriate terms," he amended. "But the sentiment stands."

"No penance?" Reed rested the side of his head against the door frame, eyes trailing down Dominic's exposed chest before moving back to the dresser and landing on his belt.

Dominic's dick throbbed—fucking *throbbed*—in his pants. He held up a hand.

"Don't," he warned, turning his back on Reed.

"Don't what?" Reed asked, his voice closer.

Dominic braced his hands on his hips and tilted his head backward to stare at his ceiling. Much to his dismay, there were no answers there. Reed's breath ghosted across his shoulder blade, and he turned sharply, reaching behind him to wipe at his skin. Reed was so close now they were almost touching.

"Don't what?" Reed asked again.

"This," Dominic answered through gritted teeth. "It's selfish of you."

"What?" Reed reeled back in shock.

"I have feelings too, Reed. And you're fucking with them."

"I didn't…" Reed stuttered. "I don't—I didn't mean—"

Dominic held up a hand again.

"Don't get me wrong. I want you. I want *this*. But I'm not going to be a tester for you so you can try how damnation feels."

"So you admit it's a sin," Reed accused.

"You think it's a sin. I don't. Don't put words into my mouth to assuage your own guilt, Reed. I won't abide that." Dominic took a step backward and fastened the button of his slacks. He yanked open a dresser drawer and pulled out an undershirt, throwing it on over his head.

"I don't know what I'm doing," Reed mumbled, working his hands through his hair, messing up the perfectly coiffed style it had been set in. He dropped his hands to his sides and blinked up at Dominic, his brown eyes pained.

Dominic took a deep and steadying breath, trying to separate himself from the moment, to pretend it wasn't Reed in front of him—in his bedroom. If it was Catherine here, or a member of his congregation, still conflicted and hurting over their inability to reconcile two important parts of themselves into a whole, what would he do? What would he say?

He searched his soul for answers, coming up with a handful that didn't truly matter, because at the end of the day it *was* Reed, it would always be Reed, and that was the heart of the problem.

ELEVEN

REED

REED COULDN'T TELL if Dominic wanted to screw him or murder him. Even worse, he didn't know which would be the better option; both of them would put him out of his misery, although one much more effectively than the other. After he'd spoken with Margaret, he'd tried to find an answer to her question about why he'd sent Catherine to Nic and not Father Cowart, and even though once he found it he wanted to ignore it, he couldn't.

That was how he found himself at Nic's house after commencement. How he found himself now in Nic's bedroom.

With Nic.

"We need to get out of here." Nic pushed Reed out of the bedroom and closed the door behind him. He retreated back to the kitchen, reaching into the sink and taking a bite of his sandwich.

Reed opened his sandwich and picked off the slice of cheese, then placed the bread back together and took another bite. They both chewed in silence, Reed thinking about why he'd come to Nic's in the first place, and Nic thinking about who knew what.

"Why are you here?" Nic asked after swallowing the last bite. His face made it clear he wasn't in the mood for nonsense, looking like being in Reed's presence was torture.

The answer was simple, but also so complicated.

While he knew his actions thus far had been hurtful to Nic, he'd never intended for that. It wasn't fair to Nic that Reed burden him with this confusion and this fear, this guilt, but he felt better around Nic. And he didn't understand how, or why. He only wanted to make sense of the battle raging inside of him.

"I just want to be with you," he admitted.

Dominic sighed. "It's not that simple for you though, is it?"

Reed shook his head and turned his back, resting his butt against the edge of the kitchen counter. Nic reached out and touched him, his hand flat against the center of Reed's spine. Reed startled and turned so fast, Nic's hand didn't move, landing flat against Reed's chest and his pounding heart. Nic flexed his fingers against Reed's chest. He tugged at his tie and his shirt. Reed closed his eyes and swallowed.

"Why can't it be?" he rasped.

"That's up to you."

Reed blinked up at the ceiling, the fluorescent of Nic's kitchen lights hurting his eyes.

"Have you prayed over it?" Nic asked.

"Of course."

"Have your prayers been answered?"

Nic's palm pressed harder against Reed's chest, fingers circling around his tie and pulling it gently when Reed didn't answer.

"No," Reed admitted. He'd been hoping for a sign, some sort of way to clear Nic out of his heart and mind, but it hadn't been presented, and so he found himself here again.

"Hmmn. Are you sure? Or have you just not been given the answer you were expecting?"

Reed snapped his chin toward his chest, eyes focusing on Nic and widening.

"What does that mean?"

Nic tugged his tie again, then laid it flat against his chest, smoothing it down with a steady hand.

"It means God always listens and always answers, but he does it in his own way. Have you been ignoring his message? Denying it?" Nic's voice was gruff, and it abraded Reed's ears.

"I thought you weren't going to preach to me," Reed countered, shoving Nic's hand off his chest.

"Fuck," Nic grumbled, storming out of the room. Reed listened to him move down the hall, his footsteps growing quieter until the stillness of the house was shattered by the slamming of what Reed assumed was Nic's bedroom door.

This was stupid.

Margaret's voice echoed in his ears. *"We always thought there was something more..."*

Had there been more? All Reed knew was he'd never felt this way about anyone else. Whenever he was around Nic, he felt like he wanted to crawl out of his skin; like his bones were too big, too awkward. Even back in high school, after he'd been adopted, no one had ever caught his eye. Margaret and James had hoped he'd develop feelings for any of the various daughters of their friends, but it hadn't ever happened. He'd appreciated them all as friends, of course, but there hadn't been a spark.

He'd always told himself he was waiting for the right person. After all, it wasn't like men turned him on back then, either. There was no baseball player or marching band member who'd ever held his attention. Reed had just existed, somehow void of all the sexual urges everyone around was exhibiting.

The last and only time he'd felt the slightest bit of sexual interest in anyone had been with Nic, and even then, it was too new, too young for him to make sense of. Nic was his friend. His best friend. They were in foster care and they'd formed a bond. It was normal to search out that affection, to miss it after it was taken away.

Wasn't it?

Reed scrubbed his hands over his face and groaned, looking around Nic's kitchen. There were no answers there, just two dirty plates. He turned the tap on and waited for the water to warm up, then soaped up a green and yellow dish sponge and washed them both. He rinsed them and slipped them into the dryer rack. He dried his hands on a dish towel that hung on the stove, then took another deep breath.

Down the hall, a door opened and closed, then another one opened. Reed backed out of the kitchen and followed the sound, all while loosening the knot on his tie. His clothes felt too constricting, and he wasn't sure he wasn't going to choke on his own spit.

Steam from a finished shower wafted out of the bathroom door, filling the hall with the scent of what he recognized to be Nic's soap. The bedroom door was open, and Reed listened to him slam around inside for a minute or two before his broad body filled the door frame. His hair was damp, hanging across his forehead and dripping down the sides of his face. He raised a towel to his head to dry his hair, then tossed it over his shoulder back into the bedroom.

Nic shifted his weight onto one side, leaning against the door, much like Reed had done earlier. He was dressed in black sweats and a white undershirt, his face marred with disdain. He stood silently, obviously waiting for Reed to do something.

"I've never..." he started to say, but stopped, the words catching in his throat.

Nic inclined his head and pursed his lips.

"I don't understand the way I feel around you," Reed admitted, looking away from Nic and staring at the floor.

"Would it help you if I articulated the way I feel around *you*?"

"Probably not."

"Fair enough." Nic huffed out a laugh.

"Would you anyway?" Reed looked up and caught Nic's stare.

"Are you sure?"

Reed nodded and shoved his hands into his pockets.

"I saw the way you looked at my belt earlier," Nic said, pushing off the door and taking a step toward him. "Not only do you want me to fuck you, but you want me to hurt you, and you don't know how to make sense of any of it."

"That doesn't sound like it has anything to do with how you feel," Reed rasped, clearing his throat and taking a step backward.

"No." Nic took another step. "But I do want to do all of those things to you. Hurt you for the way you're hurting me right now, then lick your wounds until you're mindless with want for me."

Reed tripped over his own feet. Nic's hand flew out, grabbing Reed by the jacket and pulling him forward. Their chests slammed into each other, and Reed gasped, the scent and the closeness of Dominic filling his nose. He sucked in a breath and shoved his face against Nic's chest, inhaling deeply.

Nic's arms circled him, holding him close. He kissed the top of Reed's head and turned his face, resting his cheek against his hair.

"But I won't," he said, sadly.

"What?" Reed pulled back and looked up so he could see Nic's face.

Nic slid a hand around his body, raising it slowly, as though to make sure Reed was aware of it. When he didn't flinch or shy away, Nic swiped his thumb across the arch of Reed's cheekbone.

"Consent isn't stopping when you're told no. It's not starting unless you're told yes," Nic whispered. The words settled like an unbearable weight on his shoulders. Nic was going to make him say it, and he wasn't sure if he could.

"I don't know what to say."

"I know," Nic agreed, putting space between them. "And that means it's not yes."

"Do you want me to go?" Reed looked over his shoulder toward the living room, suddenly unable or unwilling to meet Nic's heavy stare head on.

"You can stay if you want," Nic answered. "I was just going to watch a movie."

He shrugged and sidestepped Reed and walked into the living room. Nic dropped onto the couch with a huff and turned on the T.V. Reed shuffled after him, taking a seat on the other end of the couch. Nic cast him a sideways glance.

"Take your jacket off, Reed. I said you can stay, and I think I've made it clear that I'm not going to put the moves on you." Nic returned his attention to the flat screen and scrolled through the channel guide.

Reed shrugged out of his jacket and hung it over the back of the couch, taking a seat again beside Nic.

"Shoes?" Nic asked, angling a glance at Reed's feet.

Reed looked to his side, noticing for the first time that Nic's feet were bare. His toes, long and slender, were paler than the rest of his body. He looked away and kicked his shoes off, using his feet to arrange them to the side of the couch where they were out of his way.

He looked at the television and watched the opening credits for a movie he didn't recognize.

"What are we watching?" he asked.

"I don't know. I just put something on. I don't think I can concentrate on it anyway," Nic answered honestly.

"Oh."

They sat in silence, pretending to pay attention to the movie for the first half an hour. Reed's mind was racing a mile a minute, thinking about the way Nic smelled, the way his hands felt against Reed's back, the things they'd done last weekend… the way they'd cried on the phone.

"Is it lonely?" Nic asked him out of nowhere.

Reed turned to face him, met instead with the sharp lines of Nic's profile. He was staring at the T.V., the lights and shadows dancing across his face.

"Is what lonely?"

"Your life." Nic turned to face him.

"I…" Reed licked his lips. "Yes."

"Do you have friends?" Nic asked. Reed's first instinct was to be affronted, but he could see in Nic's face he hadn't meant it maliciously.

"No," he admitted with a small shake of his head. "Not really. I mean, church friends I guess."

"Are those not real friends?" Nic turned his body so he was angled toward Reed.

"No." Reed looked away. "Do you consider your parishioners your friends?"

Nic smiled. "Some of them."

"I don't even know how to make friends," Reed said with a weak laugh.

"Well, you start by being more approachable. Maybe eating some cheese on your sandwiches for one."

"Cheese isn't going to make me friends."

Nic's lips angled into a smile. "Cheese makes everyone friends."

"Whatever," Reed grumbled, turning his attention back to the movie.

"What do you do for fun?" Nic asked him a few minutes later.

Reed opened his mouth to reply, turning to face Nic on the couch. He closed his mouth, and Nic smiled at him knowingly.

"You should try it sometime," Nic said.

"Try what?"

"Having fun."

"How do you propose I do that?" Reed asked, crossing his arms over his chest and resting his head on the back of the couch.

"Same way you make friends."

"What? Cheese?"

Nic chuckled. "By loosening up. Trying new things."

"Are you a new thing?" he asked, no longer able to skirt around the tension between the two of them. He didn't know what had inspired him to speak up now, but something about the way Nic was just being so nice to him rubbed him uncomfortably. Why was Nic being this way when he'd just admitted earlier that Reed had hurt him—that Reed *was actively* hurting him?

"I could be." Nic arched an eyebrow.

The room was so dark. The sun had long ago set, and the movie was barely casting shadows across the room now. Reed could see the outline of Nic's face, of his shoulders, his hands, resting against the tops of his legs. Everything about Nic made Reed ache. He closed his eyes and said a silent prayer, reflecting on Nic's earlier words about looking for the answer he received, not the one he wanted to receive.

Reed opened his eyes and found Nic staring at him, his blue eyes studying Reed's face with a look that could only be described as interested worry.

"Would you let me kiss you?" Reed asked, voice barely louder than a whisper. Even as the words left his mouth, they terrified him. His palms were clammy, and every muscle in his body was wound tight with the growing tension.

"Yes," Nic answered, not moving from his position on the couch.

Reed muttered under his breath and closed the space between them before he could think better of it, pressing their lips together. Nic gasped in shock, like he hadn't really expected Reed to do it, then his body relaxed, his head tilting to the side so their lips could slot together like puzzle pieces.

Nic tasted like toothpaste, and he opened his mouth in the slightest, his tongue resting just behind his lips, waiting for Reed to make a move.

"Help me," Reed begged against Nic's mouth, desperate for Nic to take control of more than just this moment.

Nic's hand cradled the back of Reed's head and his tongue slipped out, sliding against the seam of Reed's mouth, encouraging him to open. He did, lips falling apart with a sigh, and Nic took him, then, licking into Reed's mouth with passionate abandon. Reed returned the kiss, his tongue exploring eagerly, his entire body pulled closer to Nic's by the sheer strength of his want.

When their chests collided, Nic pushed him backward, their bodies tumbling to the couch. Nic's erection pressed urgently against Reed's hip, and he fought the panic he felt bubbling inside of him. Reed froze. Nic broke the kiss, panting heavily, and he searched Reed's face.

"What happened just now?" he asked, putting space between them.

Reed's dick was hard, pressing at the confines of his slacks, and he palmed himself, adjusting his growing length.

"I started to think," Reed admitted. He threw an arm over his face.

"That was too much," Nic said, standing up from the couch, his own erection evident in the crotch of his sweats. "I'll be right back. I'm sorry."

Nic disappeared down the hallway. Reed assumed he was going to rub one out in the bathroom, either that or curse Reed straight to Hell. Reed couldn't handle either option. When the bathroom door clicked closed, Reed shoved his feet into his shoes, grabbed his jacket from the couch, and fled.

TWELVE

DOMINIC

IN THE BATHROOM, Dominic turned on the cold water and splashed his face, then wiped his hands dry. He braced himself against the counter with one hand and shoved his other hand down his pants, circling the base of his cock and giving a rough tug down his length to the tip.

It hurt, the pleasure arcing through his entire body like a firework, and he debated jerking off to get his erection under control before returning to the living room. He didn't expect Reed to be there when he got done to help him out with it, but he still didn't want to do it on his own. It would have been empty anyway.

Reed was the one who was in his home, still poking in him like his heart didn't mean anything. Reed was the one with the battle about his sexuality. Dominic wasn't going to give himself a shitty orgasm just to make things easier for Reed.

When Dominic emerged from the bathroom, he found Reed sitting on the edge of the couch closest to the door, his shoes and jacket on.

"You leaving?" Dominic asked.

Reed turned around, eyes searching his face before resting

on the bulge between Dominic's legs. Dominic pulled his lips between his teeth, lingering in the hallway.

"I left," Reed admitted.

"Looks like you're here."

"I came back."

"Listen," Dominic said, running a hand through his hair and glancing over his shoulder toward his bedroom. "I'll be honest. I've loved you my entire life, Reed, but I meant what I said before. I can't keep doing this with you. So either come to bed with me or leave."

Dominic shrugged and turned on his heel, padding softly toward his bedroom. He turned off the lights as he passed the threshold and crawled into bed. He flopped onto his stomach, grinding his hard cock into the mattress with an unsatisfied groan. He thought about Reed sitting on his couch, looking like a scared child, and his erection flagged. Dominic lay awake as long as he could, waiting to hear the sound of his front door opening and closing, signaling Reed's departure, but it didn't come.

Dominic fell asleep only to find himself startled awake by movement in his bed.

"It's me," Reed whispered, adjusting the covers.

Dominic tensed, his mind cloudy with sleep and memories of Reed climbing into his bed years prior. "What do you want?"

"You told me to stay or go. So I stayed."

Dominic rolled over and propped himself up on his elbow. Reed had stripped, at least partially, the tan glow of his shoulder and chest peeking out from beneath Nic's white sheets.

"I want…" Reed trailed off. "I want to kiss you."

"Then kiss me," Dominic answered, unwilling to make the move and close the distance. He'd meant what he said. It had to be Reed this time. He couldn't keep this up.

Reed lurched forward, his lips slamming into Dominic's with surprising force. Dominic's mouth parted, and Reed's tongue was there, filling the space. Reed moaned, and the sound set Dominic's body on fire. Dominic rolled, pushing Reed onto his back and pressing their chests together.

He snaked a hand under Reed's head and cradled him, his fingers tangling through the softness of Reed's hair. He shifted his face to the side and slanted their mouths together, exploring Reed's for only the third time in his life. After as many times as he'd fantasized about it, the real thing was so much better than pretend.

Reed moaned, arching up, his erection pressing against Dominic's through the cotton of his pajamas.

"Are you naked?" Dominic mumbled into Reed's mouth, changing the angle of his lips and diving back into another heated kiss.

"Underwear," Reed answered, grabbing the sides of Dominic's face and holding him steady.

"Fuck." Dominic shook himself free of Reed's hold, burying his face into the crook of Reed's neck and lapping his tongue over his throbbing pulse points, pressing wet kisses against his skin.

"It feels so good," Reed panted. "You feel so good."

"How are you here?" Dominic kissed his way down Reed's collarbone, down his sternum, sinking his teeth into one of Reed's pebbled nipples.

"Ow! Oh. Ohhhh." Reed groaned and raised his arms, burying his fingers into the back of Dominic's hair and pulling.

This was almost too good to be true. Dominic didn't trust it. Even as his cock leaked a wet spot against the crotch of his sweats and rubbed against Reed's, he couldn't enjoy it the way he wanted to because he wasn't convinced it was real. He stopped his descent, resting his forehead against Reed's rapidly-beating heart.

"Why did you stop?" Reed asked, his hands sliding lightly down Dominic's back and up his ribs. There was something familiar about the touch, while being the most foreign thing he'd ever felt.

Dominic rolled off of Reed and onto his back, flinging an arm over his face and sighing. The mattress shifted as Reed turned to face him. Reed's fingers wrapped around Dominic's arm and pulled it away from his face.

"Why did you stop?" he repeated.

Dominic scoffed. "The first time I saw you after twenty years, you ran away from me, then went home and had to get drunk to call me. Even after that, I wanted you so much. I begged you to *pretend* so you would kiss me. Fucking pretend. And you did. And you came. And then you ran away *again*. And you kept calling me, Reed, and *fuck*. You show up here again and freak out when our dicks touched, then you crawl in my bed and tell me you want to kiss me? I can't get a read on you."

"That makes me sound like a bit of an asshole."

"Yeah, well. You are." Dominic scrubbed his hands over his face.

"I don't mean to be," Reed whispered.

"I know."

"I'm in a bit over my head."

"You're not even the one trying to sleep with a straight guy." Dominic threw the covers back and got out of bed, striding down the hallway into the kitchen. He made himself a cup of coffee in the Keurig, deciding it was a better plan than cracking open the whiskey.

Reed followed a minute later, joining Dominic at the kitchen counter. Dominic passed him the steaming mug of coffee and folded his arms over his chest.

"I know that I want you," Reed said quietly, taking a sip of coffee and passing it back to Dominic. "But that comes with implications that I haven't processed yet."

"Catholic guilt," Dominic lamented, setting the mug on the counter between them.

Reed made a disagreeable noise in the back of his throat.

"To start with." Reed turned and rested his forehead on Dominic's kitchen counter. His shoulders quaked, and he gripped the edge of the countertop so tight his knuckles had turned white.

Dominic settled his palm on the base of Reed's spine, just above the elastic waistband of his tight black briefs. Fuck, those things were almost indecent. Reed's skin was clammy and peppered with gooseflesh, but he didn't shy away from Dominic's touch.

"I could lose my job, the respect of the parents at school… at church." Reed's voice was muffled by the position of his body.

"You could," Dominic agreed. "And you could get a new job."

"And a new soul?" Reed hissed, pushing up from his bent position and leveling a sharp glare in Dominic's direction.

Dominic closed his eyes and took his hand away, fisting it behind his back. He clenched his jaw and stormed out of the room, finding Reed's clothes folded neatly on the couch. He collected them in his arms, along with Reed's shoes, and marched back to the kitchen. Dominic shoved everything into Reed's chest, and backed him into the pantry.

"Go," he growled, shouldering Reed against the pantry door.

"What?" Reed blinked up at him, eyes confused.

"Go," he repeated, stepping back and putting space between them. "I told you! I told you I couldn't do this with you. I told you not to come into my home and do this to me, but you did it anyway. I'm done, Reed."

Dominic left the kitchen, stalking through the house and yanking the front door open. He held it wide open, gaze focused on the kitchen until Reed appeared, dressed, but not put together. His shirt wasn't tucked in, his tie wasn't knotted, and his jacket was flung over his arm. He shuffled to where Dominic stood, before stopping in the doorway and looking up at him with sad eyes.

"Nic."

Dominic held up his hand to stop Reed from talking.

"I get it, Reed, I do. I have a handful of former congregants from your church that sit in my pews every Sunday. I've witnessed the struggle first hand."

"You haven't lived it," Reed protested.

Dominic surged forward and grabbed Reed's chin between his thumb and finger, jerking his face up.

"Do you think I'm going to Hell?"

"No. I mean, I don't know. I hope not."

"I know what you need," Dominic sighed.

"You?" Reed asked hopefully.

"That shouldn't be a question, and until it's not, this isn't where you need to be." Dominic walked Reed backward onto the porch until he was safely outside.

"What do I need, then?"

"You need a priest," Dominic told him sadly, then closed the door between them.

THIRTEEN
REED

THREE DAYS after he'd left Nic's house, Reed found himself at the last place he expected. He'd skipped his Friday takeout—in fact, he'd skipped most of everything since he'd stumbled home after Nic threw him out. He hadn't showered, hadn't shaved, hadn't done much of anything besides nurse down his emergency vodka and worry. He should have gone to confession, but he was terrified of facing Father Cowart, and even if he had gone, he wouldn't have known what to say.

I have feelings for men.

I kissed a man.

I came for him.

None of that would do, even if it was the truth.

That was how he found himself here, at Margaret's front door, on a Saturday morning. She still lived in Cherry Grove, over one-hundred miles out of Edgewood. He raised a hand and rubbed at his smooth cheeks, finding he'd been surprisingly fond of the stubble that had grown there. He wondered if he could have trimmed it into something presentable.

"Are you going to knock?" Margaret asked, opening the peephole to tease him.

"I was," he said, shifting his weight awkwardly.

The peephole closed and the door opened. Margaret stood on the other side of the screen, hair permed, dressed in a sharp pair of slacks and a floral blouse. Reed opened the screen and stepped inside.

"Were you going somewhere?" he asked her, making note of the purse strap over her shoulder.

"Reconciliation."

Reed swallowed. "I'll see you when you get back."

"Nonsense." She swatted at his chest and pushed him back out the door. "You can come too."

"I don't..."

"We have a new priest. Did I tell you?" Margaret closed and locked the door, then stepped off the porch and retreated down the driveway to her car.

"Let me drive," Reed offered, holding out his hand. Margaret dropped her keys into his waiting palm and smiled, coming to rest near the passenger side door of her Buick.

Reed clicked the unlock button and let her inside, only closing the door after she was securely tucked in and buckled. He walked around the hood to the driver's door, feeling like it was the longest journey he'd ever taken. With a hand braced on the handle, Reed closed his eyes and took a deep breath. He'd never been scared to go to confession before, but everything was different now.

"What happened to Father Duncan?" Reed backed out of the driveway, doing his best to navigate Margaret's boat of a vehicle down the street without taking out any cars or pedestrians.

"He died."

"He what?" Reed turned to her, mouth agape.

"He was old, Reed. We all knew it was coming. Luckily, Father Morley was there to step in. I like him, and he has a lot of years left in him, too." Margaret patted her purse on her lap.

"He's young?"

Reed thought about Nic.

"Very," she agreed. "He's probably your age, maybe younger. He's like a breath of fresh air, and he's been so very kind to me."

"How so?"

Reed thought about Nic again.

"Well, after he found out I was alone, you know, without James, he came over to the house and brought me a casserole."

"He cooked for you?" Reed glanced at her from the corner of his eye. "And you're not alone. You have me."

"I do. But you're not here, are you?"

Reed thought about Nic... again.

Thought about Edgewood, and the two hours he'd put between himself and the man who was driving him to uncontrollable thoughts of lust and sin.

"I can come see you more. I will," he said.

"Don't be silly. You're an adult, and you have your own life now, Reed."

"I have the life I have because of you," he reminded her.

She smiled and patted his hand on the steering wheel.

"James and I just always tried to do what we thought was best." Her voice sounded tinged with something Reed interpreted as sad regret. He opened his mouth to ask about it, but she continued, "So, how are things with Nic?"

"What do you mean?" he choked.

"You told me he was in town. Have you seen him recently?"

"A few days ago."

"Is there... Is there anything you want to tell me?"

Reed chewed on the inside of his cheek and pulled into the church parking lot, finding a spot near the front and cutting the ignition. He stepped out of the car and jogged around to Margaret's side, opening her door and helping her out.

"Reed," she said, her voice as soothing as ever.

Once she was out of the car, he released her arm and rubbed at his chest, feeling the buttons of his shirt and the crucifix beneath. It rested cold against his skin. At the entrance to the church, he waited behind Margaret, then crossed himself with holy water and followed her inside.

"There's hardly anyone waiting," he observed, finding the pews empty.

"Well," Margaret sighed, "I said *I* liked Father Morley. Not everyone agrees with his interpretations of the scripture."

"There's only one way to interpret the scripture," Reed reminded her.

Margaret took a seat in the back pew nearest the reconciliation room and pursed her lips at Reed. "Not according to the understanding Muslims have of the Qur'an."

"I'm sorry, the what?"

"Or the Talmud."

"Margaret." Reed gawked.

She shrugged. "I'm just saying. There's so many faiths and so many interpretations of the same books."

"What have you done with the Margaret I know?" he asked, his voice light, but also serious. This wasn't anything like the woman who had adopted him and raised him. To be fair, she had lightened up, especially after James's death so many years before, but the things she was saying now weren't something he expected to hear from her.

"You didn't answer me in the car." She patted the space beside her and Reed obediently filled it, just like when he'd been a teenager.

"I answered all your questions."

"Not the last one."

"Refresh my memory."

"I asked if there was anything you wanted to tell me." She took his hand in hers. "About Nic."

"This isn't the place to discuss him," Reed bit out in a harsh whisper.

"Isn't it?" she countered, gesturing to the empty pews around them, the sacred altar before them.

Reed shook his head rapidly and yanked his hand away from hers.

"Carol had told us there was something special between the two of you," Margaret said, as if Reed had asked. His heart stalled in his chest. This was the first time he could remember Margaret even mentioning Carol's name.

"You spoke with Carol?"

"Of course. She was your foster mother."

The congregant to Margaret's left stood and entered the reconciliation room. She slid down to fill the space, taking Reed with her.

"And what did she say?" He wiped his hands down the front of his slacks. They were the same ones he'd worn to commencement, to Nic's. The thought of Nic's hands on his clothes was comforting, and he hated that. He closed his eyes and tried to push the thoughts away.

"She said you two used to sneak out and climb onto the roof together at night."

A memory from the last birthday they'd spent together filled his mind, and he forced his eyes open, focusing on the stained-glass panel of the angel Gabriel instead of his memories of the contours of Nic's jaw.

"Did she?" he rasped.

"She said you shared a room."

"We had our own rooms."

"She told me that as well."

Margaret turned and studied his face, her brows knit together with maternal worry.

"I don't understand what you're playing at," he accused.

"Watch your mouth. I'm not playing at anything, Reed Matthews." She smacked his arm. "I'm giving you an opportunity to speak with me before you see Father Morley."

Reed looked away from her, scratching at the back of his neck with a trembling hand. The church was filled with streams of rainbow light, the noonday sun casting sharp rays through the stained glass and casting the church in an ethereal glow. It was something Reed had always loved about the church when he was younger. It sometimes felt so pure and beautiful inside that there was no way to deny you were in the presence of something greater than yourself.

"Why all these questions about Nic now?" Reed turned back to face Margaret, the puzzle pieces scattered in his mind and not quite ready to click into place. There was something missing. "Shouldn't you have asked them after you and James adopted me? When the wound was fresh?"

Margaret's cheeks colored and she looked down. "Your father... well, James, he didn't think it was best."

"Didn't think what was best?" Reed asked through clenched teeth, a fear prodding at the base of his spine and threatening to sprout through his body.

"Reed," she said soothingly.

He held up his hand to stop her. "Please tell me what James didn't think was best."

"Carol gave us the impression you and Nic had a... let's say *special* relationship with one another. James thought it would be best to nip it in the bud."

"Nic was my best friend," Reed whispered.

"Is that all he was?" Margaret asked, facing him head-on.

"I tried calling him, you know. At first. When you and James were out, or asleep," Reed admitted the long-held secret. He had tried for days and weeks to call Carol's house and get Nic on the phone. But there was never an answer. It didn't even go to the answering machine. At the time, it had felt like one of his limbs had been severed. And the whole time, knowing Cherry Grove was so close to Harborsville where Nic still lived, but he couldn't get there, always under the watchful eye of Margaret or James.

"Did you now?" Margaret's eyes were wet around her lashes.

"I did."

"But you never got through." She scrunched her nose and looked away.

"How did you know that?" Reed asked, fear beginning its ascent up his spine, curling around his ribs and organs, ready to squeeze the life out of him.

"We asked Carol to block our number."

The door to the reconciliation room opened, and Margaret jumped up like she'd been bitten and disappeared, closing the ornate wooden door behind her with a deafening latch.

Reed froze, his mouth falling open in shock. He clutched his chest, sucking in desperate lungfuls of air, but unable to catch a useful breath. The stained-glass shadows he'd just been admiring turned dark and claustrophobic. The grand space of the sanctuary closed around him, the truth of Margaret's overdue confession the heaviest admission of guilt he'd ever heard.

How could they have done that to him? Simultaneously, Margaret and James had given him a place to live but taken away his home. Reed's eyes welled with tears, and they fell unrestrained down his face, pooling around his nose and filling the corners of his lips. He closed his mouth and darted his tongue out, soaking up the errant wetness.

Puzzle pieces slid into their places, with so much of Reed's life now coming into focus. He hadn't been able to get a hold of Nic because he hadn't been allowed. He'd tried. He'd tried for so long, desperate to fill the hole in his chest that had been left after his adoption. But he'd been stopped, restrained by the constraints of his new parents, of their religion.

Reed reached into the collar of his shirt, pulling the crucifix out and fisting it in his hand, the sharp points of the cross gouging into his flesh and grounding him. His mind raced, overwhelmed with confusion, and hatred, and a never-ending list of regrets.

The door to the reconciliation room opened, revealing a reluctant-looking Margaret, her face etched with worry. Reed stood, dropping the crucifix against his chest. It twisted in his tie and he left it. He exited the pew and approached the room, his eyes narrowed on Margaret the entire way.

"Reed." She clutched her purse in front of her like a shield.

He shook his head and she reached out a hand to stop him, her delicate fingers grasping for the sleeve of his shirt. He shook her off, but stopped and turn to face her.

"It was James's idea," she offered, in way of apology.

"Was it now?" Reed asked, his entire body now devoid of emotion. He'd turned numb. Frightened.

"It made sense at the time. And Father Duncan agreed it would be best."

"Did he?" Reed rasped.

Margaret covered her cheeks with her hands and implored him.

"We thought we were doing the best thing for you."

"And now?" he hissed through clenched teeth, glancing toward the open door before him.

"Now, I'm not so sure."

FOURTEEN

DOMINIC

DOMINIC SAT AT HIS DESK, scanning through his notes for tomorrow's sermon, his mind wandering away from the task at hand.

"Stop it," he ordered himself, pushing away from the desk with a shove. His chair spun in circles, and he dropped his head backward, letting the momentum make him dizzy and confused. When the chair stopped its turning, he looked up and blinked his office back into focus, not believing what he was seeing.

"You've got to be kidding me," he ground out, stare narrowed at Reed's body in the doorway.

"Didn't you ever wonder why I never called you?" Reed asked, taking a step into the office. "After I was adopted?"

"I stopped wondering about you years ago, Reed." Dominic folded his arms over his chest and turned to face Reed. He looked so small, his shoulders turned inward, his poor posture visible even through the clean lines of the dark gray suit he was wearing.

"They wouldn't let me." Reed carried on like Dominic hadn't

even spoken. His words were enough to give Dominic pause, though, and he tilted his head to the side in question.

"They asked Carol to block their number," Reed whispered. "So we'd never get through."

"Why would they do that?" Dominic asked, disbelieving. His shoulders felt tense, and he rotated them in circles to ease his muscles. He turned away from Reed and crossed his office, taking a seat on his couch and staring at the church garden out the window.

"They knew."

"What did they know?" Dominic sighed and turned his focus back toward Reed, who'd walked deeper into the office but hesitated near the middle of the room.

"They knew I loved you," Reed admitted. "Even before I knew. They did."

Dominic closed his eyes, an unexpected flow of tears forcing their way against the backs of his eyelids. He shook his head.

"No," he protested, standing. He swiped his hands in the air, still shaking his head.

"Nic," Reed pleaded, closing the space between them and fisting Dominic's shirt in his hands. Dominic tried to swat him away, but his fingers only circled around Reed's wrists and held him so he didn't go. "I did what you said."

"What did I say?" Dominic held his breath, scared to have Reed so close. His mind was at war with his cock, both wanting and despising Reed in almost equal measure.

He'd had a good twenty years. Well, the first few had been rough without Reed, but at least a good thirteen. He tried to take solace in that, knowing that after what had happened last week, nothing would ever be the same.

"You told me to go see a priest," Reed reminded him.

"No. I said you *needed* a priest."

"Same thing."

"Is it?" Dominic pried an eye open and studied Reed's face.

He looked alive, brighter and less sorrowful than when Dominic had thrown him out of the house.

"I took Margaret to reconciliation. She told me what she and James had done. What Carol was a party to, mind you." Reed raised an eyebrow, but continued, "The new priest was young. Younger than us."

"And?" Dominic interjected, not understanding Reed's point, even as his mind lingered on 'What Carol was a party to.' Carol had had a part in cutting him off from Reed, and the knowledge sent a shiver through his body, which Reed felt. His fingers tightened against Dominic's shirt.

"He made some nonsense suggestions that would probably get him removed from the clergy if anyone found out," Reed shared with a small laugh.

"Like what?"

"Like this was fine."

"What's fine?" Dominic dared to ask, his fingers slipping and sweaty against Reed's exposed wrists.

"This. Thing. Whatever this is between us."

"And a priest you don't know tells you it's fine and his word is gold? What will Father Cowart think of you?" Dominic's voice was acidic, more than he'd meant, but he couldn't keep it in. He couldn't believe that one wide-eyed priest would be enough to change Reed's entire world view.

"It's not just him. I talked to Margaret, too. After I got over my anger."

"So soon?" Dominic bit out.

"Don't be pedantic. I'm trying to talk to you here." Reed shook his hands, jostling Dominic.

"Then talk."

"Margaret said James had hoped raising me Catholic would cure me."

Dominic scoffed. The desire to be cured of one's gayness

was an overwhelming trend he saw from Catholics who'd joined his congregation after leaving their own.

"I hate to break it to him," Dominic whispered, meeting Reed's intense stare for the first time. What he saw shocked him. The look in Reed's eyes was far stronger than anything he'd seen before. Gone was the confusion from their formative years, and gone was the war inside of him that Dominic had seen on Wednesday night.

The Reed in his office now was sure and strong... and ready.

"Tell me I can kiss you," Reed begged. "I want to enjoy it. Really enjoy what it's like for the first time."

Dominic licked his lips. "There's no going back."

"I don't want to," Reed promised.

Dominic released his hold on Reed's wrists and slowly lifted his hands to cup Reed's cheeks, stroking his thumbs over the sharp lines of his cheekbones to the sides of his eyes.

"I'm serious," Dominic whispered.

"So am I."

Reed looked like he meant it, and Dominic's resolve crumbled. He pulled Reed against him, Reed's hands smashed between their chests, and he slanted their mouths together, opening his lips and allowing Reed's eager tongue to explore him for another time, even though it really was the first time.

Reed kissed him with vigor and need, releasing Dominic's shirt and sliding his hands around to his shoulder blades. His fingers scrabbled at the fabric of Dominic's shirt, clawing like he was trying to get in, or take it off, or make up his mind about one or the other.

Dominic's cock thickened from the attention, from the friction, and he groaned, pressing his body against Reed's and walking them both backward until Reed bumped into his desk. A lamp toppled onto the floor.

Dominic took over the kiss, his tongue licking over every inch of Reed's mouth until he was satisfied he'd tasted him completely. He turned his kisses to Reed's face, his jaw, his chin, finally working down his neck and around the collar of his shirt. Reed moaned and fisted his hands into Dominic's hair, his body arching toward Dominic like he was being pulled by an unseen force.

"Is this okay?" Dominic rasped, reaching between them and working the knot of Reed's tie loose.

"Yes."

Dominic pulled the tie undone and raised his trembling fingers to the tiny buttons on Reed's shirt, pulling them open one by one, until the tan expanse of Reed's chest was bare before him, save for a gold crucifix that dangled over his sternum.

Dominic flattened a hand over it and sank his teeth into the thin skin of Reed's collarbone. Reed cursed and pulled on his hair, before relaxing under his touch and mumbling, "Again."

Dominic's cock leaked against his pants, his focus torn between the way Reed had stared at his belt the last time he'd undressed for him and the way Reed was beneath him now, hard, yet pliant. Dominic licked his way to the front of Reed's throat and pinched the skin between his teeth until Reed cried out.

He took Reed's mouth for another kiss, swallowing the delicious sounds Reed gave him while reaching between them to finger at the clasp on Reed's belt. Dominic's brain was foggy with want, but he was aware enough to know this was when things had gone wrong last time, too. Kissing somehow had been okay, but once Reed's cock got involved, the line was drawn.

He stilled, resting his head on Reed's shoulder and taking a moment to catch his breath. His fingers danced around the buckle without actually removing it.

"Nic," Reed panted in his ear. His lips were wet against Dominic's skin. "Please don't stop."

Dominic pulled Reed's belt loose, tossing it onto the floor, and slid his fingertips around the elastic waistband of Reed's underwear. His skin was hot to the touch, and Dominic dipped his fingers lower, brushing against a patch of curly hair that surrounded the base of Reed's dick.

"You sure?" he asked, curling his fingers into the thick hair.

"Yes," Reed promised.

Dominic fell to his knees, taking Reed's pants and underwear with him to the floor. He buried his face beside Reed's erection, inhaling deeply and pressing kisses against his skin. Reed gasped and steadied himself with one hand against Dominic's desk and the other against his shoulder. Something else fell. Paper maybe, or a pen. Dominic didn't care. The only thing that mattered was Reed beneath him.

"I want to taste you," Dominic panted, his breath falling in harsh puffs against Reed's cock. It throbbed in his face, the crown dark pink and shiny with precum.

"Yeah," Reed managed to mumble.

Dominic took Reed's shaft in his hand and pulled it away from his body, slowly rolling back his foreskin and lapping at his slit. Reed's wetness was warm against his tongue, and his own cock leaked with want against his thigh. He debated jerking himself off while he sucked Reed, but decided against it. He didn't want anything to exist in this memory besides the feel of Reed's skin against his own.

Dominic wrapped his lips around the head of Reed's dick and sucked, lowering himself slowly until his nose was buried in the hair that surrounded Reed's base. He worked his tongue against the veiny underside of Reed's dick, then pulled off, stopping to slide his tongue under the sensitive foreskin.

"Oh, man," Reed groaned, his body folding forward and his hands grabbing at Dominic's shoulders.

Dominic hummed an appreciative sound and continued to fuck Reed with his mouth, Reed's precum leaking copiously against his tongue. Dominic took one of his hands away from Reed's thigh and reached down, circling his balls and massaging them, gently testing the weight against his palm.

"I can't," Reed started, his words slurring. Dominic stilled, convinced Reed was going to tear himself away and run out of the office with his cock hard between his legs. He pulled off, rocking back on his heels, and looked up at Reed expectantly.

"Why did you stop?" Reed asked, his face contorted in pain and guilt. Dominic saw the guilt. He acknowledged it, and he was satisfied it was a manageable amount, so he squeezed Reed's balls in his hand. "Oh, that feels good."

"I stopped because you said you can't," Dominic reminded him, rubbing Reed's erection across his stubbled cheek.

Reed winced, his eyes rolling back in his head and a pleasured moan leaving his mouth.

"I said I can't last," Reed clarified.

"Oh, but I've barely gotten started," Dominic assured him, then swallowed Reed's cock to the back of his throat.

Reed's mouth opened, and he exhaled, a shuddering sound that was followed by a full body tremor and the taste of hot salt against Dominic's tongue. He groaned and lapped his tongue in a circle around Reed's pulsing shaft, swallowing every drop that spilled into his mouth. He continued to suck, working Reed in his mouth as he softened. Reed grunted, his nails pressing sharp divots into Dominic's back, but he still didn't stop.

"It aches," Reed panted, dropping back onto Dominic's desk with a pained groan. Dominic's dick swelled against his leg and he reached down and squeezed, willing himself to not throw in the towel yet.

Dominic worked Reed through the pain until his cock was hard again, the skin hot and smooth against the inside of Dominic's mouth. He sucked him until his jaw ached and he'd swallowed another of Reed's orgasms without spilling a drop. He pulled his mouth away with a wet and sloppy pop, eyeing a sweaty and boneless Reed who was sprawled across his desk.

Dominic struggled to catch his breath, the reality of what had just happened slamming into him like a ton of bricks. He folded over on himself, collapsing against the floor of his office on his hands and knees. His breathing was coming in sharp and staggered gasps, but then Reed was there on the ground with him, a soft hand at his back and on his neck.

"Nic," he whispered. "Nic, it's okay. It's okay."

"You're still here?" Dominic blinked hard, rolling onto his back and looking up at Reed's sated face that hovered over him.

Reed smiled, and it looked like the easiest thing in the world.

"I'm still here," Reed confirmed, dropping onto the floor with his back against Dominic's desk. He reached a hand out and rested his fingertips against Dominic's hip.

Dominic covered Reed's hand with his own and closed his eyes.

FIFTEEN

REED

"I'M surprised you're still here."

Nic's voice was a quiet murmur in his ear. Reed startled, briefly forgetting where he was, but Nic's hand braced itself against his back and he settled, his head resting against Nic's shoulder.

"I deserve that."

"I know."

Nic shifted out from underneath him and stood, stretching his arms above his head and smiling down at Reed, even though his eyes were clouded with doubt and speculation. Reed pushed himself up to stand, blushing when he realized his limp cock was hanging out of his pants. He tucked himself away and righted his pants, shifting awkwardly in front of Nic.

Father Morley, as Margaret had indicated before reconciliation, was much more progressive in his line of thought than Father Duncan had been—more than Father Cowart, as well. He'd stuttered through a confession he was petrified to make, at first stopping short of coming out, while still indicating he had interests that didn't lie with the fairer sex. The priest had offered him no penance. He said Reed had done nothing wrong, said there was no sin in the confession Reed had offered. Maybe he hadn't been clear.

"I have feelings for a man," Reed had emphasized, the words falling from his mouth, heavy with the weight of their truth. It wasn't even something Reed had admitted to himself. He'd spoken the words, then clamped his hands over his mouth, stifling a sharp inhale.

Father Morley chuckled.

His laugh was delicate and sounded kind. The noise floated through the air between them, and somehow the nonchalance of it wiped away the top layer of Reed's worry. They'd talked more, Reed breaking down in tears, telling Father Morley everything from the first day he and Nic had met up to the last time they'd seen each other.

Father Morley offered him words of absolution and reminded him of Corinthians 13:13 as Reed was making to stand and leave the reconciliation room. He paused and straightened his tie, the verse a familiar one.

Reed took a deep breath and looked up at Nic, searching out his eyes. "The greatest of these is love," he whispered.

"Are we back to theology talk?" Nic raised an eyebrow.

Reed shook his head and took a step toward Nic. He walked closer, his fingers straightening against Nic's stomach until his palms were flat against the cool polyester of Nic's shirt.

"I confessed today." The tips of Reed's shoes bumped into the tips of Nic's shoes.

"So you said."

"Aren't you going to ask me about it?" Reed blinked up at Nic.

Nic raised a hand between them and slowly reached for Reed's cheek, his fingers dragging over Reed's skin so gently, he wasn't sure he'd actually felt it.

"That's between you and God. But whatever happened, I'm

glad you're here." Nic cupped his hand around the side of Reed's face, fingers stretched beneath Reed's ear.

Reed closed his eyes and wrapped his arms around Nic's back, holding their bodies together and pressing his cheek against Nic's chest. Nic tensed, surprised by Reed's affection, but slowly relaxed. He wound his arms around Reed and pulled him close, taking a deep breath with his nose buried in Reed's hair.

"I don't know what to do from here," Reed admitted a few moments later, pulling back and looking up at Nic. He felt shy now, embarrassed by what they'd done, what they hadn't yet done... what Reed *wanted* to do.

"Whatever you want," Nic assured him. "We can go home. We can go our separate ways. We can stay here."

"I don't want to stay here." Reed glanced toward the wall, eyes falling on an oil painting of Jesus.

"Alright..." Nic was waiting for Reed to make a decision, but he didn't want to. He was tired. He'd already made one huge decision for the day. All he wanted to do now was yield to Nic. Every cell in his body ached to succumb to Nic's will now that he wasn't solely focused on interpreting *God's* will.

"You tell me," Reed whispered, clearing his throat. He turned his attention back toward Nic and studied his face. He catalogued the way it had changed from when they were kids, the way it had changed from last week. Something sparked in Nic's eyes. Something Reed recognized, but couldn't quite identify. Whatever it was, though, it resonated in his bones.

"I don't know if you're ready for all that."

Nic took a step back and palmed himself, his cock thick beneath his pants. It was then Reed realized Nic had made him come, repeatedly, but he hadn't sought out his own release. His cock must be aching, swollen, hard...

Reed swallowed and returned his attention to Nic's face.

"I don't want to go home," Reed told him.

"No?"

"I want to go to your home."

Nic ran a hand through his hair and turned away from Reed, slapping his hands against his thighs with a groan. He leaned over, his back bowed and face angled toward the floor. Reed wanted to go to him, wanted to touch him, but he stayed in his place.

"This is too much, Reed." Nic turned back toward him, his face marred in conflict.

"What?" Reed was shocked.

He'd offered Nic so much already, and Nic didn't want it? Nic didn't want *him*? After he'd made his confessions and was risking so much? His soul. His heart. "You're hot and cold, Reed. And right now, you're just running way too hot, too soon."

"I'm running too hot?" Reed scoffed. "You're the one who had my dick in your mouth."

"That's the funny thing about it, Reed. I know I'm gay. I like having cock in my mouth."

Reed opened his mouth to talk back, the words stalling in the middle of his tongue, unable to be spoken. Wasn't one time today good enough?

"That's what I thought," Nic whispered.

Obviously no, it wasn't enough. "Nic."

"What I said at my house, I meant. What I said earlier, I meant. I can't survive you just using me, and I refuse to be a fuck toy until someone reminds you that you believe we're both going to Hell for what just happened."

Nic's words were bitter and acidic. They stung Reed's exposed skin. His eyes welled with tears. He pursed his lips and shook his head, blinking rapidly as to not cry.

"I meant what I said, too, Nic."

"Remind me," Nic sassed, dropping his ass onto the edge of his desk, just beside Reed, who was still standing.

It was now or never.

Reed spun on his heel and stepped into the gap between Nic's legs, taking Nic's face in his hands and holding it straight so he had no choice but to look at Reed.

"I want this." He leaned closer and, with trembling lips, pressed a kiss against the corner of Nic's parted mouth. "I want you."

Another kiss, this time his lips open, his tongue just behind. When there was no space between his mouth and Nic's, his tongue darted out, dipping between Nic's lips. Nic moaned and opened wider, letting Reed explore him again. Reed could taste himself on Nic's tongue. It was a new flavor, a new sensation, and his cock thickened again, impossibly ready for more.

"I don't know what I'm doing," he whispered against Nic's flushed skin, "but I want to do it with you."

Reed put space between them and took a breath. Nic looked wary, hesitant, but not closed off. Reed hoped that was a good sign.

"I get it," Reed said, flexing his fingers against Nic's thighs. "I know I've been... unfair to you. But I mean what I say. I'll prove it to you. I've just never done this before so I need you to be in charge here."

The words left his cock damp with arousal, the double meaning of what he'd just said flittering around his brain and setting off alarms.

"In charge how?" Nic's voice was lower than normal— deeper and scratchy. He cleared his throat.

"In all ways," Reed rasped. "But what I meant specifically was you set the pace. Until you, I don't know, believe me."

"Until I trust you," Nic corrected.

"Until you have faith in me."

Nic covered Reed's hands with his own, squeezing his fingers.

"Let's go, then," Nic finally said, standing up and forcing Reed to take a step backward. Reed's heart skipped, accelerating and slamming around his chest like one of those cartoon hearts in love.

But Reed wasn't *in* love. He couldn't be. Sure, he loved Nic, but...

Reed trailed Nic back to the parsonage, only checking over his shoulder twice to see if anyone had seen them. Closing Nic's door behind him, he realized he hadn't checked out of fear for being caught, but he'd checked because Nic was like his own secret, and he wanted to hold onto that for as long as possible.

Besides, it was one thing to be out to an out-of-town priest and the guy who sucked your dick in a church office. It was a completely different thing to be out to your colleagues, your peers, your neighbors. Reed hoped Nic would understand, but he also hoped it wouldn't come up.

"So I'm in charge?" Nic turned to face him after the door locked.

"Yes."

"Go into my bedroom and strip. Wait for me."

Reed licked his lips and nodded, turning down the hallway and letting himself into Nic's bedroom. He'd have to tell Nic the truth. It was unavoidable at this point. Things were escalating so quickly. Reed shrugged out of his suit coat and laid it across the foot of Nic's bed, pulling his already-loose tie from around his neck before discarding his shirt.

He hadn't even re-knotted his tie before they'd left Nic's office.

Reed kicked out of his shoes, pants, and briefs, then bent over and pulled off his socks. He arranged everything neatly and as out of the way as he could without risking wrinkles, and he waited. His cock was still hard from the innuendoed exchange in Nic's office and from the order Nic had just given him.

He didn't know why he liked that. He couldn't have articulated why he'd told Nic he wanted him to be in charge, other than it felt like the way things were supposed to be. Just like being with Nic felt like the way things were supposed to be.

The door opened and Nic walked in, less dressed than before. He had his slacks on still, but he was barefoot, and his shirt was off, tossed over his forearm casually. Nic dropped his own clothes onto the pile Reed had assembled on the bed and stepped back. His eyes traced fire over every exposed inch of Reed's skin, from his toes to his hairline.

Nic took a step closer and reached out, swirling his thumb around his fingers, still inches away from touching Reed's flesh. He was ready to combust. His cock ached from the intensity of Nic's appraisal, and it leaked, a cool damp spot against his stomach.

"I never thought I'd get to see you again," Nic whispered.

"Me neither."

"And here we are."

Reed's lashes fluttered and his eyes closed. When Nic's fingers skated over his stomach, he didn't startle. Instead, the slow drag calmed him, settled him. Nic made an approving sound in the back of his throat and took another step closer. The heat of Nic's skin was a tangible thing between them. Reed could feel it against his.

Nic dropped his head against Reed's shoulder and peppered a cluster of delicate kisses against his collarbone. His cock was hard, too, and it bumped and banged into Reed's dick, making him gasp every time. Nic had stopped short of touching him there again, his fingers relegated to the soft angles of Reed's stomach instead.

"I have so many plans for you," Nic rasped, his teeth nipping against Reed's skin. Reed gasped and arched upward, his body pressing against Nic's chest.

"I need you to know something," Reed mumbled.

"I want to know everything."

Nic stepped away, his fingers still dancing around Reed's stomach. Nic's eyes were leveled on him with a singular focus.

"I don't know how to say this."

"That seems to be a recurring thing with you." Nic sounded cautious. He took his hand away. Reed's hand shot out. He grabbed Nic's wrist and yanked forward, returning his fingers to the soft motions he'd been making against Reed's stomach.

When he was confident Nic wouldn't stop, Reed let go and fisted his hands at his sides.

"You're trembling," Nic observed, tilting his head to the side and studying Reed's face.

"Can I tell you later?" Reed asked, his fear getting the better of him.

Nic narrowed his eyes and took his hand away again, shoving them both into the pockets of his slacks. Reed noticed they were unbuttoned, and the movement of Nic's hands exposed the top of Nic's royal purple underwear.

"Not much later," Nic conceded.

"Not much."

Nic eyed him hungrily, then stepped out of his pants, discarding his briefs to the floor. He took a step toward Reed and pushed him backward onto the bed. Reed collapsed onto the thick duvet and panted, staring up at Nic.

"I have to be up early for service tomorrow," Nic told him, pulling back the comforter and crawling under the blankets.

Reed was confused, unsure of what Nic expected or wanted from him. Nic yanked the blankets out from underneath Reed and fanned them out over both of their bodies.

"Come here," Nic whispered, fingers pulling Reed against him. "I just want to hold you for tonight."

SIXTEEN

DOMINIC

"HOW WAS SERVICE, DEAR?" Carol spoke into the phone, her voice smooth and calm. Dominic drummed his fingers against his desk, eyes focused on a framed photo of him and her from the day he graduated from seminary.

"Good," he answered, reaching forward and toying with the gilded edges of the frame. His fingers still felt electrified from every part of Reed's skin he'd touched last night. Dominic had kept his word, holding Reed's body tight against his until his alarm went off at five in the morning.

He'd begrudgingly torn himself away and readied himself for church, encouraging Reed out of bed to do the same. He had a fleeting thought of a time that Reed might come to church with him instead of across town, but he shoved that one into a locked box in the depths of his brain. He could only ask so much of the man.

If last night was all he'd be allowed, he would hold those memories for the rest of his life. He'd take them as closure on a life that was never allowed to exist and move on. But even as the thought crossed his mind, he rejected it, unwilling to accept that was all he'd be given. After two decades alone, he was owed more than a blow job and one night of physical affection. Not that Reed owed him that. Reed didn't owe him anything, even though he seemed to now willingly offer Dominic everything. But he was still owed.

"I need to ask you something." Nic tipped the photo frame down onto his desk so he'd stop looking at the picture.

"Of course, sweetheart."

"Did Margaret…" Dominic cleared his throat. "When Reed was adopted, did Margaret and James tell you to block their number?"

Dominic was answered with silence, and that was all the affirmation he needed.

"Carol," he hissed, and in his mind, he could see her wince from the sharpness of it. Dominic took a deep breath. "Carol, please just tell me."

"Dominic," she apologized. "It didn't happen the way you're thinking."

"How did it happen then?"

Dominic angled the frame up to look at the picture again, then he yanked his desk open and tossed it in the top drawer, slamming it closed so he'd stop fiddling with it.

"It's complicated, sweetheart."

"I'm an adult now, Carol." He emphasized her name. Because he knew it would hurt. Because he was angry.

She sighed. "David and I had fought, just before your birthday. I don't know if you remember that. I hope you don't. But he'd left."

Dominic furrowed his brow and stared at his phone sitting on his desk, the screen counting out the minutes of the call.

"He was gone for work that year you'd said."

"No, sweetheart. He was… gone. We'd fought, I don't even remember over what at the time. Everything was moving forward so quickly with Reed's adoption and Margaret and

James had been to the house. I'd spoken with them both about Reed, and about you."

"What did you tell them?" Dominic folded his arms together on his desk and dropped his head against them. He knew where this was going. He knew what Reed had said was true.

"That you two were close." Carol sniffled.

"Close," he repeated.

"You were."

"We are," he countered, rolling his head to the side and resting his cheek against the outside of his forearm.

"It was James's idea to have our number blocked, and I told him absolutely not. You and Reed were near inseparable and the adoption would be hard enough on you both. I told him the phone calls would be important for you two to get through the separation."

There was a but. There was always a but.

"But," Carol continued, "James threatened to tell social services that David had left. That I was alone with you, and they would have taken you from me. Moved you to another foster home, or a state place, and I didn't want that for you, Dominic. I didn't."

Dominic closed his eyes and withdrew his arms, banging his head against the hard wood of his desk until he registered Carol's voice in his ear repeating his name over and over. He stopped and sat up, leaning back in his chair and swallowing hard.

"I see," he said.

Carol whimpered into the phone, a sound so far removed from her normal calm and smooth maternal tone that it made Dominic's eyes water.

"I'm not mad at you," he half-lied to her so she'd calm down. "I'm hurt. And I'm confused."

"I just wanted the best for you. For both of you," she pleaded for him to understand.

"I believe that."

After a long silence, she asked him, "How did you find out about that?"

"Reed told me. Margaret confessed to him yesterday."

"I wonder how that even came up. It's been so many years."

"Twenty," Dominic bit out. "And it came up because the guilt of wanting to be with me was eating him alive and she regretted what she'd done and wanted to make it right."

Dominic's heart was at battle. Part of him was shocked and hurt that Carol had deceived him, when she'd worked so hard to build their relationship on trust and respect; another part of him was so angry with her, he was afraid he couldn't contain it inside of him for much longer.

"I need to go, Carol," he whispered.

"Dominic."

"I'll talk to you later, alright?" He stabbed the end button on the phone and shoved it off the desk.

He knew, in the back of his brain, he knew he was being unfair to Carol, but he couldn't turn it off. His body burned with years of pent up... *everything* that he'd never allowed himself. He stood abruptly, his chair rolling back into the wall, and he departed his office, leaving his phone and locking the door behind him.

He drove across town, straight for Our Lady of the Mount, and pulled alongside the curb outside and waited. Mass had been over for just over half an hour, and Dominic expected Reed was the type to stay around and fellowship. It was then he realized he didn't know where Reed lived. Reed had only shown up at Dominic's when he'd felt moved enough to grace Dominic with his presence.

Dominic bristled, knuckles white against the steering wheel until Reed appeared at the top of the stairs, talking to someone over his shoulder who was still inside. Dominic unrolled the passenger side window and leaned over the console.

"Reed!" he hollered.

Reed's attention flew to where Dominic was parked, his eyes widening in what Dominic was confident to be fear. He wasn't going to have any part of that today. Not now. He gestured for Reed to come toward him.

Reed looked back over his shoulder one more time before he quickly jogged down the stairs. At the curb, he leaned into the open window.

"What are you doing here?" he asked.

"You should get in. Someone is going to see you talking to a man." As he said it, he winced, squeezing his eyes closed and taking a deep breath to steady himself.

Reed sighed and opened the door, sliding into the passenger seat. He turned and faced Dominic, his face now showing more concern than fear.

"You seem out of sorts," Reed observed.

"I am," he agreed, turning the car on. "Tell me where you live."

Reed gave him some easy directions, and Dominic drove toward Reed's in silence.

"It's this one." Reed pointed and Dominic parked.

"Do you still mean the things you said to me yesterday?" Dominic asked, glancing at Reed from the corner of his eye.

Reed worked his lips like he was trying to get them to form an answer on his behalf, finally mumbling a barely coherent yes.

"That wasn't convincing." Dominic thumped his head against the headrest with a groan. This was a mistake. This whole charade with Reed, his anger toward Carol, his confusion, his lust, his want. All of it was a mistake.

He closed his eyes and curled his fingers around his knees, doing his best to gather all the fortitude that existed inside of himself and shove Reed out of the car for good, but all of that went out the window when he felt the soft press of lips against his.

Dominic's eyes flew open, and he was met with Reed's penetrating stare. He'd crawled half across the console and had kissed Dominic. On his own. No prompting. No begging. No praying...

Dominic's lips parted on a breath and Reed's tongue was there, filling the space, exploring him again. Dominic cupped the back of Reed's head with a shaking hand and returned the kiss until they were both panting against each other.

"We should go inside," Dominic finally whispered, after Reed had separated their mouths.

"We should," Reed agreed.

Dominic was out of the car and around to the passenger side before Reed could change his mind. He opened the door and reached inside, grabbing Reed's hand and yanking him out. He guided him toward the front door and waited while Reed unlocked it and let them both inside.

Dominic did a quick inventory of the space and turned as soon as he heard Reed lock the door. He shoved Reed into the door and he landed with an oomph, and Dominic was on him, devouring his mouth, licking the salt from the skin of Reed's neck and his jaw until Reed's cock was so hard it stabbed Dominic's thigh.

He reached between them, undoing Reed's belt with one hand and tossing it to the ground. Dominic shoved his hand into Reed's pants and fisted his dick. Reed gasped and his back arched, his chest slamming against Dominic's pounding heart.

"I want you so much," Dominic whispered, his teeth nipping at the shell of Reed's ear. Reed mumbled something and nodded, his cock leaking into Dominic's hand.

"Gotta..." Reed mumbled, his head lolling from side to side. He babbled nonsensically, and Dominic swiped his thumb through the damp slit at the tip of Reed's swollen cock.

"I know," he soothed, releasing Reed's shaft and raising his thumb to his mouth. He sucked it between his lips, tasting the subtle musk that was indescribably Reed. Dominic groaned and worked on his own belt, tossing it onto the floor and yanking the tails of his shirt out of his pants. It was then, he realized he was still wearing his collar.

He reached toward his throat and pulled it off, discarding it carelessly so he could work the buttons of his shirt open. Once his chest was bare, he reached for Reed, loosening the knot of his tie and using trembling hands to smooth his way over Reed's chest.

"I've wanted you for twenty years," Dominic whispered, shoving both of their pants to their knees and closing the space between them. Dominic's cock throbbed against Reed's, the friction almost enough to send him into his orgasm.

"Nic," Reed panted.

Dominic fisted their cocks in his hand and stroked them, the tight friction of his palm only lubricated by the slickness they were both leaking against each other. This was real, and this was happening. Reed had gotten in the car. Reed had invited him in. Reed had kissed him. And now Reed was with him, cock hard and hot in the palm of Dominic's hand.

"Come for me," Dominic grunted into Reed's ear. "Come for me and then let me fuck you."

Reed cried out, his hot release spurting over Dominic's hand. His fingers crawled up Dominic's chest and ground into his shoulders while he rode out the duration of his orgasm. Dominic didn't loosen his grip, continuing to stroke Reed's well-used cock just like he'd done with his mouth the night before.

Reed's cry turned toward pain, and Dominic grunted, his own cock releasing into his hand, mixing with Reed's orgasm. He pumped their dicks one more time, letting them go and taking a step away to catch his breath.

"Gonna fuck you so good," he rasped, licking his lips and making eyes toward Reed. Everything he'd felt earlier was gone.

All that mattered was fucking Reed the way he should have been for the past lifetime.

"Nic," Reed managed to say, louder this time, so Dominic focused on it.

"Reed."

"That thing I needed to tell you last night." He took a deep breath and held Dominic's stare. "I'm a virgin."

SEVENTEEN

REED

NIC LOOKED like he'd been hit with a semi-truck.

"Please don't freak out." Reed grabbed his pants in one hand so he didn't trip and took a step closer toward Dominic.

"Virgin."

"I don't want it to be a thing. I just thought you should know."

"Uh…"

Reed sighed. "You look like you want to talk about this. Do you want to do it naked or dressed?"

At his question, Nic's nostrils flared, his stare intent on Reed's spent cock, now hanging limp against his thigh. Reed could still feel the rough abrasion of Nic's hand against his flesh, and it was enough to start to fill his cock with blood again. He'd never known this about himself; he'd never anticipated that he'd enjoy being hurt.

"Where is your bedroom?" Nic finally asked him, and Reed breathed a sigh of relief. He stumbled toward his bedroom with Nic trailing behind. Once he'd entered, Reed discarded his pants completely, tossing them toward the hamper he used for dry cleaning. He pulled his underwear back up, gently arranging his cock beneath the fabric.

Nic pulled his pants up but left them undone, loose around his hips and showing the brightness of his underwear. Reed bit back a smile, secretly loving the fact his priest wore such statement pieces beneath his vestments. He stilled, dissecting the thought.

Was Nic *his*?

His priest?

The implications were far reaching and beyond anything Reed wanted to think about. After reconciliation yesterday, for the first time in years, he felt like he'd been granted permission to *feel*, and that's exactly what he wanted to do.

"Sit." Nic gestured toward Reed's bed, and he sat on the edge, feet planted on the ground.

"How does…" Nic shook his head. "How does that even happen?"

"Do you mean, how does it *not* happen?" Reed chuckled.

"I'd rather you not be cute right now," Nic said sternly.

"I mean, I was waiting. For marriage, you know. And then marriage didn't happen. And by then I was in my mid-twenties. I'd given up on trying to hold on. I figured I'd just do it with someone and deal with the penance afterward, but I couldn't find anyone I wanted to do it with. Women thought it was weird. I got close, one time, but…" Reed trailed off, the memory biting.

"But you couldn't get hard," Nic guessed.

Reed nodded.

"So, I gave it up. Figured, it would happen when it happened, but it never happened."

"Do you…" Nic gestured like he was jerking off.

"Sometimes," Reed answered. "I honestly don't think about sex much. Or, I didn't until you showed up in Edgewood."

That made Nic straighten. He squared his shoulders like he was proud of what Reed had just shared with him.

"Don't let that go to your head," Reed warned with a small smile. He turned his attention toward Nic's bare toes against his floor.

"This sounds like you're demi," Nic mumbled.

"Demi?"

"Demisexual," Nic clarified. "It means that like... you're attracted to who the person is, not just how they look. Basically."

"Oh."

Reed scratched his chin and tested how the label felt. It seemed applicable, as he thought back to the girlfriends he'd had in high school and college. He'd been somewhat close with them, but he'd always held them at arms-length. Though, that could have been because he was denying another very important fact about himself.

"Am I gay?" he whispered, blinking up at Nic, who had leaned back against Reed's dresser and folded his arms over his chest.

"You're not straight," Nic answered with a small lift of his shoulders. "Are you attracted to women?"

Reed pursed his lips and tried to remember the things he'd felt when he'd been involved with women. When he'd had relationships with women, he'd never even let things move toward anything sexual under the guise of him saving himself for marriage. But again, now, he didn't know how true that reasoning had been.

"I don't know."

"That's fair." Nic pushed off the dresser and approached him slowly, stopping a foot away from him. Reed looked up, his eyes pulled toward the thick trail of hair that bloomed out of the elastic waistband of Nic's underwear.

"I'm attracted to you," Reed admitted.

"I'm glad for that." Nic took another step closer, his crotch inches from Reed's face. Reed inhaled, the salty smell of sweat and cum thick against his nostrils. Reed tentatively reached his hands out, fingers dragging through the coarse curls of Nic's happy trail. Nic groaned, his cock thickening in front of Reed's eyes.

"I've never done this before." He looked up at Nic. "Any of this."

Nic smoothed a hand through Reed's hair and Reed leaned into the touch, a smile flitting across his face. He closed his eyes.

"That's okay. We can go slow."

"What if I don't want to go slow?" Reed blinked Nic into focus, his fingers delving deeper under the band of Nic's briefs.

"What if I do?" Nic countered.

Reed's hands stilled.

"You're right." Reed pulled his hands away and folded them in his lap, wishing that he had a blanket to cover himself with. "I'm sorry."

"Hey, hey." Nic chuckled and pushed Reed onto his back, using his body to shoulder Reed up the bed until he was spread over top of him. "I didn't say I wanted to. I just want to make sure you understand that whatever this thing is between us, it goes both ways. Consent is a two-way street."

"Right," Reed said, gasping when Nic's teeth sank into the lobe of his ear.

"Slow is good," Nic whispered.

"Alright," Reed panted, back bowing off the bed. Nic's tongue drew a circle over the thin skin behind Reed's ear.

"School's out until fall?"

"What?" Reed was confused. "Yeah."

"Good," Nic growled, sucking a bruise into the side of Reed's neck.

Reed gasped, fingers scrabbling over the broad muscles of

Nic's back. Nic sucked until Reed's moans turned to whimpers, his cock leaking a wet spot against Nic's belly.

"I have so many ideas for you." Nic tore his mouth away from Reed's neck and leaned back. He situated himself so he was straddling Reed. Nic reached down and shoved his briefs down, tucking the elastic under his balls so it held his cock on display for Reed's enjoyment. "But there's something I need to tell you, too."

Reed nodded, hoping what Nic had to say wouldn't stop whatever was happening between them right now. Reed didn't know where this was going, or what would become of them, but he'd go down in flames to see it through.

"I'm leaving," Nic whispered, his head tilted to the side. His face was scrunched up, his eyes dark with want... and with worry.

"What?"

"I'm, uhm, I'm taking a sabbatical this summer."

Reed scrambled out from underneath Nic's weight and crawled back toward his headboard, pulling his knees up to his chest protectively. "Where?"

"Fuck." Nic looked away.

"Where?"

"Around." Nic shrugged. "I'm doing a two-week missionary trip to Honduras, then I was going to do a spiritual retreat in Arizona. The church has property out there."

"How long?"

"A month."

Reed scrubbed his hands over his face. "Starting when?"

"I leave in two weeks."

Reed looked up at Nic, searching his face for an explanation, a reason, reassurance; he didn't know what he was looking for, but he knew when he found it. Nic's face twisted into an apologetic grimace and his eyes turned to glass. His mouth opened, but no words escaped him.

"Come here," Reed whispered, stretching a hand toward Nic. Nic laced their fingers together and let Reed tug him to the head of the bed, their bodies colliding again. Reed fell beneath Nic's weight, chest heaving. He buried his face in the crook of Nic's neck and kissed him there.

"I'm sorry," Nic rasped.

Reed stroked his hands down Nic's back in a slow and soothing motion. "It's alright. We have until then."

Nic reared back. "Only until?"

"You may not want me when you're back," Reed offered. "God could… inspire you to focus your dedication elsewhere."

"Reed, I've wanted you longer than I've even known God. There is nothing he can ask of me that will take me away from you again." Nic bumped their noses together.

"You don't know that."

"I do," Nic protested. "God wouldn't ever ask something of me that I couldn't handle, and being apart from you… well."

Nic didn't finish the thought; instead, he dipped his face down, slanting his lips over Reed's and kissing him tenderly. It was different from their earlier kisses. Slower, less frantic, more measured.

Reed's cock hardened again.

"Please."

"There's no rush," Nic whispered against Reed's swollen lips. He ground his hips into Reed, their cocks dragging together and the zipper of Nic's loosened pants gouging into Reed's thigh.

"It feels…" Reed licked his lips, trying to find the word and settling on, "urgent."

"There's no denying that." Nic pulled them both up until they were sitting, keeping their fingers twisted together between them. "But you've had a big weekend, Reed. You've changed position on some important things, and I want to make sure you've thought it through before we do much more than this."

"I've thought it through," he protested.

Nic huffed out an amused laugh. "That's your dick talking."

"I want you," he emphasized again.

"If that's true, then you'll want me tomorrow. You'll want me two months from now." Nic lifted Reed's hand and kissed it.

"That's a lifetime," Reed whispered.

"No." Nic shook his head and pushed Reed onto his back. "Twenty years is a lifetime, but I'm here now, and you won't need to wait as long as I have."

Nic slid down his body, tongue drawing scalding shapes and lines over the ridges of Reed's abs and his ribs until it dipped lower, drawing a long stripe just above the waistband of his underwear.

Nic's fingers pulled at the waistband, tugging them down low enough to expose Reed's red and leaking cock. Nic circled his hand around it and stroked. Reed gasped and arched into the touch, desperate for more.

Nic tongued Reed's cock from the base to the tip, and Reed was surprised he didn't shoot off across Nic's face just like that. One of Nic's hands dragged up Reed's body and flattened against his chest, pushing Reed back onto the bed.

"Hold the headboard," Nic ordered from between his legs. Reed raised his arms and threaded his fingers through the decorative bronze bars of the bed.

Nic swallowed the head of Reed's cock into his mouth. Reed stared down at Nic and watched his cheeks hollow, the pressure and suction on his cock growing painful. He thrashed beneath Nic, and Nic's eyes flared, his efforts renewed. Reed's balls tingled, churning in their sac and lifting toward his body.

Nic popped off, Reed's cock slapping against his stomach.

"You like it when I hurt you," he observed, working his lips around the thick midsection of Reed's shaft. "But you want more from me."

Reed's eyelashes fluttered.

He wanted lots of things, most of which he didn't know how to understand, let alone articulate.

"If I ever do something you don't like, say red and I'll stop," Nic promised him.

Reed nodded.

"Repeat it. Use your words," Nic chided.

"I'll say red if I need you to stop," Reed panted, eyes coming open. "What if I don't want you to stop?"

Nic bit his lower lip between his teeth and grinned deviantly up at Reed. "Then you say green."

"Green," Reed repeated. "Green."

Nic groaned and returned his attention to Reed's cock, licking and sucking at the tender underside of Reed's foreskin. He used his tongue to push it down, exposing the flared tip of Reed's engorged cock, and then he bit down, his teeth pressing just so into the most delicate part of Reed's body.

And not much to his own surprise, Reed came.

EIGHTEEN

DOMINIC

TWO WEEKS later

Dominic bent over and braced himself on the edge of his dresser. He dropped his head down and took a deep breath, relaxing when he felt the warmth of Reed's hand make contact with his back. He straightened and turned, pulling Reed into his arms.

"Will you miss me?" he murmured into Reed's ear.

"Yeah." Reed cleared his throat. The past two weeks had been pleasantly tumultuous, if that could even be a thing. Reed hadn't quite cooled himself since Dominic had picked him up from church, but he was very clearly still hiding who he was and what they were. And that was fine with Dominic, for now, but he hadn't been in the closet for years and he wasn't interested in going back.

Either way, Dominic would miss Reed a lot while he was gone, and he hoped that when he was back from his sabbatical, Reed would be in a better place with who he was and what he wanted for his life. He gripped Reed around the biceps and kissed him on the forehead.

"I should get to the airport."

"I haven't asked, but have you spoken with Carol?" Reed looked away sheepishly.

"No."

Dominic hadn't spoken with Carol, and he didn't know when he'd want to talk to her again. He hoped that the trip would give him time to clear his head, to separate a bit from the situation with Reed and realign himself mentally and spiritually. He planned to reach out to her when he returned later in the summer. He'd pray over it, in the meantime. And Reed, too. Dominic sighed.

"Shouldn't you?"

"No." Dominic gave Reed a sharp look that he interpreted correctly, snapping his mouth closed.

"Will you have cell service?" Reed twisted his fingers together nervously and stepped back until he hit the bed.

"In Honduras, yes. Not Arizona."

"That seems backward."

"The point of being in Honduras is to communicate with other people. The point of being in Arizona is to communicate with…" Dominic pointed up.

"Tell me again about it." Reed sat on Dominic's bed, pulling one of Dominic's pillows to his chest and hugging it.

"It's a property outside of Sedona that is entrusted to the Bishop's Committee of Pastoral Development. They offer it on scholarship to priests who are applying for their sabbatical leave who wish to reflect on their spiritual development in a more natural setting."

"You sound like you're reciting something from a pamphlet."

"I am." Dominic grinned, but it didn't hold.

"So, six weeks?" Reed grimaced and held the pillow tighter.

"Do you want me to call you when I make it back stateside?" Dominic questioned, conceding that he was worried about the break in communication as well.

"Yes, please," Reed whispered.

"Come here." Dominic gestured for Reed to stand, and he did, shuffling across Dominic's bedroom until they were face to face.

"You've been so good the past two weeks, Reed. So trusting. So patient." He raised a hand and stroked Reed's cheek. Reed moaned and arched toward the touch like he was a plant and Dominic was the sun. "If you still want me when I'm back, then I'll have you."

Reed's breath stuttered and he turned his face, pressing a kiss against Dominic's palm with a calm reverence. It made Dominic hard, and he didn't have time for that now. He could tell that Reed wasn't going to let him go so easily, and he knew he needed to leave. He had to be the one to sever the connection between them.

"Reed," he whispered, even as Reed still dropped light and tender kisses against the clammy skin of Dominic's hand. Dominic took his hand from Reed's grasp, and he grimaced, shaking his head and closing his eyes. He looked like he was ready to cry.

"I know it's your house, but can you go now?" Reed asked, squeezing his eyes tighter.

"Yeah, I can do that," he agreed. "Will you lock the door behind you when you go?"

Reed nodded, eyes still screwed shut.

Dominic leaned in and kissed Reed, a chaste and closed-mouth peck on the corner of his mouth. "I'll see you soon."

He turned and exited his bedroom, leaving Reed facing the dresser with his face contorted into a pained mask.

Dominic hoped he was making the right decision. He and Reed had spent time together over the past two weeks, dancing around each other, avoiding the one thing they really wanted to do, or the one thing Dominic really wanted to do. Reed had been adamant he was ready, that he wanted it to be Dominic, but Dominic wasn't convinced. He'd sworn to Reed over and over if he was still ready when he returned from sabbatical, it could be then.

It would be then.

The cab ride to the airport was excruciating, the weakness in Dominic's bones deepening with every mile he put between him and Reed, but this was the right choice. He felt it. He'd prayed about it. He needed to re-focus himself on the things that had mattered most in his life before Reed had stormed back into it.

HIs phone buzzed in his pocket and he dug it out, surprised it wasn't Reed. Dominic answered the call.

"Bishop Jenkins," he greeted.

"Dominic." He could hear the smile in Bishop Jenkins's voice. "I'm glad I caught you before you left."

"I'm on my way to the airport right now."

"I wanted to see how the congregation took the news of your sabbatical."

Dominic's sabbatical had been a hot topic with the vestry and the bishop's council. He'd been at his previous church for nearly six years, and the sabbatical had been scheduled for months. When he'd been called to relocate to St. Paul's in Edgewood, the plans had remained in place, even though he was still new to this specific church.

"I think they were more concerned with the continuation of the Friday movie night than my leave," Dominic said with a laugh.

"It's a good thing you're doing there, Dominic. Bringing new life into that church," Bishop Jenkins mused.

"Thank you, Bishop. I appreciate that."

"I've spoken with the caretakers of the Arizona property. They confirmed it will be open upon your arrival. Everything will be stocked and they'll be gone, but contact information will be readily available if you need replenishment of any supplies during your reflection."

"That's great. Thank you."

"And I expect to hear from you when you return to St. Paul's," the Bishop reminded him.

"Of course. And I remember the written report due as well. I'm looking forward to the time and the journey, Bishop." Dominic rested his head against the back seat of the cab, the airport coming into view on his right.

"Safe travels, then, Father O'Halloran."

"Thank you, Bishop. Speak with you soon."

Dominic ended the call and tossed his phone from hand to hand. He wanted to text Reed, but Reed hadn't reached out to him, and Reed had asked him to go. The pain on Reed's face was now permanently etched in Dominic's memory. He should have known then, in his bedroom, this was real for Reed. That conflict and loss that marked Reed's face didn't come to people who didn't care.

He sighed and powered off his phone, zipping it into his bag.

The driver pulled alongside the curb and let Dominic out. He didn't have any checked bags, only a hiking backpack full of clothes and supplies as a carry-on. He'd shipped his other belongings to the estate in Arizona in advance of his departure so he didn't need to travel with them.

After he made it through security, Dominic made his way to one of the restaurants in the international terminal and had a beer. He sipped it slowly, nursing it until the call for boarding echoed over the loudspeaker, then he boarded his flight and put thousands of miles between him and his home.

NINETEEN

REED

IT WAS FRIDAY.

Nic hadn't even been gone a week, and Reed's previously mundane life felt even more barren, like the light had been sucked out of his days. With school being closed, he had nothing to do, which four weeks ago, had been a welcome prospect. But now...

He'd debated the merits of trying to get his Friday takeout schedule back on track, but he was so thrown off, he didn't even know where he was supposed to be eating. He could just start fresh, establish a new routine... but somehow that held even less appeal than staying home alone.

Reed was surprised to find he didn't want to start new routines that didn't involve Nic. And that terrified him. Against all his better judgement, he found himself on the steps of St. Paul's five minutes before movie night was scheduled to start.

"Reed?" said a voice behind him.

He turned, finding Lisa, the owner of Star Garden, at the bottom of the steps.

"Lisa. Hey."

She climbed the steps and joined him near the top. "Did you come for the movie?"

"Uhm... yeah." Reed blinked.

Lisa smiled. "Me too. Not the religion part. That's not my gig, but don't worry. I won't tell Father Cowart that you're here."

She winked.

"Thanks," he whispered.

"You coming?" She took a few steps away from him. "It's about time to start and I don't want to miss it or the food. We didn't cater it, so anything besides Chinese is a welcome switch for me."

Reed snorted, Lisa's joke shaking him out of his stupor. "Yeah. Let's go."

He followed her into the auditorium space, making a quick inventory of the twenty or so people who had gathered. They were happily eating pizza and drinking soda from red plastic cups.

"Pizza," Lisa hissed with an excited grin on her face before disappearing from Reed's side.

"Principal Matthews?"

Reed paled and turned toward the voice.

"Catherine," he greeted, a slight feeling of relief covering him. If anyone was going to say anything about him being here tonight, it wouldn't be her. She had her own secrets.

"I never expected to see you here." She laughed and looked around nervously.

"Same."

"Uhm." Catherine took a deep breath. "I wanted to apologize for my outburst before school ended. I was just... confused, I guess. Hormones or something."

"I think it was more than hormones, yeah?"

Catherine blushed. "Well, yeah."

"You spoke with Father O'Halloran?" Reed asked, even though he knew.

"Yeah, thanks for that." Catherine smiled and picked at something on the leg of her jeans.

"Did it help?"

She blinked up at him.

"Talking to him, I mean," he amended.

"Oh." Her eyes widened. "Yeah. It did. Thank you."

He stood in front of Catherine awkwardly for a minute, neither of them sure of what to say, Reed probably more confused than her, as his own war continued to rage inside of him. A part of him envied Catherine, and he wondered briefly what it would have been like to know at her age that he was attracted to men.

You did know, a voice in the back of his head reminded him.

"I saved you a seat, Reed!" Lisa called out from the corner of the room.

Reed glanced her way gratefully and offered her a wave.

"It was good seeing you, Catherine," he said, taking a step back and joining Lisa.

After he got situated and had a mouthful of burning cheese, he searched the room for people he knew, finding a surprising spattering of kids from his school clustered in another corner with Catherine.

"There's a lot of yours here," Lisa observed, leaning closer to him. The movement was almost... friendly, and it caught Reed off guard. He was close to saying something about it but realized that he didn't have friends, and he was very much alone, especially with Nic being gone. Having friends wouldn't be such a bad thing. He'd closed himself off for so many years, maybe it was time for more than one change.

"There are," he agreed, counting four plus Catherine.

"I overheard he was starting an LGBT youth group," Lisa shared.

"A what?" Reed hadn't heard anything about that. Nic hadn't told him. He supposed, Nic didn't need to tell him; in fact, Nic always did his utmost to avoid any topics regarding church or religion with Reed.

"Like, part bible study, part friends or something," Lisa shared. "I heard some kids talking about it last weekend. It's relatively new."

"That's… that's really great of him." Reed's chest swelled with pride that shouldn't belong to him for a man who wasn't his.

"I think it'll be good. So many kids in Edgewood are brought up in the church. It'll be good for them to know that they can have both things in their life."

"Both?"

"Yeah. Love of God and love of a partner."

Reed angled a look in Lisa's direction and opened his mouth to speak, only to be interrupted by someone from the front of the room announcing the movie was about to start. The lights in the room dimmed, and Reed closed his mouth. He studied the screen, wondering when he'd lost sight of holding onto the things that mattered most.

LATER THAT NIGHT, alone in his bed, Reed tossed and turned. Another night alone, another rest evading him. He threw his covers back and fisted his cock, kneeling on his mattress with his head bowed against the headboard. He jerked his dick until it was hard, then until it was hard for a second time. He worked his flesh in his fist until it ached and chafed, pretending it was Nic milking him dry.

But it wasn't.

Reed wasn't sure how he'd survive another five weeks of this.

SUNDAY of the next week marked two weeks since Nic had left. Reed had managed to make it to the grocery store on schedule, buying his normal staples and another bottle of vodka to replenish the emergency bottle in his freezer that he'd long since finished.

It was Sunday, though, and he'd just gotten home from church and stripped out of his suit. He changed into jeans, deciding to forego underwear so he could relish the way the rough denim of his jeans abraded his skin, which was raw from use. Reed had developed a new nightly habit of rubbing himself off without lube, and the fruits of his labors were finally starting to show.

If no one else would give him penance, he would offer his own.

Reed finished the sandwich he'd made himself for lunch and pushed the plate away and was debating what he wanted to do with the rest of his day when his phone vibrated across the table.

He reached for it and slid it closer, sliding the screen open. When he saw Nic's name on the screen, he nearly choked. He answered the call.

"Nic."

"Reed." Nic sounded like he'd run a marathon.

Reed's eyes filled with tears and he hated himself for wasting so much time that he'd never be able to get back.

"How was Honduras?" he managed to ask, thankful Nic couldn't see his watery eyes.

"It was good. Really good." Nic's voice scratched through the line, grating against Reed's ears so well it made his dick plump against his leg. He'd heard Nic's voice in his ear every night since he'd left, but the memory was nothing compared to the real thing.

"I miss you," Reed whispered.

"I miss you, too," Nic admitted. There was a silence between them that even over the static on the line somehow felt like it was shrouding words that needed to be said. "I just wanted to let you know I'm back in the States."

"Good." Reed sniffled. "That's good."

"Are you crying?"

"What?" Reed's hiccupped whimper gave him away.

"I'll see you soon, Reed," Nic said abruptly, before the call disconnected.

Reed pulled the phone away from his face, staring at the blank screen in shock. He tried to call back, but it went straight to voicemail. Reed covered his mouth with his hands, dropping his phone back to the table with a clatter.

Then, it buzzed again with a text.

A text with an address.

TWENTY

DOMINIC

DOMINIC DIDN'T GET a reply from Reed after he'd sent the address from the airport. It had been a rash decision, the pain in Reed's voice enough to appeal to a part of himself that was desperate to care for the man. He stared at his screen the entire ride to the house, only powering his phone down once he was out of the car with his backpack secure over a shoulder. It had been a half-baked idea anyway, built on a hope that Reed would somehow give up years of beliefs so he could lie with Dominic one more time.

Dominic dropped his backpack in the entryway of the house, and he took some time to look around the place he'd be staying for the next four weeks. The property was gorgeous— quiet and secluded. It reminded him of the time he and a friend had pulled off on Zzyzzyx Road on the way to Las Vegas, except the desert out there was almost like a salt flat.

The gravel beneath his feet had crunched, and the desert was so silent it was deafening. One of his friends yelled out his name and he looked up from the ground. They'd wandered off and were barely a speck in his vision, but he could hear their voice as if they were standing right there. He laughed quietly, and the sound reverberated loudly across the sand.

Arizona was a lot like that.

"You're a dumb shit," he whispered to himself, and it echoed back in his ears like a scream.

The house was on a large acreage of landscaped desert, short cacti in the backyard and a couple of large trees for shade. The whole affair was terribly beige and awfully hot, but it was peaceful, and Dominic immediately understood the point of being there. God was there, he could feel it, and not in the judgmental way, but in the 'sit back and look at what I've made for you' way.

So, Dominic sat. He collapsed into one of the wooden lounge chairs that someone had placed under a shade tree, and he closed his eyes and prayed. In the distance, a bird chirped, and for the first time in months, Dominic felt at peace.

When the sun grew too hot for him to bear in his industrial travel clothes, he stood and retreated back into the safety of the air-conditioned house. He navigated his way through the terracotta tiled hallways until he found the master bedroom, his suitcase already near the bed. He unzipped it, grateful for clothes not covered in two weeks of Honduran mud, then he stripped down and turned toward the en-suite for a shower.

Even though the air inside the house was cool, the heat of the water was welcome, and Dominic scrubbed away all the layers of dirt and grime from his skin. He stayed under the spray until the water cooled, then reluctantly got out and toweled off. He wanted more, searching through the other rooms of the house until he stumbled into the guest bathroom, happy to find it had a full bath.

He discarded his towel on the floor and filled the tub with hot water, lowering himself down and closing his eyes with a relaxed sigh. When he'd worked with Bishop Jenkins on the schedule, they'd agreed he'd be allowed three days of rest and recovery before he was expected to begin his self-guided study, and he planned to spend at least two of those days in this bathtub.

Dominic missed his bathtub.

He missed... a lot of things.

Long after the bathwater turned tepid, Dominic drained the tub and dried off, returning to the bedroom to pull a pair of cotton lounge pants out of his suitcase. Half-dressed, he made his way to the living room, noting happily there wasn't a T.V., but instead a huge bookcase full of books and a surprisingly modern-looking sound system. There was a stack of records, which made him laugh, and he decided to finger through the vinyl instead of the CDss.

He put on a Sidney Bechet album and curled up on the couch, quickly falling asleep.

———

"NIC." Reed's quiet voice filled his ears and a hand stroked through his hair. Dominic reached up and grasped for the hand, pulling it closer to his face and nuzzling against it. The fingers felt like Reed's, and the voice... Dominic sighed; what a welcome dream.

"Mmmn," he groaned, pressing a kiss against the palm of dream-Reed's hand.

"Open your eyes."

Dominic pried his eyes open, the voice in his dream sounding insistent about it, even though he didn't want to. He wanted to stay in this hazy space where Reed was with him, touching him...

"Hey," Reed whispered, smiling and flexing his fingers against the side of Dominic's face.

Dominic's eyes widened. "Are you really here?"

Reed nodded and passed a thumb over Dominic's forehead.

"I'm here."

Dominic couldn't explain the feeling that washed over him. It was like being stripped bare of everything—all his worry, and his need, and his fear—so the only thing that existed was the core of him. He trembled, his entire body wracked with a shiver he felt in his bones. He sucked in a breath, eyes filling with tears.

"You're here," he repeated.

Reed nodded.

Dominic lunged for him, hands clasping around the sides of Reed's face and pulling him down until their mouths slanted together and Dominic's body ignited. Reed gasped, his lips parting and his tongue sliding alongside Dominic's.

"You're here," Dominic said again, pushing himself into a seated position and hefting Reed onto the couch with him. He traced Reed's face with his fingers and dropped kisses all over his skin, landing finally back against his mouth.

"I've done a lot of thinking," Reed whispered, closing his eyes and again leaning into Dominic's touch, "and I want this."

Dominic groaned and wrapped his arms around Reed, pulling him impossibly close. He held Reed's head in the crook of his neck and worked his fingers into his hair. This couldn't be true. This was too good to be real.

"What does that mean?" he rasped, needing to know for sure what Reed meant.

Reed wiggled his shoulders and worked himself out of Dominic's hold. He braced his hands on Dominic's bare shoulders and leaned close, bumping their noses together. He stayed that way, close, just breathing the same air for what felt like a perfect eternity, before he pulled back.

Dominic focused on Reed's face, noticing the calm ease that marked his features, such a far cry from the last time they'd seen each other. He raised a hand between them and rested his palm against Reed's chest. Reed's heart beat against his hand, hard and sure.

"It means I trust you." Reed chewed his lip between his teeth before letting it go and offering Dominic a small, lopsided smile. "I'm putting myself in your hands."

"Do you mean it?"

A tear slid down Reed's cheek and he nodded. "Every word."

Dominic surged forward, sealing their mouths together and standing at the same time. Reed gasped and wrapped his limbs around Dominic. He whimpered, dropping his face into the crook of Dominic's shoulder. Dominic tightened his hold and carried Reed down the long hallway to the bedroom, laying him down gently on the bed.

He stood at the foot of the bed, somehow both overjoyed and worried. He committed Reed's comfortable pose and face to his memory, but didn't make a move. Reed watched him curiously, then sat up and reached behind him, tugging his shirt over his head and tossing it onto the floor.

"Please." He stretched an arm out toward Dominic.

Dominic crawled onto the bed, and Reed lay back down underneath him. He skated his fingers up Reed's side, and Reed arched against him, his back bowing off the bed. Dominic slid his arm between the bed and Reed's spine, pulling them both up, kissing him again. It was slow, and Dominic poured himself into it. Every ounce of want and fear that existed inside of his heart, he gave to Reed.

Reed reached between their bodies, shoving his pants and underwear down. His cock bobbed against his leg and he sighed into Dominic's mouth. Dominic pulled Reed's pants the rest of the way down, taking his lounge pants at the same time, and he pressed every inch of their naked skin together.

It felt different this time. It felt… more.

Dominic adjusted his weight so their erections rubbed together and he reached between them, but Reed swatted his hand away.

"No," he begged. "I don't want any of that right now. I just want you. Please."

Dominic groaned, dropping his hand lower and pressing the pad of his middle finger against Reed's hole.

"Are you sure?" he asked against Reed's panting mouth.

"I've never been more sure of a single thing in my entire life," Reed promised.

Dominic stole Reed's mouth in another kiss, still gentle, still easy, but he made his intent clear. Reed's moans and whimpers were his affirmation. Begrudgingly, Dominic broke the kiss and separated their bodies, leaning over to where his suitcase was on the floor. He reached inside the front zipper until he found the bottle of lube he'd brought. He'd only planned on using it to jerk off, but this with Reed was such a better application.

He coated his fingers until they were a slick and slippery mess, then he returned his hand between them, swirling a finger around Reed's hole again.

"Kiss me," he panted against the side of Reed's face, and Reed turned, sealing their lips together. Reed shoved his tongue into Dominic's mouth. He was hungry and needy, and he kissed Dominic with an urgent passion.

Dominic slid one finger inside of Reed, and Reed stilled, gasping into his mouth. He withdrew and slid it back inside. Reed's eyes fluttered and rolled back in his head. Dominic chuckled.

"That's just one finger," he whispered.

Reed moaned.

Dominic worked him with one finger until Reed was writhing against him, then he inserted a second finger. Reed arched off the bed, eyes half-closed with delirious want. Dominic worked Reed's hole, twisting his wrist and scissoring his fingers apart until he added a third finger. Reed's hips pumped against him, and he rolled his head back and forth across the pillow, a sheen of sweat across his forehead.

"Nic," he panted. "Nic, please."

Dominic stilled, three fingers deep inside of Reed, and grimaced.

"I don't have condoms," he admitted. "I wasn't planning on this."

Reed's eyes opened. "It's okay."

"Reed."

"It's fine." Reed pushed himself against Dominic's hand.

"I haven't been with anyone in years, and I'm negative," Dominic said.

"I believe you," Reed rasped. "Now, please."

Dominic pulled his fingers out and coated his cock with lube, working himself in a tight fist. He'd never gone bare before, and neither had Reed, but Reed had never had anyone before at all.

"Are you sure?"

"Now, Nic," Reed practically growled, yanking Dominic down and kissing him again.

Dominic could hardly think. Reed explored his mouth, his hands roaming over the expanse of Dominic's back and sides, and Dominic dragged the head of his cock past Reed's balls toward his ass.

He pushed his tip against Reed's hole, using his hips to thrust inside. Reed was so hot, so tight. His head popped through Reed's rim and Reed's eyes flew open. He cried out, and his fingers scrabbled against Dominic's shoulder blades.

"Sssh," Dominic soothed.

"It hurts," Reed moaned, and dropped his head onto the pillow.

"I know." Dominic pushed in deeper, another inch. Reed's breathing was coming in rough and labored pants. Dominic could feel him tremble, and he slid another inch inside.

"Nic." Reed's voice was thick with unshed tears.

"Do you want me to stop? Is it too much?" Dominic stroked Reed's hair away from his face.

"No." Reed bit his lips together between his teeth and shook his head. "I want it. I want you. God help me, I want you."

Dominic exhaled a needy breath and shifted his hips, pushing the remainder of his length into Reed. He rested his head against Reed's shoulder and stilled, giving them both a much-needed minute to adjust.

"How does it feel?" He pressed a kiss to the spot just behind Reed's ear.

"Full."

"Mmmn," Dominic agreed, lifting himself onto his forearms so he could see Reed's face.

"How does it feel for you?" Reed asked. He sniffled and opened his eyes, a tear escaping the corner of his eye.

Dominic nodded, his own eyes filling with unshed tears. He couldn't answer Reed, because he didn't know how to explain how sex could feel like an epiphany, so he kissed him, hoping he could answer that way instead, then he started to move.

HE HADN'T BEEN PREPARED for the sting, but once Nic started to move, long and slow strokes in and out of him, the pain waned and he was overcome with burning pleasure. His cock throbbed, smashed between their stomachs, and he cried out.

A tear slipped from Nic's eye and splashed against his cheek, and then Nic's lips were there, his tongue in Reed's mouth. Nic kissed him the same way he fucked him, with methodical and measured movements that Reed was sure were designed to drive him insane. He writhed beneath Nic, every nerve center in his body short-circuiting.

He'd been waiting his entire life for this moment, and he was not disappointed.

"Can I come inside of you?" Nic tore their mouths apart and exhaled the question against Reed's lips. His muscles clenched in response, and Nic groaned, his pace quickening.

"What does it feel like?" he whispered, wrapping his legs around the backs of Nic's thighs.

"Like everything I've ever prayed for," Nic answered, hips jerking hard against his body.

Reed knew in that moment, he was in love with Dominic O'Halloran.

"Yes," he said, answering Nic's question.

Nic's body bucked, and his back bowed. He grimaced and stilled, his face morphing into ecstasy, and his cock pulsed when he came. Reed could feel it test the tight muscles of his ass, then an unfamiliar heat poured into him.

Nic's cock was still hard inside of him, and he reached between their bodies, grasping Reed's erection in his fist. Nic jerked him until he came, spurting his release against their chests, then collapsed on top of him. The sensation of Nic's cock softening and slipping out of Reed's ass was strange and his entire body tightened as it happened. He inhaled a shocked breath and buried himself against Nic's chest, breathing him in.

Nic rolled onto his side and took Reed with him, arranging their bodies together and stroking his fingers lightly over Reed's arms and back. He kissed Reed's hair and whispered into his ear, "How beautiful you are, my darling."

Reed huffed out a laugh and grinned into Nic's skin.

"Am I supposed to feel like a new person now?" he asked after a time, shifting his weight. His ass burned, the muscles sore and stretched from use.

"Do you?"

"I feel…" he trailed off, searching for the words to articulate it properly. He settled into Nic's embrace and took a deep breath. His lungs felt full. His heart… his heart overflowed. "I feel whole."

"Me too," Nic agreed. "Will you rest with me awhile? I don't even know what time it is."

Reed chuckled. "It was just before lunchtime when I got here."

"What day?"

"Monday."

"I think I slept for almost twenty hours," Nic said.

"I haven't slept at all," Reed yawned.

After Nic had texted him on Sunday, Reed had debated what to do, fretting over buying a plane ticket or deleting the tempting message. He'd stayed up the entire night, pacing his living room. He didn't even remember driving to the airport, but he'd bought a ticket for an early flight and headed to Arizona. Running on nothing but adrenaline at that point, he'd knocked at the front door for ten minutes, only to be met with silence. Thankfully, he tried the knob and it was unlocked. Reed had let himself in and found Nic asleep on the couch, curled into a ball far too small for his figure.

Now, here they were.

"Close your eyes, then," Nic whispered, pressing a kiss to the top of Reed's sweaty hair.

Reed did as he'd been told and fell into a calm and easy sleep.

HE WOKE ALONE, fearful everything had been a dream.

Reed rolled over and opened his eyes, sucking in a shocked breath when he didn't recognize the room he was in, only releasing it when he remembered where he was.

He was in Arizona.

With Nic.

Reed turned onto his back and stretched out, the ache between his cheeks having faded into a dull throb. Now it felt like more of a pleasant reminder than a punishment. He felt around the bed, finding the sheets around him cold and empty. He didn't know where Nic was, but he knew he couldn't be far. Reed grabbed his underwear off the floor and stepped into them, then ventured into the house to find Nic.

He wasn't in the living room, and he wasn't in the kitchen, but there was an open door off of the dining room, and Reed went through it. The backyard was a huge desert landscape, and he found Nic there, front and center under a huge shade tree. He was reclined in a wooden lounger, his eyes closed.

"Come sit with me," Nic said, extending a hand toward the door. He hadn't opened his eyes.

"How did you know I was here?" Reed closed the distance between them and sat on the edge of the chair.

"I can feel you." Nic opened his eyes and rubbed at his chest. "Here."

"That's a little cheesy, don't you think?"

Nic shrugged. "It's true."

Nic slid over and made room for him, and Reed situated himself between the arm of the chair and Nic's side. He rested his cheek against Nic's chest and listened to his heart.

"Are you alright?" Nic asked, twirling his fingers through the ends of Reed's hair. "Any regrets?"

"I'm good," Reed promised. "I wouldn't change a thing."

Nic made an agreeable noise in his throat. "I'm glad you came."

"Me too."

"Tell me about the last two weeks."

"I went to your church," Reed admitted.

"What now?" Nic turned his face toward Reed and raised an eyebrow.

"On Friday. Lisa was there."

Nic smiled and lay his head back against the lounger. "I'm glad she finally came."

"And Catherine."

"Mmmn." Nic nodded.

"Why didn't you tell me you were starting a group for LGBT kids?" he asked.

"Isn't it the unspoken rule? We don't talk about my work, remember?"

Reed propped himself up on his elbow and looked down at Nic. "Is that all it is to you? Work?"

"It's my life," Nic corrected, turning to face him. "Or at least a large part of it. You know that."

"I want to talk about it," Reed said softly. "I want to know all those things about you."

"Alright, then. Yes, I'm starting an LGBT group. Jordan, a guy who comes every month or so, said he'd help me with it, and Catherine, of course, offered to help." Nic lay back down against the chair and closed his eyes.

Reed studied Nic's face. The wrinkles around his eyes seemed softer, his burden so much lighter under the hot Arizona sun.

"How is Catherine able to make time for that?"

"I'm not privy to her schedule. She offered to help, and I accepted."

"That's good of her," Reed mused.

Nic shrugged. "She's feeling pretty confused, a little bit lost. I think it's important for her to find some support and people she can talk to who have shared her struggles."

Nic opened an eye and focused on Reed.

"Someone like me," Reed said.

"She's fighting a lot of the same demons as you," Nic agreed. "But I'd never ask it of you. If you feel you're able to offer her guidance, then you should. If not, well, I'd never begrudge you."

"It's like… I don't know. It's not like everything I've believed for my adult life has been a lie, but I need to somehow recategorize the things I've built my life around to make room for this."

Nic shook his head. "You're not making room for *this,* Reed. You're finding room for *yourself* in a belief structure that doesn't have a place for you."

"That's… that burns a bit." Reed winced.

Nic shifted onto his side and rubbed their noses together.

"That's not what I meant." Nic kissed him. "I've read the scripture, and I know there's a place for you at the table. You just need to find it for yourself."

"I suppose you're right," Reed grumbled.

"I know I am." Nic smiled. "You'll see it eventually. Or you won't."

A dark shadow danced across Nic's face and was gone as quickly as it had appeared.

"I want to," Reed whispered, resting his forehead against Nic's chest. Nic wrapped his arm over Reed's shoulder and tapped his fingers against the bones of Reed's spine in a soothing pattern.

"I want that for you, too."

They sat in silence together, the only sound in Reed's ears the echo of Nic's fingers against his back, until the calm was interrupted by the rumble of his stomach.

"Hungry?"

"Yeah."

Nic groaned and sat up, leaving Reed reclined in the chair. He ruffled his hands through his hair and smiled down at Reed.

"I'll go see what's in the kitchen."

"I'll come with you?" Reed asked, not wanting to encroach, but also not wanting to be away from Nic.

Nic stood and held his hand out. "Come on then."

Reed twined their fingers together, and Nic pulled him up, tugging him along into the house. It was cooler inside, and Reed shivered.

"I like it outside," he mumbled.

"It's warm." Nic opened the refrigerator and pulled out some thin plastic bags that looked like they were filled with lunch meat and cheese.

"That's an understatement."

"It's far less temperate than Edgewood, that's for sure." Nic opened a few of the cabinets until he found plates and a loaf of bread.

He untwisted the top of the bag and set two slices of bread on each plate, then opened the lunch meat, laying several thin slices of roast beef on one and turkey on the other. Nic hummed and sealed the bags, before opening two more and producing cheddar cheese for the roast beef and provolone for the turkey.

Reed's breath stuttered in his throat, and Nic began to hum a song. He turned to the fridge and put the bags back inside. He pulled out the mustard and squirted a healthy amount onto the turkey sandwich, then flipped the top closed and returned the container to the fridge.

Nic opened a drawer and pulled out a knife, slathering the mustard around. He held the knife up, like he was ready to toss it in the sink, but he hesitated. Nic glanced his way with a smirk and swiped the knife across the bare piece of bread. He tossed the knife into the sink and assembled both of the sandwiches, pushing one of the plates in Reed's direction.

"You got the lunch meat I like?" Reed asked, picking up the sandwich with trembling hands.

Nic's cheeks flushed, and he used his palm to mash his sandwich down before he picked it up and took a bite. He chewed, studying Reed until he swallowed.

"I don't know what I was thinking. I gave them my list before I left for Honduras. I just hoped maybe you'd end up here," Nic admitted, setting his sandwich back down on the plate. He wiped his hands on his legs.

"Seems odd you'd go to all that trouble then ruin it with mustard." Reed took a bite and chewed thoughtfully. He'd been eating plain sandwiches his entire adult life. It had always been a safe thing; it was so easy to go wrong with condiments. Too much, and the entire taste of the sandwich would be ruined.

The flavor of the mustard hit his taste buds and he stopped chewing, assaulted with a memory he'd long forgotten when he and Nic had barely been teenagers.

"Do you remember when we used to camp out in the yard?" Reed asked, finishing his bite and swallowing.

"I do," Nic rasped.

"You'd make us sandwiches while I pitched the tent in Carol and David's yard."

"I remember."

Reed licked his lips and closed his eyes.

"You used to put mustard on my sandwiches," he whispered.

"I did," Nic admitted.

Reed blinked and lifted his fingers to his mouth, dragging them across his lower lip. The memory was so vivid it could have just happened yesterday, not over twenty years ago.

"I used to like it."

Nic nodded, looking away and reaching for his own sandwich. "Maybe you'll learn to like it again."

TWENTY-TWO
DOMINIC

"I WANT YOU."

Dominic didn't open his eyes. "Hmmn?"

A hand circled around his cock and squeezed.

"I want you," Reed repeated.

Dominic reached out blindly, his eyes heavy with sleep. He ran his fingers through Reed's tousled hair and pulled him in for a kiss.

"You're a fiend," he murmured into Reed's mouth.

Reed smiled against him and licked him. "Come on, then."

Dominic arranged himself against the pillows and opened his eyes, smiling when Reed lunged for the nightstand to get the lube. He poured it into his palm and slicked Dominic's shaft until he was fully erect.

"Do I just...?" Reed trailed off, not asking the question.

Dominic took Reed by the waist and arranged him so he was straddling him, hovering over his stomach.

"Hold it steady," he rasped.

Reed reached behind him and pointed Dominic's cock toward his ass.

"Work yourself onto it."

The head of his cock breached Reed's hole and he angled his body upward with a moan. "Just like that."

Reed lowered himself around Dominic's shaft until he was fully seated, then raised himself up again. Dominic's eyes rolled back and he groaned, digging his fingers into Reed's sides to calm himself.

"You're huge," Reed whispered, finding a rhythm that drove Dominic insane.

"You're tight," he hissed.

"No one's been here but you."

Dominic smirked, running his hands over Reed's stomach. "I know."

Reed's cock was hard and it bounced with every move he made. Dominic grabbed it, letting Reed's gyrations work his dick through his fist.

"That's it," he praised. "Take your pleasure from me. You're perfect like this."

"Talk to me more," Reed begged, moving faster. His ass was a vice around Dominic's cock, grabbing and pulling him deeper with every dip of his hips.

It had been two days. Only two days, and Dominic had lost track of how many times he'd buried himself inside of Reed. Today was the last day before he needed to start his study, and he'd already planned to take advantage of it. Reed had just started them off on the right foot on his own.

It was almost like losing his virginity had turned Reed into a new person. Dominic wasn't sure if he'd tapped into a new part of Reed, or if Reed had always been this wanton, sexual being who'd just been waiting to break out. He wasn't complaining either way, even though his dick was growing tender from near-constant use.

He wasn't in his twenties anymore.

"Nic, talk to me."

Another thing Dominic had discovered was that Reed loved

when Dominic talked to him. Even if it was something as simple as narrating what he was doing, but honestly, the dirtier the better.

"Your ass is so tight, Reed. I've never felt anything that feels as good as being inside of you," he told Reed. "I've dreamed about having you like this for years."

"Having me how?" Reed slammed himself down against Dominic's thighs.

"Sweaty and cum soaked." Dominic gripped Reed around his neck and yanked him down. He sank his teeth into the lobe of Reed's ear. "Marked. Mine."

Reed moaned and smashed his cock against Dominic's abs. "I want to come."

Dominic flattened his feet on the bed and pushed up, shoving himself deeper into Reed. He wrapped his arms around Reed's back and braced himself, pumping upward. Reed whimpered into his ear and reached between them, jerking his cock.

"I love coming inside of you," Dominic whispered gruffly. "I love painting the deepest parts of you with a part of me."

Reed cried out, sinking his teeth into Dominic's shoulder. Hot jets of cum splattered against Dominic's chest, and he growled, fucking Reed harder and faster until his own orgasm exploded out of him. He pulled Reed's hips down while pumping his own up, getting his cock as deep inside of Reed as he could manage.

Reed writhed against him, mumbling nonsense into the side of Dominic's throat. Dominic gritted his teeth and grunted, his balls finally empty, then he stilled, smoothing calm touches down the divots he'd gouged into Reed's sides.

"Nic," Reed whimpered, his arms shaking against Dominic's chest.

"I know," Dominic soothed. He adjusted himself, his cock slipping free. Reed winced, and then he settled. Dominic slid a hand around to Reed's hole. He held it there, tracing light circles over the puffy rim of his ass. It pulsed, Dominic's cum slipping out. Dominic used his finger to scoop it up, pushing it back inside.

Reed gasped and slanted his mouth over Dominic's. Dominic fucked Reed's hole with one finger until Reed's cock grew hard again between them.

"Good morning," he whispered, taking his hand away.

Reed groaned, frustrated and obviously horny. He rolled off of Dominic and onto his back, resting one of his hands against Dominic's bare thigh.

"Do you want some coffee?" Reed asked.

Dominic smiled to himself, surprised Reed had already caught on to the control Dominic took over his orgasms.

"Yes, but kiss me again first."

Reed rolled onto Dominic again and kissed him, slow and gentle, almost worshipful. Dominic's cock jumped, and he broke the kiss.

"Coffee."

Reed hummed and climbed over him, padding out of the room naked and barefoot. Dominic took his time getting out of bed, appreciative of the way Reed had unraveled for him. He stretched, cracking his neck and dropping his feet onto the floor. He followed the smell of sex into the kitchen, boxing Reed in at the counter and biting him on the shoulder until Reed bowed from the pressure.

"That hurts," he hissed, breathless.

"I know." Dominic flattened his tongue and licked the bumps and grooves left by his teeth.

The Keurig hissed and beeped. Reed turned in his arms and kissed him.

"Your coffee is ready."

Dominic stroked Reed across the cheek and took the mug of coffee to the small dining room table in the corner. It over-looked the back yard and was almost as peaceful as the outdoors. There was a cross-shaped crystal that hung over the window pane, a rainbow-colored reminder of the real reason he was here. He took a small sip of his coffee and waited for Reed to join him.

"You know that things are going to change," he said, after Reed took a seat.

God, he was beautiful like this; calm, and relaxed, and so fucking naked. More than that, though, he was comfortable in his skin, and Dominic was pretty certain that was a new feeling for him. Dominic liked the way it looked on him.

"I know." Reed eyed him over the brim of his mug.

"I shouldn't even have you here." Dominic sighed. "I'm breaking all kinds of rules."

"Do you want me to go?" Reed tilted his head.

"No. That's the problem. I don't want you to go, but I can't abandon the real reason I'm here."

Dominic looked up toward the ceiling and exhaled loudly. He looked back at Reed, who seemed like he was miles away. Dominic scooted his chair back and patted his lap. Reed pushed away from the table and came to sit on his thigh. Dominic petted him fondly, inhaling against the outside of his arm.

"You inspire me," he whispered, dragging his lips over Reed's skin.

"Do I?"

Dominic hummed and rested his forehead against Reed's shoulder. "I came here for personal reflection, spiritual growth, and study. I can't deny it, though, Reed. I see the beauty of creation in you. In the way you move. The way you fuck."

He stood and took Reed with him, laying him down over the small table. He peppered kisses over the V-shaped line that angled sharply toward Reed's cock.

"The way you discover yourself more every time you lay beneath me." Dominic licked the dried sweat from Reed's skin. He tasted like salt, cum, and a little bit of dirt. Dominic reached down and dragged his nails up the inside of Reed's legs. "What's godlier than that?"

"I can think of a few things," Reed mumbled, his cock hardening beside Dominic's cheek.

Dominic circled his fingers around Reed's cock and stroked him until he was hard, sucking the top of his crown into his mouth. Reed grunted and bucked up, pushing himself deeper in Dominic's mouth. He popped off with a wicked smile.

"I can't," he rasped.

He slid back into his seat, leaving Reed sprawled across the small dinette table between their steaming coffee mugs.

"You're welcome to stay," he continued, "but I will have work to do."

Reed took his cock in hand and started to jerk himself off.

"I don't want to distract you," he mumbled.

Dominic smacked his thigh. "You very much want to distract me."

Reed chuckled and continued to work his length in his fist. Dominic picked up his coffee and took a drink, leaning back in his chair to enjoy the show. It was like a different Reed had shown up in Arizona. The Reed he'd left behind would never spread his legs over breakfast and grind against his own palm this way. The Reed he'd left behind didn't even want to be seen on Dominic's porch. But this Reed... this Reed had hopped a flight to Arizona and showed up unannounced, offering so much more than just his body.

"Are you going to come?" he asked.

Reed's hips pumped up, his ass slapping into the wood of the table while he fucked his hand. He mumbled something that Dominic couldn't hear, then he came. Ribbons of cum coated his stomach and chest. His whole body jerked, and Dominic reached forward with his free hand to steady Reed's coffee mug so it didn't fall.

"Yes," Reed panted.

He sat up and Dominic passed him his coffee.

"You need to go get dressed. You need to stay dressed."

"Do I?" Reed took a drink from his mug.

"Starting tomorrow, yes."

"But until then?" Reed rested his feet on Dominic's thighs.

"At least put on some sunscreen," he recommended.

"Oh? Are you taking me outside?"

"I'm taking you everywhere," Dominic promised. "After I've eaten and showered."

Reed laughed. "Are you asking me to make you breakfast?"

"I wouldn't presume." He set his mug beside Reed's leg and stood up, leaving a kiss on the top of Reed's sweaty hair.

"You don't need to," Reed assured him. "I'll cook for you."

"I'll see you after my shower then?"

Reed jumped off the table and grinned. "Don't get too clean."

Dominic shook his head and retreated to the master bedroom, drawing himself a shower. The water was hot, and the scald was welcome. It was enough to shock him back into his head. He closed his eyes with a sigh and rested his forearm against the wall of the shower. The hot spray washed over his shoulders, down his back, and over his legs.

When his entire body had reached the same temperature, he grabbed the loofah, soaping it and washing himself, starting from his throat and working down to his feet. He used his palm to clean between his legs, working his cock and balls between his soapy fingers. He slipped back between his ass cheeks, prodding his hole with a slippery finger.

His muscles clenched and he pushed deeper. It had been years since he'd bottomed. The sting was unfamiliar, but not unwelcome. He added a second finger, reaching toward his prostate but not able to reach it on his own. He'd need assistance, and while he fucked his own ass with his fingers, he came up with the perfect plan to get it.

TWENTY-THREE

REED

REED ENJOYED a lazy day at Nic's side. He'd dressed, eventually, and only because it was time for dinner. He was confident he'd made the right decision by coming to Arizona, and by sharing these things with Nic. He knew he needed to find a way to reconcile his spiritual worry with his beliefs, but that could wait another day.

"This is really good," he told Nic, spearing a slice of chicken breast onto his fork and chewing thoughtfully.

"It's only chicken salad." Nic smiled at him, a light blush creeping up his neck.

Reed loved the look of Nic out here in the desert, his tan skin blending with the earth tones of the architecture and his hair even beginning to lighten under the harsh sun. Nic looked good, he looked healthy and fulfilled. It made Reed's heart full.

"Are you sure you'll be good tomorrow?" Nic asked him.

"I will."

"If you get bored and change your mind, I won't be offended if you want to head back to Edgewood." Nic pushed leaves of lettuce around on his plate.

"I don't want to go home. I was actually thinking of maybe

reading some of the books." Reed had taken a quick mental inventory of some of the titles shelved in the living room. There were a few fiction books shoved in the stacks, but most everything was specifically religious based. A small part of Reed hoped maybe he'd find something in one of the texts that would further unlock the worries he carried about his relationship with Nic.

"Good," Nic agreed. "I think that would be good."

"Are you going to get in trouble?"

"What for?" Nic rested his fork on the side of the plate and looked up at him.

"For having me here."

Nic's face darkened and he looked away.

That was all the answer Reed needed.

"I'm not trying to cause problems for you," Reed started, but Nic cut him off with a hand in the air and a shake of his head.

"If I was worried about it being an unmanageable issue, I wouldn't have asked you to come."

"But it will be an issue."

Nic exhaled and pursed his lips together. He turned his attention back toward Reed. "I don't know what the future holds. Only today. Well." His lips turned up into a smirk. "I know what tonight holds."

The way Nic's pupils expanded when he spoke was enough to pique Reed's interest.

"What does that mean?" he asked.

"I have something planned for tonight. It's something that I want to try with you."

"Do I get a hint?" Reed asked, shoving his plate to the side, suddenly more interested in dessert than dinner.

"Hmmn." Nic tapped his chin thoughtfully. "No."

"No?" Reed reeled back in mock horror. "You're just going to tease me?"

"I'm done teasing you, Reed. But don't worry. I'll tell you everything that's going to happen before I do it."

There was something dark about the inflection in Nic's voice, and it was enough to send every drop of blood in Reed's body to his dick.

"Can we just, you know, go do that now?"

Nic huffed out a small laugh and eyed Reed speculatively. He took another bite of his salad and chewed, with what Reed estimated to be the slowest swallow of all time.

"Go into the bedroom. Get naked. Lay down and wait for me," Nic instructed.

"Lay down on the bed?" Reed asked, standing and pushing his chair in.

Nic's nostrils flared. "I like that you ask for clarification, but yes, on the bed."

Reed spun on his heel and made his way back into the house, the tiled floors cold against his feet. Once in the bedroom, he stripped out of his jeans and shirt, tossing them toward the hamper and stretching himself out on the bed like he'd been told.

A few minutes passed, then Nic appeared in the doorway, his shoulders nearly filling the space and blocking the light that filtered in from the hallway. Nic looked around the sparsely-furnished bedroom before raking over Reed with a focus that made his toes curl.

"I'm conflicted," Nic told him, approaching the bedside table and pulling out the bottle of lube he'd tucked in there after their first night together.

"How so?" Reed rasped.

"I had plans about taking you on the bed, but that seems almost too comfortable for what you deserve."

Reed's cock jumped and slapped against his stomach. It felt like magic when Nic acted dominant with him. Adding words to that dynamic was an even more tactile sensation, the cruel promise of the things Nic said touching him in places his body never could.

"What part of that did you like?" Nic tapped the stretched skin of Reed's dick with the tips of his fingers.

"The end part," Reed admitted.

"I thought so." Nic slid his hand up Reed's stomach to his neck, where he circled his fingers around Reed's throat and pushed him against the pillows. Reed's mouth parted and he breathed heavy against Nic's arm.

"Get up and strip the bed," Nic ordered him, releasing his throat and stepping backward to discard his own clothes.

Reed didn't know where Nic was going with this, but he stood, his heavy balls swinging against his thighs, and he yanked the blankets and sheets off of the bed. He turned, the over-flowing mess of fabric in his hands, and presented it to Nic.

Nic fingered through the bedding, tossing the thin blanket back onto the mattress and taking the fitted sheet and top sheet from Reed. He looked over his shoulder, then pointed at the floor near the foot of the bed.

"Lay down."

"On the floor?" Reed scoffed.

"Lay down now," Nic demanded.

Reed lowered himself to the floor, his knees banging into the tile first. His skin broke out in gooseflesh and he slowly stretched out onto his back. The floor was hard and cold, the uneven texture of the tiles gouging into his shoulders and his hips.

"Cold?"

"Yes," Reed hissed.

"Good. I'm going to restrain you now."

Nic twisted the top sheet in his hands, forming something that looked like a rope. He straddled Reed, squatting over his face so his balls swung against Reed's chin, and he took Reed's hands in his. He wrapped the sheet around Reed's wrists, then ran the tails of the sheet around one of the legs of the bed, effectively securing Reed in place.

Nic walked around him and grabbed his ankles, giving him a rough tug. He slid down the floor until his shoulders were pulled taut. Nic wrapped the other sheet around Reed's ankles and stretched it backward, looping the end around the doorknob and closing the door with a click.

Reed's muscles burned, stretched from both ends, the cold floor still digging into his shoulders and legs. Regardless, his erection hadn't waned. It stood hard between his legs, pointing toward the ceiling.

"I'm going to blindfold you now." Nic reached over him for something on the bed. "But it's going to make it hard to breathe."

"What?" Reed sputtered, his heart accelerating.

"I think you'll like it," Nic assured him, angling his head and looking down at Reed, the pillowcase in his hand. "I know I will."

"How do you know?" Reed rasped.

"Because your cock gets harder when you hurt."

"Oh."

"Yes, then?"

"Yes," Reed agreed.

Nic knelt beside him and leaned over him, ghosting his mouth across Reed's lips. He kissed him, barely, his tongue dipping deep enough into Reed's mouth that he could taste the vinegar from their salad dressing, but nothing else. Then Nic pulled away and slipped the pillowcase over Reed's head.

Reed fought back his fear. It tickled at the base of his spine and crept upward.

"Your cock is leaking," Nic chuckled. "I haven't even gotten started."

"Haven't you?" Reed panted against the cotton that shrouded him.

"Mmmn," Nic agreed.

The lube bottle opened and Nic's hand closed around Reed's dick. He worked Reed's cock, the lube squelching between his fingers and out over Reed's thighs and balls.

"If you want me to stop, tell me to stop," Nic said, flattening Reed's cock against his stomach and slicking his hand from root to tip.

"Don't."

Nic chuckled and shifted around, settling his weight so he was straddling Reed's hips.

"I'm going to use you to get off now," Nic told him.

Reed gasped, his back arched, shoulders pressing uncomfortably into the floor. He tried to adjust himself but didn't find a position that alleviated the stretch in his muscles or the ache in his back. If he twisted too much, the pillowcase stuck to his face and made it hard to breathe.

"This is going to be tight," Nic whispered. "I'm going to put your cock inside of me."

"What?" Reed thrashed his head, the pillowcase secure over his face. He wanted this. He wanted this so much, but he wanted to see it. "I want to watch."

"No." Nic tisked. He dragged the head of Reed's dick through his crack, bearing down when it reached his hole. Reed could feel his muscles open up and make ready. "Maybe next time, but right now, you just focus on feeling it, okay?"

Reed nodded.

Nic's grip on his shaft tightened, and then he was enveloped in a tight heat like nothing he'd known before. His instinct to press his body against Nic was stifled by his restraints, and the bite of the sheets into his wrists when he tried to move went right to his balls. Nic's ass swallowed his cock and Nic sat on him, using his hands to brace himself against Reed's torso.

"It feels bigger than I thought it would," Nic breathed out.

His breath dusted over Reed's chest. "I'm going to fuck you now."

He moved, raising up until Reed's cock almost slipped out of him, but dropped back down before the crown cleared his tight rim.

"Your cock hits my prostate every time," Nic gasped, working himself faster over Reed's dick. Reed struggled against his binds. Tears welled in his eyes and he felt... angry.

Angry that he couldn't touch Nic even though he was right there.

Angry that he couldn't see the look of pleasure on Nic's face while he used Reed to get off.

Angry that things couldn't be this way forever.

Reed opened his mouth and a sob escaped, the cotton of the pillowcase sucking into his mouth. He gasped and panted, the material sticking to his cheeks as the tears matted into the fabric.

"What's wrong?" Nic asked, his voice level and calm even while he rode Reed's dick.

Reed shook his head, hiccupping through another sob.

Angry that he'd denied himself for so long.

Angry that he'd been forced to live a life that didn't have Nic in it.

"I'm going to hurt you," Nic rasped. He leaned over, and his breath was hot against Reed's ear, even through the pillow case. Their chests rubbed together, and Reed could feel the sweat from Nic's skin and his cock, hard as iron, between their bellies. "And I want you to come."

Nic pushed up and dragged his fingers over Reed's nipples in warning, then took each one between his fingers and pinched. He tugged them away from his body and twisted, twin points of pain searing through Reed's body, down his spine and to his cock. He cried out through a sob and thrashed beneath Nic's body.

Angry that he worried what people thought about this.

Angry for the way he felt toward Margaret, James, and Carol.

Angry that he believed in a God who wouldn't allow him this pleasure.

Nic released his nipples and it felt like fire in their place. Reed shouted, his cock thickening inside of Nic's ass.

"There you are," Nic praised, fisting the front of the pillowcase in his hand and hoisting Reed's neck off the floor. He tightened his muscles and Reed came, his body jerking furiously against his restraints. The heavy metal bed dragged across the floor and he filled Nic's ass with his release.

"You're beautiful like this, but I'm going to fuck you now," Nic panted, yanking the pillowcase up Reed's head so he could see.

Reed blinked Nic into focus, his eyes still blurred by his tears. His face was covered in spit and sweat, and in the light, his anger morphed into something bigger than him. He fought against the ties around his wrists, glowering at Nic even while his cock continued to empty inside of the man.

Nic lifted off of him and reached behind him, undoing the sheet that had bound Reed's legs to the door. He used his thighs to spread Reed's legs apart, then with no preamble or prep, he buried himself inside of Reed's hole.

"Fuck," he grunted, dropping his head against Reed's shoulder and fucking him with short and hard thrusts.

"Nic," Reed groaned, his wrists sore now from his struggle.

"What's wrong? Talk to me," Nic demanded. He reared back and hooked his arms under Reed's shoulders, pounding furiously into him.

"I'm angry," Reed sobbed. "I'm so angry."

"Why are you angry?" Nic slammed as deep as he could reach and circled his hips. Reed whimpered and wrapped his legs around Nic's back, holding him there. He reached down and pushed Reed's hair out of his eyes. He stared down at him with a calm and understanding look on his face that was at odds with the erection he sported and used to drive Reed nearly insane.

"Because it's not fair!" Reed shouted, trying yet again to jerk his hands free.

"What isn't fair?" Nic resumed his thrusts with slower, more measured movements. His dick dragged over Reed's prostate and his own cock grew hard again between them.

When Reed didn't answer, Nic adjusted himself and pounded into Reed at a merciless pace. Reed wasn't sure his shoulder blades hadn't ground down from the friction against the floor, and he was certain he'd have bruises from the way Nic was handling him so thoroughly.

There were lots of reasons it wasn't fair. The list was a mile long, but every reason was an excuse that boiled down to one singular reason that had haunted Reed since he'd caught a plane here in the first place.

"Tell me, Reed, or I won't give you what you want," Nic grunted, the pumps of his hips growing jerky and labored.

Reed turned his head, using the side of his arm to wipe the snot from his face. He was a mess—tied to the floor, covered in cum and tears and probably bruises. He wept freely, knowing he'd face no judgement from the man above him.

"I just want to be allowed to love you," he cried out.

Nic stilled, eyes widening. His mouth fell slack and his cock throbbed inside of Reed. He threw his head back and dug his fingers into Reed's hips, holding him steady while he came. Always holding him. Always touching him. Always grounding him.

Always loving him.

TWENTY-FOUR

DOMINIC

"BABY."

Dominic tore Reed's wrists out of the sheets and scooped him into his arms. Reed was gasping for air, tears staining his face and neck, his chest covered in cum. "Reed," he soothed. "Baby, calm down."

Dominic ran his hands down Reed's back, feeling indents from where the textured tile and grout had dug into his skin. He cradled Reed's face against the side of his neck and rocked their bodies until Reed quieted.

"I just want to be allowed to love you," Reed whispered into Dominic's shoulder.

"Who is stopping you?"

Reed pulled back and wiped at his face with trembling hands.

"Everyone."

Dominic took a deep breath. Reed. His poor, tortured Reed. Dominic wasn't certain if Reed had always put so much stock in what other people wanted or felt, but it was apparent now that Reed had lived a life for everyone but himself.

"I'm not," Dominic whispered. He cupped Reed's face in his

hands and bumped their noses together.

Reed's eyes watered and leaked again. He sniffled and looked down at their laps.

"I'm not," he repeated. "Who else should matter in this besides us?"

Reed took Dominic's hand and raised it between them, pressing his palm against the gold crucifix around his neck.

"What then, Reed? You're here for now, then you'll go back to avoiding me when we get back to Edgewood? I don't understand what's going on in your head." Dominic tugged the chain around Reed's neck. "This is only between us. You and me."

He heard his voice echo in his ears, and he sounded desperate. If he hadn't been able to convince Reed yet, though, nothing they'd share over the next four weeks would be of any worth in the long term.

"I'm trying!" Reed cried, his voice louder and more insistent than earlier. "I'm trying, Nic."

"I know," Dominic said quietly. "I know. I'm sorry."

He pulled Reed back into his arms and held him. The only sound in the room was their harsh and labored breathing. Once it quieted, Dominic stood, taking a wobbly-kneed Reed with him.

"Let's get you cleaned up. You're a mess."

Dominic guided Reed out of the bedroom toward the guest bathroom that had the tub. He sat Reed on the closed lid of the toilet and turned the taps on, making sure the water was warm, but not hot. While he waited for the tub to fill, he knelt between Reed's parted knees, running his hands up Reed's thighs.

"Maybe that was too much. I'm sorry," Dominic said.

"No," Reed whispered, resting his hands on top of Dominic's. "It was… it was necessary."

Reed's eyes flickered up and caught Dominic's gaze. The drain in the tub made a gulping noise and Dominic tore his attention from Reed. The tub had reached the drain line. He leaned over and turned the water off, returning his hands to Reed's legs. He patted him and stood up.

"Come on, then. Let's get in the bath."

Reed sighed and stood. He let Dominic ease him into the water without protest. Dominic climbed in behind him and arranged himself with his legs spread, holding Reed between them. He wrapped his arms around Reed's chest and pulled him backward until he was reclined in the water, his legs straight and his toes popping over the water line against the other end of the tub.

Dominic washed Reed, taking care to use his fingers to swirl through the hair of Reed's chest and belly and work the dried cum loose. He turned Reed around so they were face to face and used a washcloth-covered finger to clean the crevasses of Reed's swollen face.

"Can I kiss you?" he asked, unsure of where they stood after Reed's half-proclamation and his emotional shutdown.

Reed nodded.

"Tell me."

"You can kiss me," Reed whispered.

"Do you want me to kiss you?"

Reed swallowed. "I want you to kiss me."

Dominic leaned closer and pressed their mouths together. The kiss was a small and delicate thing, befitting a relationship far less intimate than their own. He pulled away and studied Reed's face. His eyelashes fluttered even though his eyes were closed, and his lips were parted.

Even after Dominic held the space between them, Reed didn't open his eyes. He didn't move. Another tear slipped out from his lashes, and Dominic reached up to wipe it away. In that moment, the reality of their relationship hit him like a ton of bricks. This was… this wasn't fair to Reed. He could say he wanted Dominic, but the battle inside of him was going to tear him apart.

Dominic closed his eyes and took a deep breath. When he found the courage to open them, Reed still hadn't moved except to open his eyes. He was searching Dominic's face for something, and Dominic lamented that Reed would probably not like what he found.

Dominic took Reed's hands in his, twisting their fingers together nervously.

"You need to go home, Reed."

Reed blinked at him, slowly, then his brows furrowed together in confusion.

"What?"

Dominic swallowed back the tears that were fighting to break free, and he looked away with a small shake of his head before he repeated, "You need to go home."

"Why?" Reed's eyes widened.

Dominic worked his fingers free of Reed's grasp and stood up, stepping out of the tub. He wrapped himself with a towel from the counter and left the bathroom. He padded down the hallway toward the bedroom, where he kicked his way through the tangle of sheets on the floor, dropping his weight onto the mattress with a heavy thud.

This decision might kill him, but he was confident that he could turn to his faith for guidance. Reed... Reed didn't have that safety net right now, and Dominic didn't dare to be the one who had taken it from him.

Reed appeared in the doorway, his hair damp, his body dripping. He had a towel loosely wrapped around his waist, barely obscuring Dominic's favorite parts of him.

"What are you on about? Why are you kicking me out?" Reed demanded, even stomping his foot against the tile. There was a puddle beneath him and the water splashed around him.

Dominic couldn't fight the smile, thinking of the parallels of water and rebirth he'd preached about weeks back. He focused on the steady drip from Reed's leg onto the floor instead of meeting his stare.

"I think it's best if you go home," Dominic repeated.

"Why?"

"This isn't going to work. You're not..." he sighed. "You're not ready."

Reed glowered at him and stomped across the bedroom. He dropped the towel and used both of his hands to shove Dominic in the chest. The force behind it caught him off guard, and he reeled back, bracing himself on the bed with his forearms.

"You don't get to tell me what I'm ready for," Reed leveled with a shaking finger pointed at Dominic. "That's not your call."

"I can see it in your eyes, Reed. You unravel, and you do it so well, but you're not *ready*." He emphasized the last word, hoping that Reed would understand what he was trying to explain.

"No. You know what? You're right." Reed shoved him again, this time climbing on top of him. Dominic lay flat against the bare mattress with Reed above him, banging his palms against Dominic's chest. "I'm not ready. I'm not fucking ready for this, Nic, but me going home isn't your decision to make. Send me away if *you* don't want me here, but you're not allowed to tell me to go because you *think* you know what's going on in my head."

"Reed," he tried to interject, but Reed was banging his fists against Dominic's chest again.

"I'm not done. I'm tired of you doing this. Please, Nic, please stop making decisions for me without talking to me. I want to be in this with you because I love you. And I'm not ready for that, but I can't just turn that off until I am. So, no thank you; I love you and I'm not *leaving*."

Reed shoved him again, battering his chest with shaking hands. His chest heaved with his breathing and his eyes were wild. Dominic reached up, circling his fingers around Reed's wrists to stop the assault.

"You what?" he whispered, hoping he'd heard right, but needing to be sure.

"I'm not leaving!" Reed glowered, struggling against Dominic's hold.

"The other part."

"Stop making decisions for me," Reed answered with a small smirk.

"I'll stop," Dominic whispered.

"I love you."

Dominic's heart swelled in an unexpected way. He released Reed's wrists, but grabbed him by the back of the neck and pulled him down, slanting their mouths together and shoving his tongue into Reed's mouth. Reed whimpered against his lips, parting his mouth and allowing Dominic to plunder him thoroughly.

Dominic's cock grew hard, and he lifted Reed, flipping him onto his back and lowering his weight slowly. He pressed Reed into the bed and rubbed their cheeks together, a sense of relief coursing through his veins. Somehow, he knew that Reed offering that admission was a far bigger step than just being here. It was an acknowledgement that he understood what was blossoming between them, his frustration toward Dominic's attempts to have him leave a clear sign that he wasn't interested in continuing on alone.

"You love me," Dominic rasped against Reed's ear.

"I said as much."

"Tell me again," he pleaded.

"I love you, Dominic O'Halloran."

The words landed against Dominic's ears like a rush of truth. His skin prickled and his heart threatened to burst out of his chest. He breathed in the soapy scent of Reed's skin and kissed him on the shoulder.

"Are you sure?" he whispered, adjusting himself onto his forearms so he could see Reed's face.

"I don't think I've ever been surer of anything in my life," Reed whispered, a small smile flitting across his lips. "I love you, Nic, and if you don't love me too, I think maybe then I'll go back to Edgewood."

Dominic barked out a laugh and shook his head. "You're not going anywhere."

He lowered his mouth and kissed Reed, lingering after he was through, holding their mouths together until all he could smell was the man beneath him.

"I love you, too," he promised against Reed's swollen lips. "I don't think I've ever not loved you, and I can't imagine there will come a day after today where I won't."

"So, I'm staying," Reed told him stubbornly.

Dominic chuckled and nodded. "You're staying."

"I need to make the bed," Dominic lamented, standing.

"Good, because I'm tired." Reed yawned and stretched, bruises beginning to show around his waist and hips. Dominic's cock jumped.

He clenched his jaw and turned to go, searching the hall closet for spare sheets. He found a set and returned to find Reed sprawled across the bare mattress like a starfish. He tossed the top sheet on Reed's chest, then leaned down and tucked the fitted sheet into the corner of the mattress, working his way around, shoving Reed aside so he could get all four corners attached.

Reed watched him, eyes bright, even though they were heavy with sleep. He tossed the top sheet onto the floor.

"Too hot for that," he muttered, blinking slowly.

"Alright," Dominic agreed, settling onto the fitted sheet against Reed's side.

"Top sheets are useless," Reed mumbled again. Dominic wasn't sure if he was talking in his sleep or not. He rolled onto his side and yanked Reed against his chest.

"I love you," Dominic whispered into Reed's ear.

"Mmmn," Reed agreed. "I love you, too."

Dominic twined his fingers through Reed's and raised them against Reed's chest. "We'll figure the rest out, okay?"

"I know."

A silence settled over them, far more comfortable than any blanket or sheet, and Dominic closed his eyes, resting his head against the cool cotton pillow.

"Reed."

"Hmmn?" Reed wiggled against him.

"Are you okay with everything that happened earlier?" Dominic chewed his lip between his teeth and waited for a reply.

Reed rolled over, tucking himself into Dominic's chest and kissing his sternum.

"That wasn't an answer," Dominic prompted, swatting the back of Reed's thigh gently.

"There's a lot going on inside of my head that I can't make sense of," Reed said. "But the way things are between us. The way you are with me, at least? It feels right to me."

"I don't want to go too far," Dominic explained.

"You won't. It wasn't," Reed countered quickly. "It was... I don't know how to explain it, but what happened tonight? I needed it."

"How do you mean?"

Reed shrugged his shoulders and tilted his head back, smiling up at Dominic and looking completely at ease and at peace.

"It was cathartic," Reed whispered. "Like my past was forgiven and all that I have to worry about now is what I do next."

"And what are you going to do next?" Dominic pulled Reed back into his arms.

"Love you."

TWENTY-FIVE

REED

REED WAS glad he'd decided to stay, glad he'd admitted his feelings to Nic, and glad that Nic didn't begrudge him for being a terrible cook. It had been two weeks since Nic had turned his attention toward his required study. Two weeks where Reed had entire days to himself, where he could listen to music or read, or do whatever he wanted. He'd given Nic the space he needed, finding that they quickly settled into a new kind of routine.

One thing Reed hadn't expected was to find *himself* so frequently falling into prayer. There was something about the Arizona desert that was equal parts calm and complex. The quiet and the heat provided a space where Reed and Nic could find the peace they needed, together and alone. Things were coming clearer for him, and he hoped that before their stay was over, he'd be in a place where he could find lasting comfort with the feelings he had for Nic.

"Have you read this one yet?" Nic asked, walking into the living room and waving a thin, red paperback in the air.

"I can't see it."

Reed snatched it out of Nic's hands and looked at the cover.

"I haven't."

"You should," Nic recommended, collapsing onto the couch beside him.

"Is it good?"

Reed turned to face Nic and puckered his lips for a kiss.

"I wouldn't tell you to read it if it wasn't." Nic kissed him and smiled.

"Are you done already?"

Reed looked up at the clock. It wasn't even three in the afternoon.

"I am."

"Early day," he observed.

Nic pinched his thigh. "I need a breather."

"How many days until we go home?"

"Eleven," Nic answered.

"You're counting?"

Nic looked at him from the corner of his eye and nodded.

"Why are you counting?" Reed asked, taking Nic's hand in his and kissing the tips of his fingers.

"Because I'm scared of it," Nic admitted, giving Reed's hand a squeeze.

"Because you think things are going to change?"

"I know they'll change," Nic corrected. "There's no way they won't change. I'll be back at work, and you'll still be the principal of a Catholic school. We won't live together. It won't be Arizona. Everything will be different."

"Not everything." Reed rested his head on Nic's shoulder. "I'll still love you."

Nic made an agreeable noise in his throat.

"I'll still expect you to make love with me," he whispered, cheeks blushing even though Nic couldn't see his face.

"Is that so?" Nic pulled Reed onto his lap and arranged Reed's legs on either side of his thighs.

"I want you all the time," Reed rasped, curling his fingers over Nic's shoulders and grinding against him.

"I want you always." Nic held Reed by the hips, his fingers digging into old bruises. "But it's more than that."

Reed stilled and tilted his head to the side. "What is it?"

"I love being with you, touching you, kissing you, waking up with you, but it's more than just the physical, don't you think?" Nic tweaked his nose with his thumb and forefinger.

"Obviously," Reed agreed.

"Let's go outside. Hold on."

Reed tightened himself around Nic's body, and Nic stood, carrying them both through the house and into the yard. He lowered Reed into one of the wooden lounge chairs, then took the other for himself.

Reed lay back in the chair, folding his hands together behind his head. He stared up at the sky. It was clear and blue, the sun still hanging high. The days were warm and long, and Reed had been surprised how well he'd taken to the dry heat of the Arizona desert. Adjusting to the temperature difference when they returned to Edgewood would be interesting, no doubt.

"Would you ever want to move here?" Nic asked out of nowhere.

Reed huffed and turned his head to face Nic's chair. "I was just thinking that."

"The weather is nice."

"It's hot," Reed laughed, "but the air feels good."

"Too bad our work is at home," Nic sighed.

Reed extended a hand over the arm of the chair, searching out Nic. His fingers landed on Nic's forearm, and he dragged them from elbow to wrist, enjoying the feel of his coarse, curled arm hair.

"It doesn't need to be," Reed suggested. "I could get a job anywhere, and it's not like there's not churches here."

Nic smiled at him. "I just got to St. Paul's a couple months ago. I don't think my time there is through, yet."

Reed nodded, turning his attention back to the sky. "I know. Just wishful thinking."

"Never say never."

An easy silence settled between them, and Reed reflected on what life would be like with Nic if they lived someplace like this. They were in a city, well, a few minutes outside of the city, but the property was large and secluded. It was its own private world. Nothing could touch them here. They could just exist together.

This was Reed's idea of heaven.

"You're too far away," Nic said.

"Come over here, then," Reed countered, looking at Nic with an eyebrow arched in challenge.

Nic hummed, pushing out of his chair and settling his body between Reed's legs. He folded his fingers together and rested them against Reed's stomach, his chin propped on his knuckles.

"What did you want to do with all this spare time you have on your hands today?" Reed asked. He dropped his head against the back of the chair and closed his eyes. He felt out Nic's face by memory, tangling fingers into Nic's hair.

"I can think of some things." Nic's hands moved toward the waistband of his pants.

"I think I like these things," Reed panted.

"You don't even know what these things are." Nic chuckled, working Reed's pants open. "I like this side of you by the way."

"What side?" Reed opened his eyes and glanced down his chest at Nic.

"The casual side. The jeans and no underwear side. The hair matted with sweat and cum side. The loving Dominic side." Nic pressed a kiss against his hip bone.

"I'd still love you if I was wearing a suit," he groaned.

"Would you?" Nic looked doubtful, but he swiped his tongue

across the top of Reed's cock before he was able to question it further.

"Fuck."

Nic wrapped his fingers around the base of Reed's cock and squeezed hard enough to wrench a groan from Reed's throat. His cock hardened.

"I want to try something new today." Nic's breath ghosted across the damp slit in Reed's dick. He stroked him with lazy pulls from base to tip, using his thumb to collect Reed's precum for lube. It felt good. So good. It always felt amazing when Nic touched him, whether he used his mouth, hands, or other parts of himself.

Nic hadn't let Reed fuck him since the last time, and if he were being honest, Reed hadn't really done much of the fucking then anyway, and that was fine. He liked submitting to Nic's will. The act—and the idea—turned him on more than anything ever had before.

Nic worked Reed's erection until he was seconds away from his orgasm, and then he stopped. He took his mouth away, took his hand away, and hovered over Reed's helplessly bucking body.

"What the fuck?" he panted, hips jerking toward Nic's mouth, out of his control.

"Deep breath, Reed."

Reed inhaled sharply and exhaled, his muscles settling back against the wooden chair. Nic held his stare the entire time, those dark blue eyes devious and intent. Minutes passed, and Nic didn't move, his focus maintaining the same point, then he smirked and leaned down, taking Reed's cock into his mouth.

He circled his lips around the head and sucked, hollowing his cheeks and working his mouth all the way to Reed's base. Reed fisted Nic's hair, holding him down and fucking his cock into Nic's mouth. He'd never done that before, but his body was a live-wire, ready to combust from want.

Nic palmed his balls, massaging and playing with them until Reed was ready to come. He opened his mouth, and a whimper escaped. Nic tore his mouth away and gave Reed's balls a rough tug. He flew forward, body folding in half over Nic and he cried out in shock and pain. His cock leaked copious amounts of precum, and Reed could see it shine on Nic's lips.

"I need to come," he grunted, tightening his hold in Nic's hair and trying to navigate his mouth back where Reed wanted him most.

"Not yet," Nic warned him, sucking a finger into his mouth.

He lowered his hand between Reed's legs and swirled his spit-soaked fingertip around Reed's hole. Reed gasped and spread his legs, and Nic pushed inside with one swift movement. Nic fucked his ass with a single finger until Reed's cock had turned from pink to an angry-looking crimson. His balls were tight against his body and heavy with cum.

Nic added a second finger and searched out Reed's prostate, dragging his fingers over the swollen spot. Reed's orgasm churned inside of him, building into something that was beyond his control.

"Nic," he gasped, thighs snapping up against Nic's arms.

Nic pulled his fingers out and Reed's orgasm faltered. Every nerve in his body was on fire. His balls churned, his cock throbbed, his muscles were tight with need.

"Nic, please," he begged.

"I like you like this." Nic rubbed Reed's cock against his cheek. His scruff abraded Reed's overly-sensitive skin and he mewled, writhing wildly beneath Nic.

"Please let me come," Reed panted.

"You're so desperate for it," Nic observed, sliding his tongue through Reed's slit.

"You're teasing."

"Not just you," Nic assured him, standing up and dropping his pants. His own cock was hard, engorged with blood and slick with precum. He stroked himself, pointing his cock toward the ground, only for it to bounce up and slap into his stomach.

"I want to be inside of you next time you come." Nic worked himself in front of Reed's face.

"Then please get inside of me." He reached for Nic.

"Go inside, I don't have lube out here." Nic tipped his chin toward the house.

Reed looked up at Nic, looked up at the sky, then shook his head. "I don't want to go inside. I want you here."

Nic spit on his hand and used it to slick his cock.

"Are you sure?"

"Positive." Reed flattened his feet on the lounger and bucked his hips.

"It'll hurt." He spit in his hand again and lubricated himself more.

Reed looked at the swollen member between Nic's legs and nodded. "I know."

He couldn't help but feel like whatever this was between them was somehow made more real with every sliver of pain he felt. If his body burned, or ached, or throbbed, it was a reminder of the sins of his flesh. Though as every day ticked by, Reed found it harder to reconcile anything they did as being sinful. It was practically celebratory, the way they rejoiced in their love like this.

Nic dropped onto his knees and yanked Reed down to the edge of the chair, then spread his legs apart and buried his face between the globes of Reed's ass. Nic licked his hole, dipping his tongue through the tight ring of muscle. He licked and sucked Reed's ass until he was a quivering ball of want for the third time since they'd come outside, then he reared back, spreading Reed's ass apart with demanding fingers and spitting directly onto his hole.

Reed gasped, shocked more by the feeling than the action itself, and then he was full. Nic pushed inside of him, his cock hard and stretching Reed open. It did hurt. It burned, and Nic licked his hand and rubbed it on his cock, using it to help lubricate his way.

"You're so tight," he growled, burying himself to the hilt inside of Reed.

Reed tightened his muscles, and Nic grimaced.

"Come for me," Nic grunted, dragging his cock against Reed's prostate.

Reed's mouth opened and he cried out, his orgasm tumbling through his body and exploding from him in a burst of energy. His body jerked off the chair, and Nic caught him, wrapping his arms around his back and holding him, even as his body fought against the restraint.

Nic sank his teeth into Reed's neck, and his cock swelled, filling Reed with his release. Nic's fingernails gouged divots into Reed's skin, but Reed couldn't feel anything besides the satisfaction of every cell in his body working together to do as Nic had demanded of him.

Nic lowered him onto the chair, and he swiped his hand through the proof of Reed's orgasm, then he raised his fingers to his mouth and licked them clean. He showed it to Reed, puddles of white cum against the pink of his tongue. Nic leaned down, hovering over Reed's parted and panting mouth, and he opened his lips, letting Reed's own cum dribble into his mouth.

Reed lapped it up, swallowing half of it before Nic slanted their mouths together and kissed him, using his tongue to scoop the cum back into his mouth with a satisfied groan.

"That was a good breather," Reed said with an exhausted laugh.

Nic shouldered him to the side of the chair and shoved his body into the space he'd made, pulling Reed toward him and holding him against his chest. He made an agreeable sound, then rolled onto his back, staring up at the sky in silence.

TWENTY-SIX

DOMINIC

"YOU'VE READ that book three times," Dominic observed.

He leaned against the kitchen counter and sipped his tea. Reed was sitting at the small dining table, flipping through pages of the worn red paperback Dominic had given him nearly two weeks before.

Reed looked up, his eyes wide. "Well, you know. It's amazing."

He returned his attention to the book.

"It's changed the way you relate to religion." Dominic repeated what Reed had told him after the second reading.

"I find something new each time. Some nuanced under-standing I missed."

"I'm glad." Dominic took the seat across from Reed and smiled while Reed flipped through the pages, a crease between his brow.

"Can you put it down for a second?"

Reed blinked up at him, turning the book over and resting it on the table so it stayed open on the page he'd been reading.

"What's wrong?" Reed asked, his face worried.

"Nothing." Dominic shook his head. "It's just our last day

here. I wanted to talk to you about going home. It's not some-thing we've really discussed in detail."

Reed pursed his lips together and nodded. Dominic was right with what he'd just said. They'd always known they had to return to Edgewood, to their normal lives, but even when Reed had booked a plane ticket home, they hadn't talked about what it all meant.

"How do you think things are going to change?" he asked, making a deliberate attempt to leave the ball in Reed's court. After Reed had properly dressed him down about making deci-sions for both of them, Dominic had been making an effort to school himself from doing so.

"Well, you have your place at the church, and I have my place." Reed reached across the table and picked up Dominic's mug, raising it to his lips and taking a sip. "So we won't be together as often."

"I don't need to live in the parsonage," Dominic offered, testing the waters. He didn't think he was ready to cohabitate long term with Reed, but he was more interested in seeing where Reed was with that idea.

"Where would you live?"

Dominic chuckled. "Nevermind. So, we won't share the same living space anymore. What else?"

"I mean…" Reed scrunched his mouth together and angled a look toward the ceiling. "That's it, right?"

"I know we haven't done it here, because we haven't left the house, but when we're home, would we go out on dates?" Dominic queried, pulling his coffee mug back to his side of the table so he'd have something to do with his hands.

"I don't know, Nic," Reed whispered, sounding sad.

"What don't you know about it?"

Dominic worried that Reed was still wrapped up in his own feelings of guilt and treachery over their relationship, although he had shown a shift toward more open acceptance since he'd undertaken reading about the gospel of Thomas. Dominic picked the red paperback up from the table and scanned the page Reed had been reading. He closed it and set it between them.

"I don't think Father Cowart would be too pleased if he saw us on a date." Reed looked away.

"Is he the only person you're worried about?"

"Mostly," Reed agreed.

"I'm not asking you to scream it from the rooftops, Reed, but I don't want to hide the way I feel for you. I don't want to worry about you sneaking in and out of my house or being seen sitting too close to me at a restaurant," Dominic explained.

"I know."

"What do you think happens if Father Cowart finds out you're gay?" Dominic asked.

"You know, there's tons of gay educators and administrators. The schools just don't ever find out about it," Reed half-answered.

"That's true, but what if someone does find out, Reed?"

"I'd probably be terminated," Reed answered with a helpless shrug.

"And what would you do if that happened?"

"Then I'd probably have to move in with you because the other schools in town all have principals and I won't have a job." Reed pulled the paperback he'd been reading back to his side of the table and clutched it against his chest.

"That seems extremely fatalistic."

Reed looked up at him and raised an eyebrow. "What would you suggest I do if that happens, Nic? You said yourself that you're just getting started at St. Paul's, you're not going anywhere. If I'm not employable, then what is there for me to do?"

Reed's voice grew louder. "This is all I've had. My job and the church. And the church is quickly turning into something that doesn't fit into the box it used to, and if I lose my job too, then I don't know what I'd do, Nic! That's my whole life, up and gone, and all because of the person I love? How is that right?"

Reed threw the book onto the table. It bounced and fell open on a well-worn and highlighted page. Dominic folded it closed, using the opportunity to try and gather his thoughts.

"It's not right," he agreed softly. He held a hand out for Reed, and he took it quickly, grabbing Dominic like he was a lifeline. "I'm sorry if you feel like I've been responsible for any of the upheaval in your life."

"You've been responsible for all of it!" Reed tore his hand from Dominic's grasp and looked over his shoulder, but quickly turned his attention back and took Dominic's upturned hand between both of his own. "But I can't see that as being a bad thing anymore."

"It's a lot."

Reed offered him a tight smile. "I think I knew. Back when I saw you at Lisa's restaurant for the first time."

"What did you know?" Dominic asked.

"That my life as it had been was over."

"I wanted you, Reed. I've always wanted you, but I never meant to make things hard for you," Dominic told him honestly.

He'd always understood the implications of pursuing anything with Reed. That was why he'd told him to stop calling; that was why he'd tried so hard to steer their course to any point besides the one they were at now. His own life would face little change as a result of his love with Reed, but Reed's life? Everything for Reed was going to change as soon as they landed back in Edgewood.

"I know what I signed up for," Reed assured him, pushing his chair back from the table. He walked over to Dominic and stood before him. Reed reached into his hair and tangled his fingers through the strands. Dominic closed his eyes, enjoying the weight of Reed's uninvited attention.

Dominic lifted his hands and rested them on the curve of Reed's hips. He leaned in and used his nose to lift up Reed's shirt, and he kissed him just above his navel.

"I love you," he whispered against Reed's skin.

"I'm glad for it," Reed answered. "I'm glad for you."

"I don't want to go home," Dominic admitted, holding his cheek against Reed's stomach. Reed circled his hands around the back of Dominic's head and held him.

Dominic heard the words Reed had been saying to him, felt the things he and Reed had shared over the past four weeks, but he couldn't click it all into where he wanted it. He didn't believe they'd get home and things wouldn't change. Every outcome of every worst case scenario ran through his head on a loop. All the different ways Reed would break his heart assaulted him, and the fear crept up his spine until it spread through his whole body.

This had been too good. It couldn't be over.

"You're shaking," Reed whispered, smoothing his hands down Dominic's back.

"Am I?" He didn't even realize.

"Let me take you to bed," Reed suggested, lifting Dominic out of the chair. Reed guided him to the bedroom, where he divested him of his clothes before laying him back against the cool sheets.

"I love you," Reed whispered, crawling onto the bed and taking one of Dominic's bare feet in his hands. He kissed his heel, the slope of Dominic's arch, then the pads of his toes.

"I love you," he repeated, pressing a kiss against Dominic's ankle bone.

He rubbed Dominic's calf against his face and kissed his way to Dominic's knee, sucking the thin and rarely-touched skin of the backside into his mouth. Dominic gasped and fisted the sheets. Reed stilled and waited until he was calm again, then resumed his ascent up his body, kissing his favorite parts and ones he'd never even paid attention to before.

By the time he reached Dominic's hip, both of their cocks were fully hard, but Reed paid Dominic's erection no attention, instead choosing to lave his tongue over the fold of skin where his thigh turned into his groin.

"I love you," Reed said again, sinking his teeth into that tender patch of flesh.

Dominic arched against Reed's mouth, a thin layer of sweat already slicking his body. He rocked his head from side to side against the pillow and stretched his fingers out toward Reed. He threaded his hand through Reed's hair, but fought the urge to control his movements. He relaxed his muscles and let the touch of Reed ground him firmly in the present.

When Reed's mouth was level with Dominic's chest, he adjusted his weight, laying himself over Dominic's body and dragging his stomach over his cock. Dominic clenched his teeth together, and Reed dragged the tops of his teeth across one of Dominic's hard nipples.

"I love you." Reed licked from Dominic's sternum to the dip in his throat. He used his tongue to pull the skin into his mouth and sucked. Dominic struggled against the bite of pain, but Reed flattened a hand against Dominic's hip and held him still. Reed sucked and sucked, then pulled away with a pop. He looked up at Dominic with a surprisingly satisfied grin.

"No one will know what's under your collar but me," he rasped, returning his face into the crook of Dominic's neck and sucking a bruise just above his clavicle.

"Reed," he panted.

"Mmmn?" Reed trailed his nose up the arch of Dominic's neck to his ear. He pressed light kisses down his jawline until he reached Dominic's parted and desperate lips.

"I love you." He breathed the vow into Dominic's mouth.

Dominic grabbed him, flipped them both over, and slanted their lips together. He shoved his tongue into Reed's mouth and devoured the hungry cries that left it. Dominic rutted against Reed, their cocks both hard and slick, leaking against their bellies, and Dominic squeezed his eyes closed, coming within minutes and coating their flesh with his orgasm.

Reed forced a hand between their bodies and grabbed his dick, jerking himself less than four times before grunting and bucking into Dominic's body. The heat of Reed's orgasm spurted across his skin, and Dominic growled, cupping a hand around the back of Reed's neck and kissing him until they were both senseless from their need.

"I love you," Reed promised, raising a cum-soaked hand to Dominic's face and holding him steady.

Dominic nodded. "I love you, too."

"This is what I want to come home to, Nic." Reed wrapped him in his arms.

"Me too," he agreed.

"So we'll figure out a way to make it happen," Reed said, his tone matter-of-fact.

Dominic couldn't stop the chuckle that escaped his lips.

"What's funny?" Reed asked.

"You," he answered, rolling onto his back and pulling Reed against his side. "This is better."

"You're a proper caveman, aren't you?" Reed tucked himself into the nook made by Dominic's armpit and sighed happily.

"I want to take care of what's mine," Dominic mumbled.

"And am I yours?" Reed bumped Dominic's ribs with his nose.

"Aren't you?"

"Yeah," Reed answered with a happy yawn. "I'm yours."

TWENTY-SEVEN
REED

BEING BACK in Edgewood was awful. It wasn't so much that he didn't feel comfortable in his relationship with Nic, it was more that Edgewood was just *not* Arizona. The bubble was gone. Now there was traffic, and work, and people, and things that weren't just him and Nic. Reed flipped through his desk calendar and scowled. It was almost August, and almost time for him to return to work. He loved his job, but he wasn't looking forward to facing Father Cowart and the other administrators. It wasn't like they knew he was gay, but *he* knew he was gay, and he was worried about always wondering if he'd give himself away by doing or saying something...

Reed shook his head and mentally chastised himself. He wasn't ashamed of being gay, and he most certainly wasn't ashamed of his relationship with Nic, but he was aware there were people who might be. People who controlled his paycheck.

His phone rang, and he snatched it, grateful for a distraction.

"Hello?"

"Hey, you." Nic's voice oozed through the line.

Reed smiled. "How are you?"

"I'm finally done with my report for Bishop Jenkins," Nic answered with a groan.

"Does that mean things can go back to normal now?"

Since they'd gotten home, Nic had kissed him on his porch and promised they'd see each other soon. He'd needed to draw up a written report for the Bishop and the vestry about his sabbatical. Reed had asked teasingly if he'd include all the hot sex they'd had in the cliffs notes version, but Nic had only rolled his eyes and asked for three days to decompress and evaluate.

"We don't even know what normal is." Nic chuckled. "This is our first time to do this here. I don't know what it looks like, do you?"

"I know what I want it to be," Reed answered.

"And how is that?"

"With you."

"You've turned emo on me."

Reed grinned even though Nic couldn't see it. "I just like how I feel with you. I want to be with you. I told you that before we left."

"Let me take you to dinner then," Nic purred into the phone.

Reed looked at his calendar. "When?"

"Now."

He laughed. "I don't even know what day it is. I've been staring at my calendar trying to make sense of the days."

"It's Saturday."

"Do you preach tomorrow?" Reed asked.

"No. I'm going to church, but I'm not preaching until next week. Why? Did you want to come and watch me?"

"I go back to work on Monday," Reed continued, avoiding Nic's question.

"All the more reason for us to go on our first official date tonight, then."

"Seems backward that we're in love even though we've never

been on a date." Reed closed his calendar and leaned back in his chair.

"I don't think there's much about us that's conventional, Principal Matthews."

"You're being particularly feisty tonight, Father."

Nic growled, the sound shooting straight between Reed's legs. He gasped, the unexpected arousal heavy.

"Call me that again and I'll show you feisty." Nic's voice was rough and low, and it made Reed shiver.

Reed cleared his throat. "Dinner?"

"If you like," Nic responded, his voice still thick with promise.

"Should I meet you?"

"I'll pick you up," Nic said.

"What time?"

"Now."

"I need to get ready," Reed countered.

"Hurry up, then. I haven't seen you in three days and I miss you."

"I'll hurry," Reed promised, standing up and popping open the fly on his jeans.

"I'll see you soon, Reed." Nic ended the call.

Reed tossed his phone onto his desk and ran into his bathroom, taking a quick shower and toweling off on his way to his closet. He didn't know what to wear, still used to being far more casual than he normally was. He reached for a collared shirt and hesitated, his fingers dancing over the pressed cuff.

He'd always been so worried with the way he was seen, the way he was perceived. Hell, even his fears over being outed all made their way back to other people's perception. He swallowed, pulling his hand out of the closet. It was impossible that people would think less of him for wearing jeans to dinner on a weekend. He looked over his shoulder at his dresser and groaned.

Reed reached for a drawer on his dresser, pulling it open and digging around for a pair of dark blue jeans. He tossed them onto the bed and turned his attention back toward his closet. He wavered between a plaid button up that Carol had gotten him for a birthday a few years ago that he'd never worn and a plain white button-up.

He chewed his lip between his teeth and took the white shirt out of the closet. He shrugged it on and rolled the sleeves so they landed just below his elbows. After he put on his jeans, he left the shirt untucked, and he opted for a pair of black sneakers instead of his oxfords.

It was a fair compromise.

There was a knock at his door. He turned off the lights in his bedroom, taking one last look at himself in the mirror before he went. His hair was a mess, he hadn't put product in it, and he stalled, running his fingers through the unruly strands to try and tame them.

Another knock.

"Coming!" he hollered, detouring into the bathroom. He scooped some pomade from the small plastic tub on the sink and fingered it through his hair, rinsing his hands quickly and finally making his way to the living room.

He yanked the door open just as Nic lifted his hand to knock again.

"Sorry," he blurted. "I had to do my hair."

Nic raised an eyebrow and scanned Reed from head to toe, eyes lingering longer than necessary at the fly of Reed's jeans.

"Look at you," Nic assessed. "You're practically naked."

"Shut up." Reed smacked his chest.

"Are you sure you don't need a blazer?" Nic smirked.

"I didn't wear one in Arizona."

"You didn't wear a lot of things in Arizona."

Reed's cheeks heated from the reminder. "Did you want me to go change?"

"No," Nic answered quickly. He reached out and grabbed Reed's bicep, pulling him closer. "You look great. I promise."

Nic's lips skirted over his, and his mouth opened, a small gasp filling the space between them. Nic deepened the kiss, dipping his tongue into Reed's mouth and sealing their lips together. He pulled back when Reed whimpered.

"I missed you," Nic said against his mouth.

"I missed you."

"Are you ready for our date?" Nic crowded his space and lowered his head, his breath hot against Reed's ear.

"I'm ready."

Nic hummed and stepped back. "Let's go then."

Nic led him to the car, tucking him into the passenger seat safely before slipping into the driver's seat.

"Where are we going?"

"Puck's."

"I've never even heard of that," Reed said with a laugh.

"It's pretty new, on the edge of town, but I'm not surprised you haven't heard of it. It's no Star Garden."

"That's not the only place I eat," Reed grumbled. Nic reached out and snatched his hand, twisting their fingers together and leaving a kiss against Reed's knuckles.

"I know," Nic agreed, driving them to the other end of the city and pulling up in front of a valet stand.

The drive had been mostly silent, but Reed hadn't minded. Sharing space with Nic after three days apart was all he'd wanted.

Once inside, a hostess led them to a tall-backed booth near a window, leaving them with menus before she disappeared. Reed smoothed his hands over the royal purple tablecloth.

"This place is nice." He made note of the small tea-light candles in gold-flecked holders and the single red rose in a vase near the salt and pepper.

"I've been wanting to try it, but it seemed like more of a date kind of place." Nic placed his napkin in his lap and held his hand out, palm up.

Reed slipped his fingers against Nic's palm and twined their fingers together.

"Tell me about your debrief," Reed said, after the waiter had come to take their food and drink orders.

"It's mostly boring theological speak." Nic took a sip of his water. "But I advised them I'm going to actively pursue bolstering the LGBT program at St. Paul's. I know people who have suffered discrimination at the hands of church believe that all organized religion is to blame, but I'd like to be a beacon for those who still struggle to reconcile the two parts of themselves."

Nic leveled a knowing look across the table at him.

"I'm not struggling," Reed said.

"There's so much focus on retaining people in the church. I think that to stay relevant, we need to realize that we can't force people to stay. We need to offer a welcoming environment with no expectations or restrictions. I fully expect many of the kids in the LGBT group to leave the church." Nic shrugged. "If at least one stays, then maybe that means I've done well. Like I've shown them a way to maintain their spiritual beliefs in addition to their emotional and sexual needs."

"You're a good man, you know?" Reed found himself in awe of the way Nic spoke about his plan. His mind drifted back to Catherine, from the interactions they'd had at school, to the easygoing and friendly way he'd seen her at the St. Paul's movie night.

"Am I?" Nic tilted his head to the side. "I'm just doing my job. Doing what I'm called to do."

"You downplay it."

"I'm humble," Nic said with a laugh.

"Hardly."

Their food arrived, steak for Reed and mushroom pasta for Nic, and they fell into an amenable silence while they ate.

"Do you want to try mine?" Reed asked, slicing into his steak.

Nic nodded, spearing some pasta onto his fork. He held it up for Reed to try, and he laughed while they reached across the table and tried each other's food. Nic leaned closer and raised his hand, swiping some stray sauce off the corner of Reed's mouth. Reed rubbed the place Nic's finger had just been and smiled.

"Thank you."

"You're wel—"

"Principal Matthews." A booming voice from behind him turned his blood cold.

Nic looked over his head before turning his attention to Reed's face. Reed patted the napkin in his lap, eyes locked on Nic.

This was it. He knew this was a test. Nic studied his face, not making a move or saying a word. Reed looked at the half-eaten steak on his plate and took a deep breath. He turned in his chair and looked over his shoulder.

"Mr. Ollingham. How are you?" he asked.

"Quite well." Evan Ollingham, Catherine's father, shifted his attention from Reed to Nic, then back to Reed.

"Did you have a nice dinner?" Reed fisted his napkin in his hands, hoping it was obscured beneath the tablecloth so his tension wasn't clearly visible.

"It was...tolerable," Evan answered.

"Is your wife with you?"

"No. It was a business dinner."

"I'm not sure we've met," Nic interjected, standing and holding out his hand. "I'm Dominic O'Halloran. I'm the priest at St. Paul's."

Evan narrowed his eyes and took Nic's hand, shaking it

briefly. "I know who you are, Father. I've been dropping Catherine off at St. Paul's every Friday and every other Wednesday since she got out of school."

Reed's breathing accelerated.

"Ah." Nic smiled and took his seat. "Movie night."

"And...the other thing," Evan added.

Nic nodded and offered Evan an understanding smile. "That's very good of you, Mr. Ollingham."

"Evan!"

All three of them turned their attention to a man a few tables away. He had his hand raised and was calling for Evan to join him.

"I need to get going." Evan smoothed a hand over his tie. "Enjoy the rest of your meal."

As quickly as he'd appeared, he was gone, but Reed's heart was still stuck in his throat. He leaned back in his chair and exhaled loudly, offering Nic a relieved smile. That hadn't been anything like he'd imagined it would be. There was a part of him that had assumed, ignorantly and incorrectly, that people would somehow *know* about him and Nic just by seeing them out together. He knew that was ludicrous, but it was still an impossible feeling to shake.

"You with me?" Nic asked, taking a sip of his wine.

Reed nodded, asking the question he was fairly certain he already knew the answer to. "What's every other Wednesday?"

Nic smiled at him and took his hand, rubbing his thumb across Reed's knuckles. "It's the LGBT youth group."

TWENTY-EIGHT

DOMINIC

"HAVE you talked with Carol since we've been back?" Reed asked, undoing the top button of his shirt.

It was Wednesday. The week had crept by, starting with returning to St. Paul's on Sunday. He hadn't delivered the sermon, instead sitting in the pews with the other congregants, and it had been...weird. Not that being in church was weird or seeing some of the people he'd grown to call friends was weird, but he was struggling to adjust to life again post-sabbatical.

Dominic wasn't sure how much of that struggle was due to his separation from Reed or how much of it was a result of returning from the trip with wide eyes looking toward all the things he wanted to do. The one thing he didn't want to do right now was talk about Carol's betrayal.

"No," he answered sharply, slipping his phone into his pocket.

"Shouldn't you?"

Dominic pursed his lips.

"Maybe," he agreed.

"I'm sure she has her reasons for what she did." Reed approached him and pressed his hands against Dominic's chest, sliding them up to his white collar. Reed rubbed his fingers over the exposed material, and his cheeks turned crimson.

"We don't need to talk about her right now," Dominic whispered, catching Reed's fingers in his hand. He pulled Reed closer and leaned in for a kiss.

Reed's mouth tasted like chocolate, and Dominic licked against his tongue, sealing their lips together so he could explore Reed further.

"What did you eat?" he mumbled into Reed's mouth after pulling back.

"I had a mocha before I left work."

"You taste sinful." Dominic swiped his tongue across Reed's lower lip.

"Mmmn," Reed moaned. "Forgive me, Father?"

Dominic shoved him away, palming his cock and gritting his teeth. Reed chuckled, his own cock hard and bulging in his pants.

"You're trouble." Dominic shook his head.

"Punish me?" Reed raised an eyebrow.

"I have obligations or I would take you over my knee."

Reed's nostrils flared and he licked his lips. Dominic rolled his eyes.

"You're insatiable. Can you please get your erection under control for now so we can go to church?" Dominic shoved a hand down his pants and adjusted his cock so it pressed against his leg instead of busting toward his zipper.

"You should call Carol."

Dominic's cock went soft and he rolled his eyes. "Thanks for that."

Reed grinned and checked himself in the mirror one last time, rubbing his hands over his pink cheeks.

"Are you sure it's okay for me to come with you?" he asked Dominic's reflection.

"It's more than okay," Dominic promised. "Are you worried about someone seeing you?"

When Reed had asked if he could come to the LGBT youth group, Dominic had been surprised. Reed had been making an effort to not necessarily hide their relationship, but he hadn't anticipated Reed wanting to be somewhere *so* public with him, especially after the false alarm at Puck's over the weekend.

"No," Reed answered quickly before adding, "yes, maybe. I don't know."

Dominic took Reed's hand in his.

"At work all week, I've been so nervous, just waiting for the ball to drop," Reed continued. "I haven't figured out which is worse, though, the fear of being outed or what the outcome will be when it happens."

Dominic lifted Reed's hand and kissed his knuckles.

"I wish I could answer that for you," he said sadly. "Maybe you should pray over it."

Reed scoffed. "Are you serious?"

"Of course, Reed. I am a priest."

AFTER A SHORT WALK across the church grounds, they reached the small room where the LGBT group met. Dominic was pleased to see nearly a dozen teenagers gathered in the room, including Catherine Ollingham.

He greeted them all and took a seat. The kids all pulled their own chairs around, forming a good attempt at a circle. Dominic patted the empty chair beside him and Reed slipped into it. He looked a little nervous, but Dominic wasn't sure if it was because of where they were or the fact Reed wasn't wearing a blazer. He laughed to himself, then turned his attention to the group.

"Hey everyone, thanks for coming."

He was met with a chorus of greetings in return.

"How did everything go while I was away? Can we go around the circle? Just catch me up." Dominic rubbed his hands down the legs of his slacks and leaned back in his chair.

Catherine started talking about something, but Dominic missed what she was saying because his phone had started to vibrate in his pocket. He ignored it, trying to focus on Catherine. His phone vibrated again. He shoved his hand into his pocket and pulled it out, silencing the call.

Before he could return his phone to his pocket, it vibrated again. Reed glanced toward the phone and gave him a look indicating he should answer it. Dominic shook his head and turned the phone upside down in his lap.

"I have a book you might like," Reed said.

Catherine smiled. "Really?"

"Definitely," Reed answered. "I read it earlier in the summer and it changed my life."

Dominic angled a look in Reed's direction and raised an eyebrow. Reed shook his head, indicating they'd talk about it later.

Dominic's phone buzzed again and he groaned. "I'm sorry. I obviously need to take this. Can you all excuse me?"

He stood up and flipped his phone over, not recognizing the number on the screen. He walked toward the door, stepping outside and answering the call.

"Hello?"

"Dominic?"

"Yes. Who is this?" he asked, growing exasperated.

"This is Geraldine from your mother's bridge club."

Dominic scrunched his brows, pulling the phone away to look at the number before returning the handset to his ear.

"Geraldine. What can I do for you? I'm in the middle of a meeting."

"I'm sorry to bother you, dear, but there was... oh, God."

Geraldine trailed off.

"What's going on?" Dominic asked. He clutched the stair rail with a clammy hand, a terrible feeling taking up residence in his gut. He closed his eyes and waited.

"Carol was just taken to the hospital. She collapsed at bridge." Geraldine sniffed. "I'm not sure what happened. You should come down, though."

"Oh," he answered, "right."

"She's at Providence General," Geraldine told him.

"Alright."

Dominic blinked and ended the call, not completely able to process the information Geraldine had just given him. Reed's voice echoed in his head.

You should call Carol.

You should call Carol.

You should call Carol.

Dominic tightened his fist around his phone and opened the door, but before he could step foot inside, it vibrated in his hand again. He looked down, expecting to see Geraldine's number again, but instead was met with another number not in his contacts list.

He stalled in the doorway, Reed across the room looking at him with worry in his eyes. A car screeched into the parking lot behind him, and he answered the phone.

"Hello?" He let the door close in front of him.

"Ah, yes. I'm trying to reach Dominic O'Halloran."

"This is."

A car door slammed and Dominic turned to face the parking lot. A frenzied-looking woman threw her car into park and was in the middle of the parking lot before Dominic could make sense of it. Another car door opened, and Catherine's father, Evan, who he'd met at dinner with Reed over the weekend, was on his way to intercepting the woman before she reached the stairs.

"Mary!" he hollered.

"Yes, hi," the voice on the phone greeted. "I'm calling from Providence General about your mother, Carol Creighton."

"Right," Dominic said blankly. "One of her friends just called. I'll be down there as soon as I can get away."

"That's good, Mr. O'Halloran. I'm terribly sorry for your loss, but in the meantime do you have any information about which funeral home we should contact?"

Dominic's breath caught in his throat. The woman in the parking lot, Mary, stormed past him with Evan hot on her heels. She threw the door open and stormed into the meeting room. Dominic made to stop her, but his mind had latched onto something the voice on the phone had said, even though he couldn't make sense of it.

"I'm sorry. Could you repeat that?" he asked.

"Which funeral home should we reach out to for your mother?" the person asked.

"Funeral home?" Dominic's heart stopped.

You should call Carol.

You should call Carol.

You should call Carol.

"Oh, dear. Mr. O'Halloran, you said someone had told you."

"Geraldine told me Carol had been taken to the hospital."

It sounded like a bomb had gone off in the meeting room— even behind the closed door he could hear chairs falling and raised voices.

"She was brought in, but unfortunately we weren't able to resuscitate her. Your mother has passed away, Mr. O'Halloran."

The door swung open and Mary was there, her fingers tight around Catherine's arm. She started screaming at him, something about heathens, going to hell, improper sinful urges. He could tell she was upset, but nothing was sticking.

You should call Carol.

You should call Carol.

You should call Carol.

"I, uh... I don't know." Dominic laughed, and he knew it was inappropriate, but he couldn't stop it. He turned his back on Mary.

"I understand this is a lot, and I'm sorry about the miscommunication of the notification, Mr. O'Halloran. You can reach me back at this number when you have her affairs in order."

Dominic ended the call without saying goodbye.

Mary was still behind him shouting, and Catherine was crying, but Dominic just stared at the trees in the garden beyond the parking lot.

You should call Carol.

You should call Carol.

You should call Carol.

Reed's face appeared in his vision, his hands on Dominic's shoulders.

"Nic, what's going on?" he asked, his eyes narrowed in concern.

Dominic dropped his phone. It clattered to the ground, the screen shattering. Mary was still yelling about something, and Dominic lifted his arms, covering Reed's hands with his own. Reed's skin felt warm. It felt alive. Dominic's eyes widened and he choked out a sob, slapping one of his hands over his mouth.

"Nic, baby. Talk to me," Reed tried again, this time cupping Dominic's face in his hands.

"Carol's dead," he whispered.

"Nic." His name left Reed's mouth on an exhale, then Reed's arms were around him, pulling him close and holding him tight. "I'm so sorry."

"I should have called her."

"You didn't know. You couldn't have known." Reed kissed the top of his head and stroked his hair back.

Dominic rolled his forehead against Reed's shoulder. He was sure he was choking, the collar suddenly far too tight around his throat. He reached up and worked his fingers between the material and his skin. He was sweaty, his throat was on fire. He tugged it away from his shirt and tore the top button loose. He fisted the white strip of plastic in his hand and pressed his knuckles against Reed's hip.

He wasn't aware of anything that wasn't the comforting slide of Reed's fingers over his trembling body. He didn't notice the commotion around him dying down. He didn't notice the sun dipping in the sky. All he knew was Carol was gone, and he hadn't made things right.

Reed's hand dipped into his pocket.

"Let me get the kids out and lock up, and we'll get you home," Reed whispered, stepping away from Dominic to lock the door. Reed spoke to some of the kids who hadn't fled from Mary's fury, but Dominic couldn't make out the words. He became painfully aware of Reed's absence, then the awareness of Carol's absence constricted around him like a vise.

"Let's go." Reed guided Dominic down the stairs and back toward the parsonage. He opened the door and moved Dominic into the bedroom, sitting him on the bed. Reed knelt and removed Dominic's shoes and socks. He stood up and worked loose the remaining buttons on Dominic's shirt, then pushed it down his shoulders and off his arms. He helped Dominic to stand, then removed his pants, leaving him in his underwear.

Reed pulled the blankets on the bed back and tucked Dominic under the covers, dropping a soft kiss against his forehead.

"Don't go," Dominic whispered, reaching a hand out.

"I'm not leaving you," Reed promised. He arranged himself on the bed behind Dominic, slipping under the covers. He wrapped an arm over him and pulled him close.

"Close your eyes and rest," Reed said against his ear. "I'll be here when you wake."

TWENTY-NINE
REED

REED WOKE to find a cold spot where Nic had laid all night. The news of Carol's death was a particularly hard blow to him, since he hadn't taken the time to make amends with her for what she and Margaret had conspired to do when they'd been kids. Reed stretched and blinked the bedside clock into focus. It was just after six in the morning, which meant he wasn't running behind. He threw the covers back and stood up, stretching again, before padding out into the living room to find Nic.

"Hey," Reed said tentatively after finding Nic staring out the kitchen window.

"The view was nicer in Arizona," Nic answered.

Reed walked up behind him and slipped his arms around Nic's bare stomach and rested his face against his back.

"It was," he agreed.

"Are you late for work?"

"No, I've got a bit of time."

Nic turned in his arms and dropped his head against Reed's shoulder. Reed stroked his back and hair with steady fingers.

"Do you want to talk about it?" Reed asked.

Nic shook his head. "I need to go out there and get her affairs in order. Find the funeral home information for the hospital and shit. I'll have to call Bishop Jenkins, too."

"Baby," Reed interrupted after Nic started to trail off and mumble about flowers and caskets.

"No," Nic answered softly. "I can do it. I promised David before he died that I would make sure everything was in order for her."

"Are you sure?"

Nic sniffled. "Go get ready for work. I don't want you to be late."

Reluctantly, Reed left Nic in the kitchen. He showered and dressed quickly, returning to the kitchen to find Nic where Reed had left him, staring out the window.

"Nic, are you sure?" Reed asked again, stroking his hand down Nic's spine.

"I'm sure," he promised, forcing a smile.

"Will you call me if you need anything?"

Reed didn't like the idea of leaving Nic alone, but he also didn't want to force himself onto Nic while he tried to process and grieve Carol's death. This wasn't something Reed had dealt with in years. Not since James had passed away and left Margaret alone, but that was almost ten years ago. He found himself out of practice with the emotions of this kind of loss.

"I will." Nic cupped his face and pressed their mouths together. He tasted like salt and sleep, his tongue moving desperately against Reed's lips.

"It feels like you want me to stay," Reed mumbled against him.

"No." Nic broke their kiss. "I want you to come home after work, after I've done what I need to do, and I want you to remind me that I'm still alive."

Reed's heart cracked. He stroked a hand down Nic's cheek and smiled sadly. "You're very much alive, Dominic O'Halloran."

"Remind me later?" Nic's voice was nearly a plea.

"I'll be back before dinner," Reed assured him, taking a step back before turning to go.

———————

CONCENTRATING on anything work-related was agony. Reed stared at his computer, thankful he didn't have any meetings scheduled until the following morning, because all he could think about was getting home and making sure Nic was okay. His phone sat beside him on his desk, and he tapped the screen to wake it up, just to make sure he hadn't missed any calls or texts from Nic.

He hadn't.

There was a knock at his door and he glanced up as it opened, only to see Father Cowart in the doorway. He stood up and moved to smooth his tie down, only to remember he hadn't put one on today.

It was summer, after all.

"Father Cowart," he greeted, gesturing to one of the empty chairs in front of his desk.

Father Cowart tipped his head in greeting and took a seat. Reed stepped around him to close the door, finding a nervous-looking Susan hovering between her desk and his office. Reed's adrenaline spiked and he closed the door, returning to his desk.

"What can I help you with?" he asked, taking his seat.

"I had a meeting with Mary Ollingham this morning." Father Cowart folded his hands together in front of his chest and looked at Reed expectantly.

"What did she have to say?"

"She told me a very interesting story about running into you last night."

Reed closed his eyes, his fear and worries settling heavier on his shoulders. This was the moment he'd feared, the outing he wasn't quite ready for.

"Did she?" he asked, hoping any delay would give him the opportunity to bolster himself for this conversation.

"She said you were at an LBTG meeting at St. Paul's." Father Cowart looked at him with judgement in his eyes.

"LGBT," Reed corrected.

"That doesn't matter very much, does it?" Father Cowart raised an eyebrow.

"It's the same marginalized group no matter what order you put the letters in," Reed snapped. His eyes widened at his own outburst, and he bit his lips between his teeth.

"She said that you coerced her daughter into attending."

Reed scoffed. "Catherine? No. She came to me just before school was out." Reed stopped himself. "Nevermind. That's not my place to tell you about that conversation."

"Mrs. Ollingham told me all about the conversation." Father Cowart propped an ankle on his knee.

"How could she? She wasn't there for it."

"Catherine told her."

"What did Catherine tell her?" Reed sighed, resting back in his chair. His nerves had settled somewhat, but he found himself uneasy now with the delay. The burden of his secret was jagged and painful inside of him. Maybe if it was out in the open, maybe if the uncertainty was gone, it wouldn't be such a struggle.

"That you encouraged her to seek out the counsel of Father O'Halloran." Father Cowart looked smug.

"I did," Reed agreed.

"Why didn't you send her to reconciliation? Or even to my office?"

"I didn't think she'd be best served in that manner."

"How would she not be best cared for in the counsel of our Lord?" Father Cowart held his hands out beside him.

"I felt Catherine would be well served with additional perspective," Reed sighed. He knew how the mothers at Our Lady of the Mount could get, and he knew Mrs. Ollingham wouldn't rest until she'd placed some level of blame for finding Catherine where she had.

An odd sense of relief washed over him. In this moment, it wasn't that he was scared to be outed to his boss, but he was glad if he lost his job, it wouldn't be because of his love for Nic. It seemed absurd to him now that being persecuted for his sexual identity would ever be an option. He could take no issue with losing his job for doing it to the best of his ability, which he had done when he sent Catherine to Nic.

His phone buzzed, and he looked down. It buzzed again, Nic's name lighting up the screen. His phone silenced and he rested his hand on top of it.

"Am I in trouble?" he asked, directing his attention back to Father Cowart.

"I think we could have overlooked you leading young Catherine astray, but Mary tells me that wasn't the only thing she witnessed last night."

His phone buzzed again. He raised his hand and saw Nic's name still on the screen.

"Right." Reed let out a deep breath. His phone quieted. He drummed his fingers over the top of the screen.

"She said she saw you with Father O'Halloran," he continued, "in a manner not becoming a Catholic man."

His phone lit up again.

"Can you excuse me a moment?" he asked, holding up his phone.

"This won't take long, Reed."

Reed curled his fingers around his phone nervously. He gritted his teeth together and narrowed his eyes.

"The impression she had was that you're in a relationship with him." Father Cowart nearly spat the accusation.

His phone vibrated again and Reed looked at the screen. He pushed his chair back and stood up, taking a deep breath. This was a test. He knew this was a test of his will, of his heart, and he refused to make the wrong decision.

He answered the call and whispered into the microphone, "I'm sorry. I'm sorry. Hold on."

Reed turned his attention back to the man sitting across from him. This man who he'd interviewed with, and offered confession to, and feared for years. He took a deep breath and held the phone to his side.

"I am," he answered. "And he needs me."

"Pardon?"

"I am in a relationship with him, and he needs me right now, so I need to go."

"Reed. This is serious."

"I know," Reed raised his phone. "It is."

Reed stepped out from behind his desk and grabbed his jacket from the coat rack. He opened the door and had one foot into the main office when Father Cowart spoke. "If you walk out that door, you don't need to walk back into it."

Reed stalled. Susan was still hovering between her desk and his door, her eyes frantic. She blinked at him, shaking her head, and held up her hands like he was a nervous horse. He tightened his grip on his phone and looked over his shoulder. Father Cowart had stood up and was waiting for him to make his decision.

"If it were my wife on the phone?" Reed asked.

"It's not your wife."

"If it were?" Reed pressed.

Father Cowart gestured toward the door. "Obviously you could go deal with your marriage, then."

Reed lifted the phone to his ear, the timer on the call ticking on. "I'm still here. Wait for me."

"Principal Matthews," Susan coaxed.

He exhaled a trembling breath and shook his head.

The decision was clear. It had always been clear, he just hadn't seen it. He hadn't wanted to see it. The pressure of his phone against the palm of his hand and the side of his face grounded him, much like the way Dominic's skin always did.

"I'll come back tomorrow to clean out my desk," he said. "I'd do it now, but I really need to go."

"What?" Father Cowart's jaw fell.

"You gave me a choice, and I've made it. Nic is more important than this. He's more important than everything, and I need to go to him. If I can't continue to work here because of my relationship with him, then there's no need for us to finish this conversation."

"Reed?" Nic's voice sounded worried in his ear. "What's going on?"

"Two minutes, baby. I'm sorry."

"If it's true, you'll no longer be allowed to participate in communion. I'll also no longer take your confession unless it's to repent your sins, Reed."

Reed's stomach flipped and time stalled. He was aware of Nic's voice, frantic and worried in his ear, and Father Cowart's accusatory glare, narrowed on his phone.

"I don't have time to debate this." Reed shrugged. "I love my job. I love my faith. I love him."

The words were leaving his mouth and he didn't even recognize them. His body felt light, as if the weight of the world had been lifted from his shoulders and his heart.

"I really need to be going." Reed turned on his heel.

"Susan will pack your office. You're not welcome on campus," Father Cowart spat.

Reed nodded and strode out of the office. He waited until he reached the parking lot before he returned to his phone call.

"Nic?"

Reed opened his car and dropped into the driver's seat,

pulling the door closed and banging his head onto the steering wheel repeatedly.

"Did you just quit your job?" Nic asked.

"I got fired," Reed corrected. "But that's not important right now. Are you okay? I'm sorry it took me so long to answer. He was talking about Catherine. I didn't know he was going to say anything about us."

"I'm sorry."

"What? What are you sorry for?" Reed turned his car on and backed out of the spot, pulling onto the road.

"You lost your job," Nic said sadly.

"Better than losing you," Reed countered. "Now tell me. What's going on?"

Nic chuckled into the phone, a sad and watery sound that pulled at Reed's heart.

"I need you," he answered. "I can't do this alone."

"Where are you at? I'll come to you."

THIRTY

DOMINIC

"I'M SORRY ABOUT EARLIER," Dominic mumbled, taking a sip of water from the bottle Reed had shoved into his hands after they'd left Carol's house.

"You don't need to apologize," Reed assured him, navigating them both back toward Dominic's house.

He closed his eyes and rested his head against the seat head-rest, crunching the plastic bottle in his hands. He'd really tried to take care of everything on his own today. He'd made it to Carol's house without incident. He sat down at her desk, pulled open the drawer she'd pointed out to him years ago, and opened up the well-worn manila folder marked "Affairs" in her delicate script.

He'd managed to read through everything she'd left, which had taken hours. He called the hospital with the funeral home information, then called the funeral home. He'd been fine up until the point the woman on the other end of the call asked about Carol's final wishes.

"Should we plan for cremation or ground burial?" she asks.

"My mother was terrified of being buried," Dominic answers with a laugh. It catches in his throat and turns into a sob.

"I know this is difficult," the woman soothes him in a tired voice. He's sure she's done this a thousand times.

"My mother," Dominic repeats. "My mother."

It was the first time Dominic's brain had defaulted to thinking of Carol as his mother and it was too late to tell her, too late to dial her up and say, "Hey Mom, I love you."

Too fucking late.

"Do you want to talk to me about it?" Reed asked him.

"I'm not sure what to say." Dominic didn't open his eyes.

"That's fine. You don't need to." Reed continued driving in silence, pulling to a stop when he reached Dominic's house.

"Do you want me to come in?" he asked.

Dominic nodded, unbuckling his seatbelt and forcing himself out of the car. He counted the steps to the front door and opened it, stepping inside and leaving it open for Reed.

The door clicked closed. The deadbolt locked. Dominic heard it all, but nothing registered.

"Let's sit." Reed's voice was in his ear, and Reed's hands on his arms. Reed tried to guide them to the couch, but Dominic resisted.

"I don't want to sit," he whispered, his fingers circled tight around Reed's arm.

"What do you need?" Reed turned to face him, his face worried and creased.

"You."

The lines of Reed's face softened, and he nodded.

"Come on, then." Reed led him into the bedroom, divesting them both of their clothes with a quick and silent efficiency. "How do you want me?"

Reed held his face between his fingers and waited for Dominic to decide. Dominic closed his eyes, and Reed dragged his fingers down to his throat. Dominic tilted his head back, face pointed toward the ceiling. Reed continued down his chest to his stomach, then lowered himself to his knees and took Dominic's soft cock into his mouth.

Reed licked and sucked him until he grew hard, then buried his nose against Dominic's stomach. Reed grabbed Dominic's hands and rested them on his own head, waiting for Dominic to take the lead.

He flattened his tongue against the underside of Dominic's shaft and swallowed, the muscles of his throat constricting around the tip of his cock. Dominic grunted and bucked, pushing himself further into Reed's throat. Reed groaned, then hummed, holding onto Dominic's thighs and letting Dominic fuck his face.

Tears slid down Reed's cheeks, and something in Dominic snapped. He hauled Reed up by his hair and threw him on the bed. He sprang into action, tearing open the bedside table and opening the lube. He coated his cock and crawled onto the bed.

"Turn over." He tipped his chin up.

Reed obliged with no complaint, rolling onto his stomach and pushing his ass into the air. He rested his cheek on the pillow and looked back at Dominic with nothing but eagerness in his eyes. Dominic didn't see a hint of pity or sympathy, and he loved that. His blood burned with the desire to separate himself from his life, and Reed was ready to give him that escape.

"I don't need prep," Reed rasped, spreading himself apart. "You can hurt me."

"I don't want to hurt you," Dominic countered, lining himself up with Reed's hole.

"I like when you hurt me. You know that."

Dominic thrust in, his cock stretching Reed's hole with one sharp snap of his hips. Reed's eyes rolled back in his head and he bared his teeth.

"That's good," he hissed.

Dominic pulled out and slammed back in, the sound of his

skin smacking against Reed's reverberating through the otherwise silent room. Dominic fucked Reed with reckless abandon —long and hard thrusts meant to stretch and burn—until they were both covered in a layer of sweat.

"Come on, Nic," Reed begged. "More."

Dominic fell forward, using his forearm to hold Reed against the bed and his legs to push Reed flat into the sheets. He fucked Reed like his life depended on it. His orgasm slammed into him with an unexpected ferocity, unfurling through his body with such force he feared his bones would break.

Beneath him, Reed cried out, thrashing beneath Dominic's restraint. He didn't let up, pounding Reed until his body was drained and his heart didn't feel like it weighed ten tons. He collapsed on top of Reed and bit the back of his neck. Reed bucked him off, and Dominic tumbled onto his back freely, his body limp from his release.

Reed crawled on top of him, cock in hand and fire in his eyes. Reed straddled him and fisted his cock, working his length until he came, spurts of hot, white cum spraying over Dominic's sweat-soaked chest. Reed fucked his hand until his body trembled with pain, then he fell onto the bed, half his body over Dominic, the other half on the sheets.

"Kiss me," Dominic pleaded, pulling Reed onto him.

Reed attacked his mouth, kissing him with as much need and want as Dominic had fucked into him earlier. The reciprocity revitalized him, and he speared his fingers into Reed's hair, holding their mouths together. He pushed them both into a sitting position, never breaking the kiss, only slowing it, turning it more worshipful.

Reed groaned into his mouth, and Dominic stilled, pressing a kiss against the corner of Reed's lips and opening his eyes. He panted, his breath coming hot and heavy with every inhale.

"Thank you," Dominic whispered against his cheek.

"What for?" Reed chuckled. "I liked it, too."

"I know." Dominic cupped his hands around the back of Reed's neck. "But I meant thank you for not looking at me like you felt sorry for me."

He'd had enough of it today. The lady from the hospital, the funeral home, Geraldine, who'd shown up on Carol's porch with a casserole Dominic didn't need or want. He needed to be treated normal so he could carry on as normal. There was a time to mourn, and it wasn't over urn options or flower choices.

Reed tilted his head and pursed his lips.

"Don't say it." He stopped Reed before he could verbalize the sentiment.

"I'm here for you," Reed said instead of whatever conciliatory offering he'd planned to make.

"I know," Dominic agreed. He exhaled and kissed Reed again. "Can we talk about something that isn't me, please?"

Dominic flung his legs over the side of the bed and rested his elbows on his knees. He stared at the floor. Reed arranged himself to Dominic's left, mirroring the pose.

"I lost my job today," Reed told him.

Dominic turned his face to the side and studied Reed for signs of regret or concern, but found none.

"I heard bits and pieces. Was it because of me?"

"No." Reed shook his head. "Not because of you. Not because of us. Because of them. Their ideas and their fears."

Dominic raised an eyebrow. "I thought you were one of them."

Reed reached up and fingered the gold crucifix he always wore, then he popped the clasp open and tossed the necklace onto the nightstand.

"I don't think there's a place for me there anymore." Reed shrugged.

"Your place is here," Dominic assured him, bumping their legs together. "With me."

"I know."

"What are you going to do?"

"Find another job, I guess. Maybe I'll move to Arizona, who knows." Reed's lips tipped into a sad smile.

"You'll do no such thing," Dominic warned. "I need you here."

"I'm here," Reed answered.

"You can come to St. Paul's, you know. If you want to go to church still." Dominic's eyes drifted to the gold chain and crucifix next to the bottle of lube on the nightstand.

"Maybe after a while," Reed whispered. "But thank you."

"Will you come with me? For the funeral, I mean."

Dominic closed his eyes and grimaced. Carol had written in her requests that Dominic be the one to perform her funeral. It was such a very Carol move, he knew he wouldn't be able to ever deny it. He held his hands out in front of him, tracing the lines of his palms and knuckles with a trembling finger. He circled his finger around the thin gold band he wore, twisting it around.

"I never asked," Reed said softly.

"Hmmn?"

Reed touched the ring, touched Dominic's finger.

"The ring."

"Oh." Dominic huffed, pulling it off for the first time in nearly ten years. He held it in his palm, a perfect golden circle representing everything it was ever meant to.

"I always assumed it was from someone special," Reed blurted out, the silence of the moment obviously making him nervous.

"It was, but not the way you're thinking."

"Don't leave me in suspense," Reed deadpanned.

"It was David's," Dominic explained. "He gave it to Carol after he'd left that time around when you got adopted. He came back and gave it to her, saying that he didn't deserve it and he wanted her to hold it until he'd earned it back."

"She never gave it back?"

Dominic took the ring between his fingers and held it between them.

"She tried," he answered. "She wanted to give it back, but he wouldn't take it. He said he hadn't earned it, and he wanted to work the rest of his life to be worthy of the commitment it represented."

Reed opened his hand and Dominic set the ring in his palm.

"When did you get it?" Reed asked.

"After he died. So, right after I graduated from seminary. Carol told me to keep it as a reminder of how I'd need to work my whole life to deserve the love of the person I wanted to be with."

"That seems extreme." Reed handed him the ring back. Dominic pushed it back onto his ring finger, obscuring the pale band of skin that hadn't seen the sun in years.

"I think it's admirable." Dominic turned his attention to Reed. "I'd spend my whole life proving to you that I love you. That I'm worthy of being allowed to love you, rather. That's all it is."

Dominic's cheeks heated with embarrassment at the admission, and he looked away.

"You are," Reed assured him. He took Dominic's hand in his and kissed the gold band.

"My thoughts on the matter have shifted," he admitted, squeezing Reed's fingers. "The moments I have with you are a gift. I don't want to take them for granted."

Reed turned Dominic's face toward his and slanted their mouths together. He swung a leg over Dominic and straddled him, holding his shoulders under his sure and strong fingers.

"Then don't."

THIRTY-ONE

REED

"I HAVE SOMETHING FOR YOU," Nic announced, his stare focused on Reed in the reflection of the mirror over his dresser. He straightened his collar and aligned the buttons on his black button-up, then turned to face Reed.

"For me?" Reed tied the laces on his shoes and stood up, his tie loose around his neck. He began to knot it, but Nic stopped him with a quick grab of the hand.

"For you."

He shoved a hand into his pocket and produced a silver chain with a round medallion at the end. It spun in the air between them, coming to a stop before Nic passed it his way.

"A St. Jude?" Reed asked with a tilt of his head. He backed the medallion with the palm of his hand to still it, noticing the traditional pose of St. Jude with one hand raised and script beneath that read, *pray for us.*

"Patron saint of lost and forgotten causes."

"I know." Reed took the chain in his hand. "And this made you think of me?"

Nic scrunched his mouth. "It made me think of me."

Reed chuckled. "You're not a lost cause."

"I've felt a little aimless the past week."

"I know," Reed soothed, fastening the chain around his neck. He tucked the medallion into his shirt before buttoning the top button and rubbing instinctively at the pendant.

He hadn't put his crucifix back on since Thursday night, when he'd removed it after they'd had sex. It hadn't felt right for him to wear it. He didn't think he'd have ever identified himself as a lost cause, but he definitely felt more directionless than he had in the past.

"Thank you," he told Nic, offering him a small smile.

"I love you."

"I love you," Reed reciprocated. "Are you ready for this?"

"I think so," Nic said with a strangled laugh.

"It's okay to cry, you know. If you want to."

"I don't." Nic forced a smile. "I really don't."

"THAT WAS A BEAUTIFUL SERVICE, DOMINIC."

Reed froze, his fingers tightening around Nic's hand. They both turned and came face-to-face with Margaret.

It was the first time Reed had seen her since they'd gone to reconciliation together, before Arizona, before Reed's entire life had been turned upside down. They'd spoken, of course, but the air between them was thick with unspoken apologies.

Dominic's voice was cool and collected when he answered her. "Thank you, Mrs. Matthews."

"You look well, Reed," she continued, turning her attention toward Reed.

"Thanks." He swallowed.

Nic squeezed his hand.

"Are you having a reception?" Margaret asked, clearing her throat and turning her attention back toward Nic.

"No." He shook his head. "My mother didn't want anything fancy."

Reed dipped his head and smiled. It was unfortunate that it had taken her passing for Nic to reconcile his feelings toward his foster mother, but every time he referred to Carol as his mother instead of by her name, it seemed to give him a sense of peace that Reed envied. His own feelings about Carol were mixed. He'd always remembered her fondly, and he mourned her passing, but his memories of her were nothing compared to Nic's.

"I didn't know Carol adopted you." Margaret worked her fingers around the handle of her purse.

"She didn't," Nic said. "She didn't need to. She was more mother to me than anyone else ever was."

Reed watched Nic from the corner of his eye and recognized the slight wobble of his lower lip that always preceded a bout of tears.

"Father." A voice behind them interrupted Reed's assessment, and he watched Nic swallow back the unshed tears and plaster a smile on his face.

"Would you excuse me?" He turned and pressed a kiss against Reed's temple, shifting his attention to whomever had greeted him.

"Things are good with him?" Margaret asked softly.

"Yeah." Reed nodded. "This is hard for him, though."

"I'm sure it is, dear," Margaret agreed. "It's hard to lose someone you love."

"I lost my job," he blurted, rolling his eyes at his own lack of decorum. He took a step away from Nic and gestured for Margaret to walk with him.

"What happened?" she asked, falling into step beside him.

"I'm sure you can guess." Bitterness laced his voice.

"Sweetheart," she consoled. "I'm sorry."

"I'm not." He discreetly patted the St. Jude against his breast bone. "This is better."

"When did that happen?"

"Thursday."

"Was mass on Sunday awkward for you?" Margaret asked.

They'd reached a tree in the corner of the church property, then turned to trace their steps back toward the crowd of people in front of the church. His eyes immediately searched out Nic, his tall form standing out in the crowd of well-wishers.

"I didn't go," he admitted, following Margaret's steps. "Father Cowart told me he wouldn't hear my confession or offer me communion."

"Reed—" Margaret's voice was thick with sorrow.

"It's fine," he interrupted her. "I've prayed over it, and I'm in a good place with it."

He'd debated going to another church, confessing to another priest, but he had nothing to confess. The covenant he shared with Nic was not sinful. If there were things he needed to repent for, it was not loving someone, and it was not for demonstrating that love.

"If you say so, sweetheart."

"I do," he said sharply. They reached the outskirts of the gathering of people at the bottom of the church stairs and stopped. He sighed, turning to face Margaret. "I'm sorry. I didn't mean to be so snappy just now."

"I know." She smiled, giving him that tender maternal smile he'd grown so used to. "It's alright."

Reed had done a lot of thinking—since Arizona, since Carol passed—and things had shifted to a new perspective for him. One where it was okay to be with Nic, where it was okay for him to have love for God and for a man in his heart. It was scary some days, but he knew he could navigate it.

"I don't know if I ever thanked you." He stared at the back of

Nic's head in the crowd. He could feel Margaret's eyes on him, but he couldn't force himself to look at her.

"What for?" she asked gently, reaching out and slipping her hand into the crook of his arm.

"Adopting me. I was mad about the thing with Carol and Nic, and I think a part of me always will be, but you were always a really great mom." He cleared his throat. "You *are* a really great mom."

"Oh." Margaret covered her mouth with a gloved hand. "Reed. I love you so much."

Reed nodded. "I love you, too."

Nic turned, and his eyes searched the grounds until they landed on Reed. He smiled, but even from this distance, Reed could see the pain in his eyes.

"I love Nic," he told her, patting her hand. "And he needs me right now, so I need to go."

"I know you do," Margaret assured him, taking her hand away. "Don't be a stranger, Reed, okay?"

Reed nodded, leaning down and kissing her forehead. "I won't... Mom."

She smiled at him, her eyes shining with tears. She nodded, then turned, walking back to her car. Reed waited until her door closed, then he made his way back through the crowd, taking his place beside Nic. He tangled their fingers together and squeezed Nic's hand.

"Are you ready to go?" he asked.

"Please."

"Okay, let's get out of here."

"I just..." Nic looked around. "I need to find Janice."

Reed searched the crowd for Nic's secretary, finding her leaning against the stair rail, talking with an older-looking man with a collar that matched Nic's.

"She's over there." Reed pointed.

"Of course." Nic sighed.

Janice was talking with her hands rather animatedly to the man, who nodded every few seconds without speaking.

"Janice is a wonderful secretary, but she's a huge gossip," Nic said, leading Reed toward the couple.

"Oh?"

Nic grunted, coming to a stop a few feet away from the stairs.

"Janice, Reed and I are going to go. Do you think you can lock up, please?" Nic asked her, his voice sounding more tired than it had all week.

"Of course, Father." Janice smiled.

"Bishop Jenkins, I don't mean to be rude, but it's been a terribly long day and I'd like to get home." Nic turned his attention to the man. Reed hadn't met him before, but he recognized the name and knew the man talking with Janice was effectively Reed's boss. His face paled, a familiar fear that spiked his adrenaline, as he was faced with yet another boss at another church alongside the man he loved.

"So you're Reed Matthews," Bishop Jenkins said, a sly grin on his face.

Janice's face turned bright red and she took a step back. "I'll go start locking up."

She bolted up the stairs, caught in the middle of her own gossip.

"I am," Reed confirmed.

"You're Dominic's boyfriend, then?" the Bishop asked.

Nic rubbed his forehead and sighed, watching Janice disappear into the church. He knew Nic's church was more liberal than his had been, but he didn't want to say the wrong thing.

"He is," Nic interjected, so he wouldn't have to.

"Janice was telling me you'd recently left your position at Our Lady of the Mount."

"You could say that," Reed answered.

"I'm sorry to hear that."

"I'm not." Reed's voice was sharper than he'd intended. He took a deep breath. "I'm sorry. I didn't mean for it to come out that way. It's been a really long week, and I think we both need some time to rest."

Reed looked to Nic, who nodded.

"Would you excuse us?"

"Of course." Bishop Jenkins nodded and stepped to the side. "Although, Nic, when things settle down, I'd like to discuss the summary you submitted for your sabbatical. You had some interesting ideas in there."

Bishop Jenkins's eyes darted toward Reed before they returned to Nic.

"Of course. Thank you for coming, Bishop. I appreciate it."

Nic exhaled and pulled Reed into the parking lot. They navigated through the parked cars in silence, reaching Nic's house a few minutes later. Nic opened the door and stepped inside, kicking his shoes off before Reed had even gotten the front door closed. He looked weary and bone-tired. Reed wasn't sure what to do for him, but he had to do something.

"Go take a bath," he told Nic, hoping to buy himself some time.

"Hmmn?" Nic pulled his collar off and undid the buttons of his dress shirt, pulling the tails free and revealing his bare chest.

"Go take a bath," he repeated. "You need to unwind for a little bit, and then we're getting off the church grounds."

Nic nodded and disappeared down the hallway. He listened while Nic filled the tub and waited until the taps turned off. He walked quietly to the bedroom, where he changed out of his suit and into a pair of worn jeans and a dark-green Henley.

He'd started to keep clothes at Nic's since he stayed there so often, and not a morning went by where he didn't think about what it would be like for the two of them to have their own home. He'd even researched the feasibility of using desert landscaping to try and mimic the serenity they'd both loved so much in Arizona.

Reed arranged himself on the bed, his back against the headboard and his legs crossed at the ankles. He played on his phone and scrolled aimlessly through the news for almost an hour, even searching for jobs and applying for them, until Nic appeared in the doorway. He was wet and naked, with dripping hair and pruney fingers, a towel loose around his waist.

He didn't look revitalized, but he didn't look like he was ready to drop either.

"Do you want to just stay in?" Reed asked, rethinking his plan.

"No." Nic shook his head and dropped his towel. He pulled a pair of briefs from the top drawer of his dresser and turned his back to Reed.

"Are you sure?" Reed asked a second time, his voice a little more lascivious than he'd intended.

Nic cast a glance over his shoulder and raised a brow.

"Alright." Reed laughed, standing up and stretching.

"What should I wear?" Nic asked, hands limp at his sides.

"Whatever is comfortable," Reed told him. "You won't be in it long anyway."

THIRTY-TWO
DOMINIC

DOMINIC HATED the way he felt, like his entire body had been blanketed with a weight he couldn't shake. He was simultaneously aware of the restraint, but somehow also numb to everything outside of it. He'd barely been aware of Reed's fingers against his skin while he'd stripped him down and sent him to bathe.

After his skin had absorbed as much water as it could bear, he'd forced himself out of the tub, only to find a fully-dressed Reed resting in bed. Reed had instructed him to get dressed, which he had, then Reed shuttled him into the car.

Regret over the way things had ended with Carol churned in his stomach, and he stared out the window, watching the lights of Edgewood blur as they drove past. "Where are we going?" he asked, rolling his head to face Reed in the driver's seat.

Reed glanced at him, but quickly returned his attention to the road.

"You need a reset," was his only reply.

Dominic closed his eyes while Reed drove, only opening them when the car came to a stop. They were one town over, in the carpark of a boutique hotel that had been open less than a year.

"A hotel?" he asked, raising a speculative brow.

"Don't judge me," Reed shot back. "I was working on short notice with a limited budget."

Dominic's cheeks flushed from shame. "That's not what I meant."

Reed smiled and patted his leg. "I know. Let's get inside before it gets too late."

Dominic opened the passenger door and joined Reed in front of the lobby door. He looked down, noticing Reed had a carryon bag.

"I didn't pack," he mumbled.

"I know." Reed stepped forward, and the large glass doors slid open. The cool lobby air whooshed into their faces, and Dominic followed Reed to the front desk.

He checked in.

One room for one night.

Reed took the plastic keycard and turned without a word. He strode toward the bank of elevators and Dominic jogged to catch up, feeling slightly annoyed that Reed had taken off without waiting for him.

In the elevator, Reed didn't look at him, instead choosing to stare at the instrument panel. They traveled to the top floor and the doors opened. Reed exited the elevator, again without a word, making a sharp left and walking down the entire length of the hallway. Dominic lingered outside the elevator after the doors closed and grit his teeth together when Reed slipped the room key into a door at the end of the hall and disappeared inside without even giving Dominic a second look.

Dominic narrowed his eyes at the now-closed door and stalked down the hallway. He knocked, waiting for Reed to answer.

He knocked again, his heart rate quickening.

Finally, Reed opened the door, a glass of wine in one hand. He pulled the door back and stepped away. It began to fall closed, only stopping when Dominic shoved his hand out to wrap around the handle.

"What is your deal?" he hissed, letting the door close behind him with a deafening click.

Reed was in front of the window, his back to Dominic, and he shrugged, looking over his shoulder with a bemused expression.

Dominic closed the space between them, using his chest to push Reed against the floor-to-ceiling glass window with a little more force than was necessary.

"Why are you being this way?" he bit out, lips against Reed's ear.

Reed raised his wine glass and took a large drink, swallowing noticeably before he answered.

"Because I know you."

"Oh, you do? You think this is what I need from you right now?" Dominic leveled a glare at him.

"Not this specifically." Reed finished his wine and set the glass on the standard-looking hotel desk beside the open bottle and another full glass.

"What, then?" Dominic pressed.

Reed practically rolled his eyes. He pulled the long sleeve t-shirt he was wearing over his head and threw it on the floor.

"Did you want to sit down and talk about it, Father?" Reed tilted his head, a deviant glint in his eye.

"Talk about what?"

"You buried your mother today," Reed reminded him.

Dominic clenched his jaw. "I know."

"Did you want to sit down, Father, and talk about your feelings?" Reed popped the button on his jeans and kicked out of his shoes.

Dominic bristled, fisting his hands at his sides so he didn't lash out. Reed was acting to impartial to him right now, and the only thing keeping him from losing his mind was the spark in Reed's eye that shrouded any malicious intent in his words.

"No," Dominic answered succinctly.

"I know you don't," Reed agreed, shoving his pants to his ankles and stepping out of them. "But you've got to do something with the feelings inside your heart right now."

Dominic swallowed, and Reed removed his socks, leaving himself completely bare.

"So, what's it gonna be, Father?" Reed fisted his cock and stroked himself from root-to-tip.

Dominic sucked his teeth and narrowed his eyes. "Don't touch that."

Reed's nostrils flared and he held his hands out at his sides, palms up with his fingers splayed apart.

"Forgive me, Father." Reed licked his lips and angled his head back to expose his throat. "It appears I've sinned."

Everything clicked into place. Dominic immediately realized what Reed was doing, and his heart swelled with love for the man before him who was trying to bring him back to the living the only way he knew how.

Dominic's cock bobbed to life between his legs, any memories of the day locked in the back of his mind. His lips twitched with the makings of a smile, and he rubbed at his throat, devoid of his collar.

"How long since your last confession?" he asked, taking a step toward Reed.

"I didn't think Episcopalians did that sort of thing," Reed rasped, eyes locked on Dominic.

"For you," Dominic said, stripping out of his shirt, "I'll make an exception."

Reed's pupils were the size of saucers, and he swayed on his feet as Dominic approached him.

"Nearly two months," Reed whispered, his erection standing strong.

Dominic made a disapproving sound in the back of his throat and fisted Reed's hair with a steady hand. Reed gasped, first shocked, then aroused. He went malleable under Dominic's grasp.

"I lie with a man," Reed panted.

Dominic tossed Reed's naked body onto the bed and stripped out of the rest of his clothes.

"And I love him," Reed continued. He fisted the sheets in his hand, and his cock slapped against his stomach, a shiny trail of precum visible in the light of the hotel room.

"That doesn't sound sinful to me," Dominic countered, crawling onto the bed and kneeling near Reed's ankles.

"I used to think it was." Reed leaned forward and matched Dominic's positioning on the soft mattress. "That was my real sin. Denying how much I loved him, how much I wanted him. Pretending that what we shared together could ever be anything less than godly."

Dominic swallowed, his breath catching in his throat. "He feels the same way."

Reed smiled, his face coloring a vibrant pink. He looked down, and Dominic turned his attention to the space between their bodies—their cocks both hard and swollen.

"I know that now." Reed rolled his eyes, then sobered. "But I didn't then, and I caused this man more pain than I intended."

"Did you now?" Dominic fisted their cocks in his hand and squeezed. Reed's body angled in, and he winced, then straightened, eyes searching out Dominic yet again.

"I did, Father." Reed's eyes rolled back in his head, and not of his own free will.

"Then you'll need to perform a penance." Dominic released their erections and shoved Reed backward onto the bed. "Get on your hands and knees."

Reed scrambled into position, his ass proudly on display. Dominic circled his hands over the round globes of Reed's ass. He kneaded Reed's flesh, pulling, pushing, and manipulating, digging in harder every time Reed winced or moaned.

"Twenty spankings, then," Dominic decided. "One for every year your absence tortured this man you love."

"Thank you, Father," Reed whispered, his head hanging low between his shoulders.

Dominic rubbed his right hand over Reed's ass and spanked him—not too hard, but not soft. He reached between Reed's legs and grabbed his balls, circling his fingers around the base of his sac and tugging downward roughly. Reed cried out, and Dominic spanked him again, again, again, again.

Dominic's own dick hardened further, the skin stretched uncomfortably tight around the swollen head of his cock. He continued to strike Reed's ass, his skin turning a beautiful red. Reed writhed beneath him, alternating moans of pleasure from Dominic's punishment and pain from the bondage between his legs.

His breath was coming in harsh and heavy pants by the time he reached twenty, and he released Reed's sac, pushing him flat onto the bed. The thick down comforter puffed around Reed's body, looking even brighter and whiter against the bruising on his ass.

"I'm sorry with all my heart," Reed mumbled into the sheets.

Dominic slapped his ass again.

"You're not finished," he growled, flipping Reed onto his back. "Did you pack lube?"

Reed nodded, but also shook his head. "Don't want it."

Dominic hesitated, taking his dick in hand while he stared down at Reed.

Reed blinked at him, his eyes watery with unshed tears. He shook his head again, repeating his plea, and Dominic realized this was as much for Reed as it was for him. Reed genuinely felt he'd wronged him and was trying to atone for his own sins while helping Dominic work through his feelings of guilt.

Dominic crawled up Reed's body and raised himself, pointing his cock downward and dragging it over Reed's trembling lips.

"Open up," he commanded, tapping against Reed's mouth.

Reed opened his mouth and stuck out his tongue. Dominic plunged his length inside, the tip of his cock slipping straight into Reed's throat. Reed gagged and bucked beneath him, the unshed tears now falling freely down his cheeks. Dominic growled and fucked his cock in and out of Reed's mouth, the wet and sloppy noises of his pleasure filling the room.

"Is this how you want it?" Dominic asked, lowering his weight so he was fully seated in Reed's mouth. He watched the way Reed's face turned pink, then red, the way his eyes bulged and his pupils turned into solid black circles against the brown of his irises. Reed looped his hands around Dominic's waist and rested them flat against his back, his fingertips flexing against Dominic's muscles.

"Is this too much?" Dominic circled his hips, sliding a hand behind Reed's head and pressing Reed's nose deeper against the hair that surrounded his cock.

In answer, Reed removed his hands, lowering them to the mattress and fisting the sheets.

Dominic growled, tearing his cock out of Reed's mouth. Reed gasped, spit flying over his cheeks and mixing with his tears. Dominic maneuvered down Reed's body, using his shoulders to spread Reed's legs apart and hoist them up. He grabbed his cock and buried himself with one rough thrust.

Reed cried out, the pain in his voice overshadowing the pleasure. His chest slammed into Dominic's, and he buried his face in the dip of Dominic's shoulder. Reed gasped and sobbed, his body vibrating with his want. Dominic held him steady until he calmed, then he started to move, pulling out slowly and

gliding back in, fighting against the opposition of Reed's unpre-
pared channel.

"Oh, fuck." Reed sank his teeth into Dominic's shoulder.

Dominic fisted his hair roughly and yanked his mouth away.
His shoulder burned. Reed's lips pulled into a sly smile, a drop
of blood barely noticeable in the corner of his mouth.

"You made me bleed," Dominic assessed, touching his fingers
to the spot where Reed's mouth had been.

"I'm sorry for all my sins, Father," Reed rasped. His head fell
back and Dominic dropped him down to the bed, pounding into
him at full force. He came quickly, his orgasm exploding
through his body and out of his cock.

He roared, body arched over Reed's limp form, and he
poured everything into the man beneath him. Every ounce of
pleasure, pain, guilt, contrition, forgiveness, understanding,
desire… he offered it all to Reed, and Reed took it without question, his own cock spurting against his chest.

Reed's fingers scrabbled against his chest, and Dominic
collapsed on top of him. Reed searched out his mouth, kissing
him with all the feelings Dominic had just given him and more.
Time blurred, their bodies meshed—the fluids between them, a
bond.

"It's alright," Reed whispered into his ear. "You're alright. I've
got you."

Dominic's brain muddled and he blinked in confusion. His
face was wet, his lashes clumped together. He braced himself on
a forearm and reached up, rubbing at his eyes, only to find them
wet with tears. When had he started to cry?

"You're okay," Reed continued, using his weight to roll
Dominic onto his side.

Dominic opened his mouth and sobbed. He covered his
mouth with both hands, looking to Reed for guidance. Reed
watched him with a calm contentment and a knowing but sad
smile.

"Let it out, Nic."

Dominic twisted himself into a ball and pressed himself against Reed's chest, unable to stop himself from weeping. His entire body shook with the intensity of his breakdown, and he cried even harder. He mourned the feelings he'd never allowed himself to feel in his past—the love he'd not shared when he had a chance to do so—and he gave thanks for the promise of a future that wrapped him in understanding arms and held him until he fell into an exhausted sleep.

THIRTY-THREE

REED

"IS THAT A CACTUS?" Nic's voice was muffled by the pillow. He rolled over and studied Reed's face with an arched eyebrow.

"It is," Reed confirmed.

It had seemed to be a silly thing when he'd booked the room the night before, but he'd asked the concierge to bring a cactus to the room, in addition to the wine. He knew he'd been yearning to return to the private bubble they'd shared in Arizona, and a hotel room with a cactus outside of Edgewood was the best he could do on such short—and necessary—notice. "It's not Arizona, but it'll have to do." He stroked Nic's sweaty and tangled hair away from his face.

"That's very... thoughtful." Dominic stretched, and Reed took the opportunity to admire the long, sloping lines of his body.

"Can we talk about last night?" Reed scrunched his nose.

Nic blushed and looked around the room. "Coffee first?"

"Of course. You wait here." Reed slipped out of bed and filled two paper cups with water from the sink in the bathroom, using the small machine to brew them two single-serve cups. He returned to the bed and passed one to Nic, then arranged himself cross-legged on top of the covers.

Nic took a small sip, testing the temperature. He pushed his back up against the headboard so he was sitting.

"What did you want to talk about?" Nic asked him.

"Are you mad with me?"

Nic looked horrified. "Why would I be mad?"

Reed's shoulders relaxed and he grinned awkwardly. "Because I sort of forced you into that, and then you kind of had a meltdown."

"First off," Nic reached out and rested his hand on Reed's bare knee, "you didn't force me. I knew what you were doing. Thank you for it, by the way."

"You knew I was driving you to a complete emotional meltdown?" Reed chuckled.

"I knew you were trying to pull me out of myself, and I needed that. The other part…" Nic sighed. "Well, that was just, I don't know. Top drop maybe."

"What's that?"

"It's like… sometimes it's just exhausting to be the way I am with you. Not that you're exhausting. It happens to other people too."

"I shouldn't have pushed." Reed stared at the dark brown liquid in his cup.

"You're not understanding," Nic said softly. "It's not a bad thing. It just happens sometimes. I think I needed it. Like a reset."

"Are you sure?" Reed chewed his lip between his teeth.

"I promise." Nic crossed his heart. "I feel better today than I have since we got back from Arizona."

Reed let out a nervous breath. "Good. I'm glad."

Nic licked his lips. "Besides, I'm not the only one who got something out of that."

"Yeah." Reed adjusted himself. "I got a sore ass from it."

"Inside or outside?" Nic chuckled.

"Yes."

Nic grinned and reached for him, pulling him closer, but slowly as to not spill his coffee. Reed reached past Nic and set his cup on the nightstand, taking Nic's face between his hands, and kissed him gently.

"I didn't mean to hurt you," Nic mumbled against his mouth. "Not in the bad way at least."

"I know," Reed assured him. "I'm good. I swear."

"Alright."

"Are you okay?"

"I'm perfect," Nic whispered, wrapping his arms around Reed's shoulders and holding him close. "I have everything I need."

Reed hummed happily.

"We have to check out soon?" Nic asked after a brief pause.

"We do," Reed confirmed. "Sadly, life goes on without us."

Nic thumped his head against the headboard. "I have a lot to do."

"Let me help you. It's not like I have a job or anything to keep me busy." Reed huffed an annoyed sound, but smiled to let Nic know he wasn't upset about it.

Nic took a breath and held it, searching Reed's face for something, finally nodding. "Thank you," he whispered.

"It's nothing," Reed assured him.

"I want to talk to you about the job thing, though."

Reed unfolded himself from Nic's arms and stretched, the tips of his toes sticking off the bed, his cock heavy against his thigh.

"Did you want to make me a kept man?" He rolled onto his side and propped his head in his hand. "I'm not against the idea."

Nic widened his eyes, incredulous. "I don't know how much

money you think a priest makes, but you might be in for a rude awakening when you find out."

"I'm just kidding." Reed sat up and reached for his coffee, taking a sip.

"I know. You'd go insane not working with kids, and that's something I'd meant to talk to you about anyway, before all of this happened."

"Uhm…" Reed furrowed his brows together. "Go on?"

"I know I told you about the LGBT program I started at St. Paul's, right?"

Reed nodded.

"I haven't spoken to Bishop Jenkins at length about it yet because of everything that happened." He waved his hand around the room. "But he was interested in the idea and wanted to set it up as a regional program, you know, pulling in other churches in the state."

"That's great," Reed enthused, not sure what any of this had to do with his unemployment.

Nic looked at him expectantly, and he shrugged helplessly.

"We'd need an administrator," Nic elaborated. "Someone who is good with kids, who wants to see them succeed, but someone who also understands the struggle they're facing while reconciling their religion with their sexual preferences and identities."

"I've never done anything like that," Reed countered weakly.

Nic scoffed. "Haven't you? You sent Catherine to me."

"That's one kid," he protested.

"You saw the need, and you took action. That's what we need. Plus, you have the administrative experience from being a principal for so long. It ticks all the boxes necessary for the position as I'd outlined it in my proposal." Nic looked smug.

"The way you outlined it?" Reed narrowed his eyes. "Were you anticipating me losing my job?"

Nic glanced away. "I was afraid it would happen, but that didn't have any bearing on the program I want to start or the positions we need to fill as a result of it."

"Do you promise?" Reed questioned.

"I promise." Nic smiled. "I didn't want you to lose your job, Reed. But their loss can be my gain."

"Is it that simple?"

Nic shrugged, looking far younger and more carefree than he had since they'd reconnected. "Isn't it?"

"I guess I'll brush up my resumé, then."

Nic smiled and threw himself on Reed, flattening him against the mattress. He kissed the curve of his throat, and Reed moaned, pushing their bodies together.

"Are you too sore?" Nic breathed into his ear.

Reed shook his head. "I'm fine, but lube this time."

Nic laughed and jumped off the bed, returning with the lube from Reed's suitcase faster than should have been possible. Nic's cock jutted out from between his legs, hard and thick in the morning light that filtered through the window.

"Pull back the curtains," Reed rasped. "I want to see you."

Nic stroked himself with lube and walked to the window. He pulled the curtains open, and light poured into the room. He turned back to Reed, the rays of the sun reflecting through the glass like they radiated out from Nic's body and not the sun itself.

"I love you," Reed whispered, awed by Nic's beauty.

"I love you, too."

Nic returned to the bed and crawled between Reed's legs. He lowered his lube-slick fingers to Reed's hole and prepped him, pushing two long fingers inside and scissoring them apart. The stretch burned, but it was welcome, a reminder of the carnal nature of the covenant they shared together—their love made whole.

"I'm ready," Reed sighed. He danced his fingers up Nic's back, pressing into his skin when the head of his cock pushed past Reed's rim.

"You feel so good," Nic groaned, sliding deeper inside. "You always feel perfect. Like I'm meant to be here."

"Aren't you?"

Nic slanted their mouths together, his tongue delving into Reed's mouth as leisurely as his cock entered Reed's hole. Nic made love with him in ways he never had before, the truth of their bond now bare between them.

Reed's entire body vibrated with desire. Gooseflesh broke out across his skin and he couldn't stop his hips from circling and gyrating against Nic's. His lashes fluttered and his eyes closed as Reed gave himself over to the pleasure Nic was giving him.

"I want to come," he panted, the need unexpectedly over-whelming.

Nic nodded, a rough grunt escaping his lips. His eyes were wild, but his movements measured. He adjusted himself and circled Reed's cock with his fist, letting the momentum of his thrusts work Reed's cock through his hand.

"Come for me," Nic whispered. "Show me how good I make you feel."

Nic's words sent him over the edge, his cock spurting jets of cum against their chests. He jerked, his back arching off the bed and his lips parted on a silent cry. Nic slammed their mouths together, somehow giving Reed permission to verbalize his pleasure, so he did. Reed cried into Nic's mouth, his eyes squeezed shut, even while he could feel the weight of Nic's stare on him.

After his orgasm passed, his eyes fluttered open in time to watch Nic's widen. His cock thickened inside of Reed and he growled, fingers digging into the hollows of Reed's hips. Nic came, filling Reed's ass with his release and Reed's mouth with his pleasure.

Nic jerked, falling onto Reed with a sigh.

"You're heavy," Reed gasped, pushing Nic off of him.

"That's so mean," Nic panted. His cock slipped out of Reed as he let Reed push him onto his back. "I thought you loved me."

"I do," Reed promised him. "More than anything."

They lay on the sweat-soaked sheets, shoulder to shoulder, until their breathing returned to normal.

"What now?" Nic asked, turning his head to face Reed.

"We check out. We go home."

"Does the cactus come with us?" Nic's eyes sparkled.

"Of course."

"Who gets to keep him? Do we need to have a custody agreement?"

"It's a him?" Reed laughed and closed his eyes.

Nic touched his face, his fingertips light and delicate against Reed's cheek. Reed smiled and pressed a kiss against Nic's palm.

"I think you need him more than me," Nic decided. "He can stay with you."

"I'll bring him with me when I come over." Reed opened his eyes and smiled at Nic.

"I'm glad we've settled that." Nic cupped the back of his head and pulled him close, leaving a gentle kiss against the corner of his mouth.

"And the rest?" Reed asked, returning to Nic's original question.

"I don't know. I've never done this before," Nic admitted.

"Me neither." Reed grinned sheepishly.

"Then I suppose we're in this together."

Reed hummed appreciatively. "I'd hope so."

"Another thing settled, then." Nic nodded like he'd actually accomplished something. He opened his mouth like he had something else to say, but snapped it closed. His eyebrows worried together and he opened his mouth again.

"You look like a fish," Reed offered with a teasing grin.

Nic glared at him playfully, then relaxed. "I feel like I have everything I've ever wanted."

"Good." Reed sat up and cracked his neck. He poked Nic in the ribs. "I meant to tell you, I want to start coming to St. Paul's."

Nic raised his eyebrows. "Yeah?"

Reed nodded.

"I do. And to be honest," he leaned in conspiratorially, "I'm very excited about the prospect of you giving me communion."

Nic's nostrils flared.

"Don't," he warned.

Reed threw his head back and laughed. Nic's arm flew out and wrapped around his side, yanking him back onto the sheets. He laughed, and Nic's fingers tickled his ribs while he struggled.

"No erections during the service," Nic demanded, his eyes light with amusement.

"No promises." Reed laughed, stilling in hopes that Nic would stop tickling him.

"Are you sure?" Nic asked, his palms flattening and dragging up Reed's chest to his heart. He rubbed his fingers over the St. Jude medallion.

"Never been surer about anything in my life," Reed said, tipping his chin up and delivering a blistering kiss that left them both breathless.

"We really need to get going," Reed panted after tearing their mouths apart.

They showered together quickly, hands lingering, but never for too long. Once they were dry, Reed unpacked the small suitcase, handing fresh clothes to Nic, then dressing himself. He tucked their dirty clothes away and zipped up, finding Nic standing at the door of the hotel room, cactus in hand.

"Are you ready?" he asked, holding the door open so they could both exit.

Reed smiled at Nic and nodded, ducking out of the room with the suitcase behind him.

"I'm ready."

THE END.

ABOUT KATE HAWTHORNE

Born and raised in Southern California, Kate Hawthorne woke up one day and realized she had stories worth sharing. Now existing on a steady diet of wine and coffee, Kate writes stories about complicated men in love that are sometimes dirty, but always sweet. She enjoys crafting hard-fought and well deserved happy endings with just the right amount of angst and kink.

From estate sale shopping to shoe worship, there's something in at least one of her books that'll tickle your fancy. Visit her website at
www.katehawthornebooks.com

Sign up for Kate's newsletter
http://www.katehawthornebooks.com/extra

ALSO BY KATE HAWTHORNE

Secrets in Edgewood

A Taste of Sin

The Cost of Desire

A Love Made Whole

Giving Consent

(now on audio!)

Worth the Switch

Worth the Risk

Worth the Wait

Worth the Fight

Worth the Chance

Room for Love

Unfettered (a standalone)

Reckless

Heartless

Fautltless

Fearless

Limitless

The Lonely Hearts Stories

(now on audio!)

His Kind of Love

The Colors Between Us

Love Comes After

Until You Say Otherwise

Carver County Vampires

A Thousand Lifetimes

COLLABORATIONS

With E.M. Denning

Irreplaceable

Future Fake Husband

Future Gay Boyfriend

Future Ex Enemy

With E.M. Denning and E.M. Lindsey

Cloudy with a Chance of Love

With J.R. Gray

May the Best Man Win

Made in the USA
Las Vegas, NV
24 June 2021

25372040R00148